THE FIRE OF HOME
A POWELL SPRINGS NOVEL

THE FIRE OF HOME
A POWELL SPRINGS NOVEL

by

ALEXIS HARRINGTON

Montlake
Romance

Published by Montlake Romance, Seattle

www.apub.com

Amazon, the Amazon logo, and Montlake are trademarks of Amazon.com, Inc., or its affiliates.

ISBN-13: 9781477826034
ISBN-10: 1477826033

Cover design by Kerrie Robertson

Library of Congress Control Number: 2014909530

Printed in the United States of America

I'd love to squeeze in everyone who is a big boost to me and my job but space won't allow.

Thanks always to Lisa Jackson, Margaret Vajdos, Penny Lainus, and my cerebral party buddies, the Book Club Babes.

Thanks also to Amazon editor Helen Cattaneo for her infinite patience, and most especially to my development editor, Charlotte Herscher. Charlotte has magic in her keyboard!

NMK and WAB,
Thanks for bringing Amy and Bax to life on the page.

CHAPTER ONE

Powell Springs, Oregon
March 1922

Bax Duncan bounced along in the county-owned Model T, trying to see through the rain and mud splattering the windshield, wondering if his kidneys would be jarred loose. Under his breath he cursed both the weather and the motorized contraption. At least on horseback a man's hat kept some of the rain out of his eyes. But on the glass there was no way to wipe it off unless he pulled over and dragged out the same wet, muddy rag he'd already used more times than he could count today. A horse didn't need nearly as much tending. But he'd been sent out on official business this morning, which included a trip to the county courthouse in Portland, and that was too far to go on horseback. He hated the courthouse visits. He was certain that everyone in the building was staring at him and saw through his flimsy disguise.

The same train that came through Powell Springs also went to Portland, but there were too damn many stops in the getting there. When he wasn't working in his official capacity as deputy, he still reported to Sheriff Whitney Gannon and served as kind of a law clerk for both Whit and the circuit judge who passed through town from time to time.

Court was a pretty informal rural event—when the judge came to Powell Springs, he commandeered the City Hall, which consisted of only Mayor Cookson's office, a small room where the town council conducted its meetings, and the corner of the building where Birdeen Lyons ran the town's switchboard and managed Cookson's doings.

Wind lashed the rain across the road and over the plowed fields where it gathered in runnels between the rows. The only birds that lacked the good sense, or maybe the fear, to seek shelter were crows. They perched on the power lines overhead, squawking at him with rough, strident voices as he passed. Now and then the temperature would drop, and lightning would sizzle in the southern sky, followed by deafening thunderclaps. The storm was rolling in this direction to cross the Columbia River and head to Camas in Washington.

Though trying his best to avoid them, Bax thumped into an especially deep pothole, clacking his teeth together and splashing mud on the windshield again. This time he did have to pull over and wipe it off. In the process, he got nearly as much mud on his coat as he did the rag. He sighed. Even though the trees were leafing out and the sedge along the roadside loved the wet, except for a few nice days here and there it would be gray or raining until the middle of June. It was almost noon, but without good light it was hard to tell. He'd grown up with this weather, but that had been a lifetime ago in Cedar Mill, twenty-five miles west of here. That Bax Duncan was gone. Now the rain would always make him remember standing knee-deep in water, huddled against sandbags or wooden timbers in the trenches of western France, bullets whizzing close enough to make his ears ring. He'd been a sergeant then, a battlefield promotion that made him proud, until November 11 . . .

Back on the road, he peered ahead, and in the distance he saw a figure walking ahead of him. Though the person was obscured by the veil of rain, he thought it was a woman, based on the clothes and the umbrella bobbing over her head. She carried some kind of bag or suitcase.

What a day to be out on foot, he thought. The low-slung clouds were heavy with what had been an endless downpour.

As he pulled alongside her, the true misery of her situation became more obvious. Her gray coat was thin and wet where her umbrella had failed to cover it, she was muddy from her shoes to the hem of her navy skirt, and she trudged along like someone who had walked every step of a long journey. From beneath a sorry-looking hat, her hair straggled in dark-blonde hanks.

"Ma'am," he called, slowing to a crawl.

She trudged on.

If she'd only look up, she'd see the county name painted on the Ford's door and know that he wasn't just some skirt chaser, or worse.

"*Ma'am!* I'm headed to Powell Springs. I work in the sheriff's office. I can take you there."

No response, but she stiffened.

He tried again, louder now. "Do you want a ride?"

At last she lifted her head and looked at him from beneath her umbrella. He felt a catch in his chest—he'd seen that resigned, world-weary expression before. He'd worn it himself for a long period in his life, and still felt the cause. Then her features hardened into a mask of superior detachment.

She stopped, and he stepped on the brake. "I'm going to—"

"No. Thank you." Her voice was almost girlish, but like tempered steel. Though she was plainly a grown woman.

He gestured at the road ahead. "It's another mile and a half. I can take you into town so you don't have to walk, especially in this weather."

She looked at the road ahead, then she raked him up and down with her eyes. Under her insulting, distrustful gaze, Bax felt his face redden. "Thank you, but *no*. I'll manage."

She lifted her chin and began walking again, showing him a haughty profile that could have curdled the milk in a cow's udder. It was almost distracting enough to make him forget that she looked as worn as a washerwoman from a hospital laundry. But not quite.

"Suit yourself, lady," he called. "Maybe that high horse of yours will grow legs and carry you into town." He jammed the car into first gear with a loud, grinding protest from the gearbox. The Model T lurched forward and he went on, giving her a wide berth when he passed.

Amy Layton Jacobsen watched the car splash off down the road, her legs unsteady and her insides quivering along with her lower lip. It had taken every bit of what little acting ability she had to show that man an imperious demeanor, which she knew was at glaring odds with her appearance. It was certainly the complete opposite of the terror she felt. She dared not trust anyone in her present situation, and when she saw *Multnomah County* painted on the car's door, her stomach had dropped. She had no idea if Adam would inform the authorities that she'd gone. Given his own circumstances, she wouldn't think so, but there was no way of knowing what he might do.

She adjusted her hand on the grip of the suitcase and let her shoulders droop as she watched the Ford grow smaller in the distance. If someone else had stopped, someone not affiliated with the sheriff's office, she might have accepted the offer. In fact, she'd looked wistfully after the few cars that had passed her during this wretched trek. She'd been able to spare only enough money for a train ticket to Twelve Mile. She had been walking for almost two hours, and still had nearly another hour ahead of her. Except for a short nap in the gently swaying rail car, she'd been awake since early morning yesterday.

No one in Powell Springs knew she was coming, not even her family. Almost four years earlier, she and Adam had left town under the dark wing of night to avoid scandal and ostracism. She had been a pampered, privileged innocent then. Since that night, she had seen things—the stinking underbelly of life—that she never could have imagined existed, not even in a nightmare. Now she forced herself to keep putting one foot in front of the other to return.

Amy Jacobsen was a frightened woman with a broken spirit. But beneath her fear and within the fragile husk of the person she had once been, a small flame of determination gleamed. It had burned brightly once, and it would again.

CHAPTER TWO

"Right now the house has two lodgers living in it. I've been collecting their rents since Laura Donaldson passed away four months ago, as she requested. My fee is coming from a fund she set up for that purpose. You are the only heir designated in her will. She must have been very fond of you." The lawyer pushed some ledger sheets and a check across his polished desk toward Amy. Daniel Parmenter was a pleasant-looking man. Although gray dusted his temples and lightly sprinkled his hair, his brows were still dark. Behind him, journals and leather-bound law books lined glass-fronted shelves. "The house on Springwater Street and its contents were all she had."

All she had. It was a king's ransom to Amy. Her gaze riveted on the check made out in her name alone. Money, and it was hers, only hers. She wouldn't have to give it to anyone or account for how she spent it. It was all she could do to keep from swooping up the piece of paper and jamming it into her pocket. Instead, she leaned forward and looked at the itemized debits and credits without really seeing them. At the same time, she did her best to maintain a semblance of dignity, despite her appearance. She had changed clothes in the ladies' room at the rail station before coming here to the attorney's office with the letter he had sent her. Her muddy skirt was in her suitcase, but she owned just the one coat and a single pair of shoes. Her wet feet were numb with cold. To distract herself from that discomfort, she explained to him why she knew Laura Donaldson.

"I boarded in her house for two or three years after my sister had to sell our childhood home to pay the property taxes. Mrs. Donaldson was like an aunt to me. And she was my only link to Powell Springs after I left. She had no other relatives, as far as I know."

He continued. "I've hired a woman to do the cooking and cleaning. She looked after Mrs. Donaldson until she passed away, too. Deirdre Gifford—maybe you remember her?"

Amy thought for a moment. "Deirdre O'Connell? Wasn't she from Montana or somewhere like that? I think she married Charlie Gifford before he enlisted."

Mr. Parmenter nodded. "He was part of the American Expeditionary Force sent to Siberia to help deal with the civil war after the revolution. He died there in 1919 and was never brought home. She was a vivacious young woman, but with Charlie gone, Deirdre might not be the same person you remember."

Who was? Amy thought. She wasn't the same. Who could have lived through the last four or five years and come through unchanged? Her own problems loomed large before her, and she had neither the time nor the energy to waste on those of others. Still, the lawyer's veiled description of Deirdre sharpened her curiosity and her questioning. "I hardly knew her. Do you mean to say she is unhinged?"

A slight frown appeared briefly on his forehead. "No, no, certainly not. She is more than capable of the work she does around the house. She's a bit timid."

Amy nodded, satisfied for the moment.

"No formal notice is required, but it would be a courtesy to give Mrs. Gifford and the boarders time to find other living quarters."

She looked up. "Other quarters—why?"

"I supposed you'd want to turn it into a private residence again."

"No, I'm very grateful to Mrs. Donaldson for her bequest. She was the only person I stayed in touch with after, well, after Mr. Jacobsen and I eloped. But I plan to keep renting out the rooms for the time being—to honor her memory, you might say, unless someone should make an offer on the house or another opportunity presents itself."

Daniel Parmenter sat back in his chair and considered her. His assessing gaze lasted so long, she was on the verge of squirming in her seat. Her last remark was a weak explanation—she knew it and she saw it in his face. Finally he said, "I confess that I'm a bit surprised by your decision to come back to Powell Springs after everything that preceded your elopement. To be frank, I thought you'd sell the property instead and maintain your distance."

Amy turned a handkerchief she clutched in her fist. She had anticipated this sort of conversation. Of course, the subject of her leaving—and other matters—were bound to come up. But she needed a roof over her head *now*. No one had to know about her plans for the future, not that she had any. "I found that I missed my hometown, especially after living a somewhat transient existence."

"So Mr. Jacobsen will be joining you shortly."

"Oh, God, no!" She cleared her throat. "I mean I don't believe he can get away from his current responsibilities in the immediate future." She hoped desperately that he would not have the courage to show his face in Powell Springs. Although she'd left him no letter of explanation, she feared he would look for her. After all, she had something he owned, something he'd want back. But not here, please, not here. At least not until she was on solid footing, both emotionally and financially.

"Lots of things have happened since you were last in town. The population has almost doubled and we have another hotel, too. Of course, I haven't told anyone who Laura Donaldson named as her heir—if she did, I'm not aware of it. But I'm sure your family will be glad to see you. Did they know you're coming?"

Amy felt her face grow hot and she began strangling the hanky in earnest, uncomfortable with this interrogation. "Not— no—really, Mr. Parmenter, I don't mean to be rude, but could we finish our business here? I've been traveling since yesterday and I'd like to get settled. Aren't there papers I need to sign or something?"

He opened the center drawer of his desk, from which he plucked a set of house keys. "Of course. I didn't mean to pry. The deed will be transferred to you. I just need to have it filed with the county clerk's office. There are one or two other minor details but I can take care of those as well."

She bit back a relieved sigh and took the pen he handed to her to put her signature on a couple of documents.

Mr. Parmenter rolled a blotter across the wet ink. "It will probably take about three or four weeks for the final deed to come through. I'll let you know when I have it."

She thanked him and stood up to leave.

He saw her to the door and shook her hand. "Welcome back to Powell Springs, Mrs. Jacobsen."

Amy stepped outside and eyed the street and the businesses that lined it in both directions. They were tidy and well-maintained, clean with new paint and the glimmer of the improving postwar economy. New concrete sidewalks replaced many of the old wooden ones. Some things looked the same—Bright's Grocery; Tilly's Soda Shop; the saloon that wore the laughably thin veneer of respectability to comply with Prohibition; the blacksmith shop and its next-door neighbor, her own sister's office with its shingle, *Jessica Layton, MD*. Her throat tightened.

Some things looked different.

Things *were* different. She was, certainly. What would life in this town mean for her now? She had run away to hide, and now she had run back for the same purpose.

Welcome home, indeed.

• • •

Bax thumped around the sheriff's small office in a frayed temper, opening and slamming cabinet doors and drawers. His own desk consisted of two barrels with a door for a writing surface. Whit had submitted a requisition to the county for something more substantial, but so far nothing had happened. Bax had a report to write about the theft of Merle Lloyd's chickens, a job that he anticipated with groaning disinterest.

To top it off, Winks Lamont was sleeping off a two-day drunk in their only cell, and although the door to the holding area was closed, Bax could still smell him. He'd known worse odors, but not on a living human.

He banged the last door shut, at a loss.

Whit turned his swivel chair to look at him. "What the hell are you up to? This crappy old furniture can't take that kind of punishment."

"I'm looking for a bottle of ink!"

"Here, come and get this one. I'm not using it."

Bax stomped over and took the bottle.

"Got a pen?" Whit asked.

"No," Bax grumbled.

Whit gave him a narrow-eyed once-over. "What's stuck in your craw? All afternoon you've been acting like someone stole your lollipop and left a dog turd in its place."

Bax gave him a sour look, then sighed. He hated to admit that his encounter with that puckered-up female on the road had put him in this lousy mood. He'd been on the receiving end of that kind of treatment too many times . . . when people found out about the past he worked so hard to keep secret. But she couldn't have known about that.

"Nothing. It's nothing."

"That's a lot of racket for noth—" Whit stopped midsentence and sat up straight to look at something beyond the window. "Well, I'll be damned."

Bax followed his gaze just in time to see the same woman he'd met coming into town before she disappeared from view.

Whit pushed his wiry frame out of his chair and went to the glass. "I can't believe it."

"You know her?" Bax asked.

"Yeah. She's Dr. Jessica's sister, Amy Layton—well, I guess Amy Jacobsen now."

"She is, huh?" That explained a lot to Bax. He'd been in Powell Springs for just three months, and the fierce scandal Amy Layton and Adam Jacobsen had stirred up in 1918 still surfaced now and then. He didn't know many details, but the story carried enough sensationalism to keep it alive even to this day. He guessed that her years of exile hadn't done much to change her high-handed attitude. "I talked to her on the way back here today. She was walking toward town with a satchel."

Whit's frosted brows rose. "Really?"

Bax told him about his conversation with her. "It was like talking to a porcupine with a toothache."

The other man's chuckle rose from deep in his chest. He went back to his own desk and tossed a pen to Bax. "I guess that accounts for your argument with the storage cabinet. It'll sure be interesting to see how this is going to play out. I think we're in for some stormy times around here." At that moment, a clap of thunder rolled over Powell Springs, low and rumbling. "Uh-huh." Whit nodded once and turned back to his desk.

• • •

Amy put down her suitcase and umbrella on the porch of the house she'd once lived in on Springwater Street. She had first stopped at the bank to open an account with the check Mr. Parmenter had given her. The whispering and sidelong glances had canceled any hope that enough time had passed to let her slip into town unnoticed. News of her return would probably be the topic of every dinner conversation tonight.

Glancing around, she noticed the yard looked a little straggly. It was still early in the season, but the shrubs were already budding with little evidence of shaping or trimming, and weeds were gaining a foothold in the flower beds. She supposed that gardening had been given low priority on the list of chores Mr. Parmenter was overseeing. She had the key he'd given her but no one in Powell Springs bothered with door locks during the day. At least that was what she remembered.

She knocked and turned the knob. The door opened. "Excuse me," she called from the entryway. "Is anyone home?"

No answer. Leaving the suitcase there, she tiptoed around, feeling like a trespasser. In the living room she saw the sofa where she had spent so much time wrapped in a shawl while she recovered from the influenza that had almost taken her life. This was also the place where Adam had begun his campaign to win her after—well, *after*.

A shiver ran through her at the memory—he'd fed her his smooth, soothing charm and concern as if they were a spoon of warm honey laced with laudanum. His criticism and outrage over Jessica's treatment of her had been his white steed and flashing armor to Amy's ego. She had easily believed that his attentions were sincere, and she'd already thought that she had done nothing to deserve the condemnation of her neighbors. If only she had known then how much worse her life would become . . .

She continued through the house and found the kitchen tidy, with dishes washed and draining next to the sink. The floor looked swept and mopped, so Deirdre Gifford seemed to be doing well at the job she was hired to do. Amy realized that except for Deirdre, she didn't know who the other two boarders were. The lawyer had shown her a list but she hadn't paid attention to the names. Based on the chambray shirts and long underwear hanging from the line on the enclosed back porch, at least one of them was a man.

A Maytag washing machine, so new the paint still gleamed, stood in one corner. An amazing luxury she had never seen before, this appliance would provide an additional source of income, she thought. She could charge extra for laundry service, something that Mrs. Donaldson hadn't been able to provide when she lived there.

She walked back into the kitchen and poked around in the cupboards, finding the same dishes, glassware, and silver she remembered, which now belonged to her. What a welcome change from the meager utensils and mismatched dime-store table settings she'd known for the past few years.

Amy was about to head for the back stairs to check the bedrooms on the second floor when she heard the front door open. She bit back a sharp breath, worried about how her presence, uninvited, might look.

"Deirdre? Are you here?"

Amy froze. She knew that voice. Light footsteps crossed the living and dining rooms, drawing closer to the kitchen.

"Deirdre? I'm just on my way to the druggist's to pick up—"

With nowhere to escape to, Amy found herself face-to-face with her sister, Jessica.

"Oh, my God," Jessica uttered, the color draining from her face. "Amy? What are you doing here?"

She pulled her shoulders back. "I—I own this house now, Jessica. Mrs. Donaldson left it to me when she died."

"What? When did you come back?" Her arms dropped straight to her sides. The tension between them arced like St. Elmo's fire.

Amy intertwined her fingers into one tight fist, trying to hide their trembling. "Today. I stopped to see Mr. Parmenter about the deed."

"And your . . . husband?" Jess's loathing for him was unmistakable in her voice. "Is the good reverend fleecing a new flock?"

Though she both feared and now loathed him as well, she refused to let her sister know that. She dodged Jessica's sarcasm and replied, "Adam is involved in important business in Portland now. He might join me—"

"*Really?* In Powell Springs?"

Amy backtracked at the horror of the idea. "No!" Her sister's appalled incredulity made Amy's insides wither like an old bouquet. "I-I mean we haven't made any firm plans just yet."

Jessica looked her up and down, taking in her dilapidated appearance. "What has happened to you?" she whispered, as if viewing the astonishing aftermath of a gruesome roadside accident.

Pity was an attitude that Amy could not bear. This conversation only made her more aware of how far she had tumbled from the respectable, sheltered young woman she had been, loved and befriended by all, including her sister. She had squandered everything and everyone, and sacrificed her once-promising future through a series of selfish, ill-conceived plans that had backfired. Again she was made aware of her thin, charity-barrel clothing and wilted hat. Amy had never looked like this until she married Adam.

"The train trip wore me out." She fingered the glass knob on the cupboard door. "You are looking tidy and prosperous." Jessica's dark-blonde hair was swept into a practical but attractive style beneath a smart wool hat, and she wore her striped clinic dress under a fashionable camel coat. She seemed to have suffered no damage from the events of four years earlier. "You married Cole, I assume. But your office shingle still says Layton."

Jessica gave her a hard, sharp look. "Yes, we were married just after the war ended. I've never bothered to have it repainted." Her expression softened. "You have a niece, you know. Her name is Margaux. She's eight months old."

Strange that Mrs. Donaldson hadn't mentioned it. But perhaps by then she'd been distracted by her own failing health. Amy tried to swallow around the lump that formed suddenly in her throat. "No, I—I didn't know."

"Do you have children?" Jessica asked. The conversation was stilted and uncomfortable. Two sisters who'd been close—different, but close—now knew nothing about each other. They could have been strangers who stopped in the street to chat.

Amy shuddered at the thought of having children with Adam. An image of a Lysol bottle flitted through her mind, along with a red rubber water bag. A woman in the neighborhood had told her it was a surefire way to avoid pregnancy. Adam had exploded when he'd learned she was using it, and she'd heard some frightening stories about the harsh chemical, but it didn't stop her. "No, but we've moved around so much it's probably best . . ."

"Hello?" a new voice called from the entry hall.

"Here in the kitchen, Deirdre," Jessica called.

Red-haired Deirdre Gifford walked in carrying a package from Bright's Grocery. She took in the scene, and it seemed as if she might turn around and walk out again. She blanched and looked like a trapped rabbit searching desperately for an escape. "Oh . . . I'm sorry, I didn't mean to—it's Amy Layton, isn't it?" she asked.

"Yes, I'm the new owner of this house. I don't know if Mr. Parmenter told you about that."

"He did—"

"We should probably talk about what the new arrangements will be."

"And I'll be going," Jessica said. "I stopped by to see if you needed anything, Deirdre, but I guess you've already been out."

"Um, yes, I—"

"Good-bye, Amy." Jessica turned and, walking out, left a faint scent of vanilla and carbolic in her wake.

Amy ran a self-conscious hand over her rumpled clothing and nodded without a reply.

• • •

Jessica Braddock stood before her glass-fronted supply cabinet, making an inventory. She'd opened the doors to see around the red crosses painted on the panes. Gauze, morphine, sutures— some of the things she'd already gotten directly from Powell Springs Drugs this afternoon, but others had to be ordered and she needed to allow time for shipping.

She tried to keep her mind on her work, but it was impossible to concentrate. Seeing Amy had almost jolted her out of her skin. Beyond the utter surprise of discovering her in the Donaldson kitchen, she'd hardly recognized the pale waif dressed like a scrubwoman. The Amy Layton she knew had skin like rose petals and cream, never went anywhere without gloves, and wore well-made clothing. The woman she saw today was a worn-out stranger with gray circles beneath her eyes and hands that were chapped and fiercely red. She hadn't expected her sister to have a fairy-tale life with Adam, but this—it looked as though things had gone even worse than she'd imagined.

Seeing her also brought up a lot of memories she'd successfully pushed to a dark corner of her mind. Now they seemed as vivid as if they'd happened last week. The scandal . . . the betrayal . . . Adam Jacobsen's attempt to assassinate her character. The list was long.

So lost in thought, she stared at her inventory list without really reading it and barely noticed the overhead bell ring out front in the waiting room. It was just after six o'clock, past clinic hours, so she imagined her husband, Cole, had come by to give her a ride home. Jess had her own car, but it was at Jarvis Automotive after suffering another mysterious engine ailment. She swore that car was jinxed. She'd had nothing but trouble with it from the first day Cole brought it home to her.

"I'll be right there," she called absently, but quick footsteps sounded in the hallway, and they weren't Cole's.

Granny Mae Rumsteadt, as breathless as a winded old nag, appeared in the back room with Jessica's daughter, Margaux, in her arms. The baby's cheeks were rosy with the chill, but she'd been dressed well, bundled in a blanket, and tucked inside the old woman's shawl. Granny Mae owned the café across the street from the clinic and often took care of Margaux when Jess's sister-in-law, Susannah Grenfell, could not.

"I thought Cole was going to pick up Margaux. Is anything wrong?"

Granny Mae had grown more rangy and rawboned over the past few years, and her white hair had thinned enough to show her scalp, but she was as strong and as opinionated as ever. Occasionally the two of them still clashed over Jess's modern medical training versus Granny's home-remedy approach. Right now, though, she looked as if she'd seen the bottom of her own grave. Jessica took her daughter into her own arms.

"God in heaven, Jessica, I can't believe it. I just can't—"

Jessica's heart felt like it flipped in her chest. "What? Has something happened to Cole? Is someone hurt?" She looked at Margaux, but the baby gurgled and smiled.

Granny shook her head, still trying to catch her breath. Although trained to remain calm in emergencies, panic began to creep up on Jess. "What's happened?"

"Amy . . . it's Amy. She's back in town."

She sighed. "I know. I talked to her."

"What?"

"I was on my way to the druggist's, so I dropped by to see if Deirdre needed anything. She doesn't get out much, you know, and running that house keeps her busy. Instead I found Amy in the kitchen." She went on to describe their conversation and her sister's appearance. "How did *you* learn about it?"

"This is a small town. You know news like that travels fast. Virgil Tilly saw her not more than two hours ago walking toward Laura Donaldson's place."

Margaux squawked and waved her arms, reaching for the pencil tucked behind her mother's ear. Jess pulled her hand away and settled the baby on her hip.

"It doesn't sound like Adam is with her. At least Virgil Tilly didn't see him."

"He isn't yet—she says they have no firm plans. I don't know how that horrible man could show his face in this town again. I couldn't bring myself to speak to him after what he did to me and so many other people."

Jess sank down on a stool at the worktable and settled the baby on her lap. It wasn't that she'd never expected to see Amy again . . . well, maybe she hadn't. Their parting had been bitter, fueled by deceit and disloyalty that had left her feeling as if she'd been kicked in the chest.

"I knew that Laura willed her house to Amy. She'd hinted that it was her plan." Granny sat on the other stool.

"You didn't think to tell me?" Jess snapped.

"I didn't think much of it at all. Just because she inherited the property didn't mean she'd come after it. I didn't suppose anyone even knew where Amy was." The old woman retied her apron and adjusted her shawl—she was becoming as thin as her hair. "What are you going to do?" Granny asked.

Jess pushed a pair of forceps out of Margaux's reach and began fiddling with them herself. "I don't know. In all the time she's been gone, I've never heard from her. You're right, I didn't know where she was, either. She said they've moved around a lot."

Granny Mae put in, "Probably always one step ahead of the law."

Jess shrugged. "Maybe. I thought she might at least send a note to apol—to let me know—I never—I just didn't—" She was at a loss for words. The sister she had cared for and supported, and sent money to while Jess was working as a public health doctor in New York, had returned the favor by fabricating a story to make Cole and Jess each believe the other no longer wanted to marry. Then Amy had moved right in to have Cole for herself. She went so far as to win an engagement ring from him. But the truth was discovered during the influenza epidemic, which, for all its tragedy, forced the postponement of Amy's wedding, and Cole and Jessica learned how they had been maneuvered.

"I'm as surprised as anyone else," Granny Mae said. "There has already been grumbling about her, and especially about that humbug Jacobsen. They left a lot of hard feelings behind them when they ran off in the middle of the night. It's hard to believe he was the minister here. His father must be turning in his grave."

Once again, Jessica's voice dropped, as if she were talking about someone who had died. "Mae, Amy looks awful. She's so thin and worn looking. She's dressed like a washerwoman. I don't know how people will react to her."

The woman folded her bony arms across her chest. "Yes, you do. She's a disgraced outcast and she'll be treated like one."

Jessica sighed again. The past few years had been busy ones in Powell Springs. Progress, Prohibition, an epidemic, war, and even peace had brought killings, births, deaths, marriages, and mayhem to a town that had once been little more than a sleepy rural village. The population had grown, and now Amy had come home to throw her own as-yet-unknown trouble into the mix. Unknown perhaps, but trouble, surely.

The bell out front rang again and Jessica recognized immediately the long strides of her husband's boots on the hardwood floor. "Jess? Are you back here?" He carried with him the familiar scents of horses, rain, hay, and leather, scents that would let her find him even if she were blindfolded. "I went by Mae's but she and—" He stopped and eyed them suspiciously. "What's going on?"

She supposed there was no way to sugarcoat it. "Amy has come back."

He stared at her, obviously as dumbstruck by the news as she had been. "Where is she?" He looked around, as wary as if Jess were hiding a rattlesnake somewhere in an examination room or her office.

"Not *here*, for heaven's sake," Jess said. "I saw her." She told him about the brief meeting.

"Oh, damn it to hell." He yanked off his hat and beat it against his thigh. Flecks of straw flew. "If I have to speak to her or that weasely, pissant Adam Jacobsen—"

"If you don't mind, this is a medical office, you know, not a corral," Jess reminded him, gesturing at the dust. "Anyway, she's alone. For now."

Granny Mae added, "Tilly said she looked as scraggly as a hen locked out of the coop in the rain, hauling a battered old suitcase down the street."

"She does," Jessica agreed. She went on to tell him about Amy's inheritance.

"Did you know about this?" he asked.

She shifted the baby on her lap, who held out chubby arms to her father. "Me? No, I haven't heard from her since she left."

Already anticipating misery, he groaned, "Oh, God, I suppose I'll have to sit at the same dinner table with her and pretend that everything is nicey-nice and—"

"No, you won't! Let's not borrow trouble."

"We never have to borrow it. It volunteers," Cole grumbled. He took Margaux from Jess, and motioned her and Granny toward the door. "I should have known it was too good to last. Well, come on, let's all go home and enjoy the peace while we can."

CHAPTER THREE

After Amy introduced herself to Deirdre and explained that she intended to keep the boardinghouse in operation, she dragged her bag up the back stairs and chose the bedroom that doubled as a sewing room. It was the same one she'd occupied when she'd lived in this house before. The walls were papered with a pattern of tiny pink rosebuds, and lace curtains made the room feminine and almost sweet. It had always reminded her of her girlhood bedroom, when life had been simpler and she hadn't yet been scuffed and dented by mistakes and circumstances.

She hoisted her suitcase to the bed and opened it. Although it held no more than it had when she'd packed it, it seemed twice as heavy. At least she had enough money to buy some proper underwear, and fabric to make a dress or two.

Beneath it all, she saw the item she'd found beneath the loose floorboard in the closet in Portland, something that Adam might be desperate enough to kill for. As long as it was in her possession, it would both protect her and put her in danger. She needed to find a safe place to hide it, but for the time being, she put it in a dresser drawer, beneath some lengths of fabric that had belonged to Mrs. Donaldson.

The enticing aroma of cooking floated up to the second floor and she remembered that she'd eaten nothing but a stale cheese sandwich since leaving Portland. Quickly, she chose the only long-sleeved blouse of the three she owned and took off the one she'd been wearing for two days. In the full-length mirror, she caught a glimpse of four finger-shaped purple bruises on her upper arm and wrist. No wonder it ached. Lightly, she ran her dishwasher's chapped hand over the marks and was horrified to feel her eyes sting with tears. She'd forced herself to learn not to cry. Her tears had only fueled Adam's twisted pleasure in knowing he could break her spirit and make her cower. She swiped at her eyes with the back of her hand and did her best to fix her hair. After putting on clean stockings, she pulled her wet shoes back on. A longer look in the mirror, though, revealed a glaring bruise right next to the hollow of her throat, exactly the size and shape of Adam's thumb. She hadn't noticed it until now.

At least for the time being she felt safe—the first time in four years.

She closed the collar of her blouse and pinned it in place with a cheap glass brooch to hide the angry, plum-colored mark, then went downstairs to meet her boarders.

• • •

Whit had gone home a bit early to surprise his wife, Em, with her birthday gift, so Bax closed the office and then went home himself. Powell Springs was a pretty quiet town, and if trouble should come up, everyone knew how to reach him or Whit. He went around to the back door of the house, a habit he'd learned in childhood, when his mother had had six boys, often muddy, always dirty. He scraped the dirt off his boots on a clever gadget someone had constructed out of scrub brushes and screwed to a thin square of iron to keep it upright. It worked better than plain metal boot scrapers.

At least it had finally stopped raining. But the ground was sodden and he glanced back to see his boot prints grinding the spring grass into the mud.

On the back porch he washed at the concrete laundry tub with a piece of white soap and tried to make himself presentable enough to sit down at a dinner table. He was still getting used to that, even though he'd lived here for three months. Compared to the last few years, even the simplest meal in this house seemed like Sunday dinner every night of the week. In the evenings, they sat in the dining room instead of at the kitchen table, ate from flowered dishes, and by deliberate example Deirdre Gifford prevented him and the other boarder, Tom Sommers, from leaning over their plates, elbows on the table, and gobbling the food like wild hogs in a logging camp.

When Bax walked into the dining room, he noticed that Tom was in his spot at the table, but another place was set at a spot that was usually empty.

"Mr. Duncan, take your seat," Deirdre said, balancing serving dishes on a tray. "We have someone new joining us." She put down a large platter of roast chicken and sweet potatoes, with a bowl of vegetables and a gravy boat. Bax was in his chair and in the middle of tucking his napkin into his shirt collar when Deirdre looked up and inclined her head, making him follow her gaze. In the doorway he saw the same woman he'd talked to on the road that afternoon, the one Whit had identified when she'd walked past his office window. The napkin, without enough hold to stay put, fell out of his collar into a heap on his plate. She came closer, and when their eyes met the spark of mutual recognition almost jumped across the table like a lightning bolt. Color rose in her pale cheeks and he felt a flush work its way up his neck.

"Mrs. Amy Jacobsen, this is Baxter Duncan, one of your boarders. He's been Sheriff Gannon's deputy for what, three or four months now?" She glanced at him for confirmation.

"Yeah, something like that." He lurched out of his chair to shake her hand, but he'd barely touched it before she snatched it from his grip, as if he were a leper. She didn't have much to be so uppity about. Hers were not the hands of an idle front parlor lady, or a society wife who visited the poor and sick with baskets of soup and bread. She had done some hard work.

"Mr. Duncan," she acknowledged, her jaw tight. At least she looked almost as uncomfortable as he felt. That high horse of hers must have pulled up lame.

"It's just Bax, ma'am."

Deirdre Gifford said, "And this is Tom Sommers. He works at the sawmill on the east end of town." To them both she added, "Mrs. Jacobsen owns this house now. Mrs. Donaldson was the owner, but she passed away just before you got here."

Tom also stood and mumbled a bashful greeting. Though he had the husky build of a woodsman, he was still young enough to blush, and color suffused his face. Then he turned a brief, calf-eyed look on Deirdre, but she seemed not to notice.

Damn it, wasn't this just a dandy turn of events? Bax simmered. The porcupine on the road was now his landlady.

"Bax and I met briefly this afternoon," Amy said. She pulled out her chair and sat. "Nothing much will change here except that I'll be living and working in the house too, and I'll be collecting the rents now instead of Mr. Parmenter. The rent will stay the same. But I understand that Deirdre has been doing the washing here with the new washing machine. Since there's a laundry in

Powell Springs, that service won't be included in the price of your room and board. There will be an extra charge, or of course, you can take your wash to Wegner's Laundry."

"So in a way, the rent is going up," Bax said, trying to snag a sweet potato with his fork.

Deirdre passed the platter of chicken to Her Highness while she explained this, and he wondered what other things might change that were supposed to stay the same.

"No, not really. I don't think it's asking much." She took a piece of chicken from the platter, then paused with her hands folded in her lap while she stared at her dish. "I hope you'll all stay on here. I—I'm grateful to have this home and I appreciate your being here."

Bax's brows rose in mild surprise. Maybe there was a different woman beneath that haughty exterior. When she looked up again, he saw the same careworn expression he'd noticed this afternoon, as if someone had kicked her down the road in an old bushel basket to this point in her life. There was probably a pretty face under there somewhere, too. Dr. Jessica, what he'd seen of her anyway, glowed like a buttercup. This one was too pale and thin, but he heard she hadn't always looked like this. Then she tightened her jaw again, and the softness was gone.

She stretched out an arm to pass the serving dish, and in doing so the collar of her blouse gapped away from her throat. He saw a purple, thumb-shaped bruise that she'd obviously tried to hide. Her left wrist looked like someone had clamped it in a cruel grip as well. He'd seen a few women in his life with black-and-blue marks who'd claimed to have walked into doors or fallen down steps. It made him wonder what, or whom, Amy Jacobsen was really running from.

When he realized he was staring, he made a point of paying attention to his dinner and to stop speculating about her. His own circumstances were tenuous enough.

Amy felt Bax Duncan's curious gaze resting on her, and she struggled to keep from fidgeting in her chair. Self-consciousness about her own dishwasher's hands had made her pull away from his handshake. His dark hair and smoke-gray eyes were the features she'd noticed first and remembered most. He was nice-looking—handsome, if she were to be honest with herself, and at least as tall as Cole Braddock. But that didn't matter to her. She knew all about men now, and she realized they couldn't be trusted.

What were the chances that she'd have to cross such close paths with him again after their first meeting? And dear God, he worked for Whit Gannon. If Adam came looking for her here, would the sheriff protect her or consider her to be Adam's property to be returned to him?

Just the possibility caused a mist of perspiration to bloom on her temples. Maybe he wouldn't come here, Amy thought. How could he? Around her, the sound of silver on china clinked and the buzz of intermittent small talk hummed between Bax and Deirdre. She was safe here, surely.

When Adam got mad, she was the reason he lost his temper. Everything else that had happened was her fault. Hadn't he told her that often enough? She *made* him say cruel things and pound her confidence into dust as fine as face powder. Wasn't that what he always said? He worked so hard (although she wasn't sure at what), day and night, to achieve something, but that wasn't enough for her, ungrateful, nagging—

Amy tried to block out the memory. She didn't suppose that life here would be easy—it would depend upon how long people held grudges and memories. Still, this was her chance to start over, here in this house that had once been a haven to her. Here she could make up for everything she'd done wrong. As long as people would let her.

• • •

At three in the morning, Adam arrived home and looked around the dull cracker box of a house that he and Amy rented in the working-class Portland neighborhood of Slabtown. Feeble light from the one street lamp outside penetrated the clean, wavy window glass. He hadn't seen her for a day and a half. Because they both came and went at different hours, it wasn't all that unusual that they might have missed each other. But she was always home at night. He, on the other hand, was often out trying to drum up some donations for his ministry. At least that was what he told Amy, and she finally knew better than to question him.

She was a decent housekeeper, he had to give her that. Everything was neat and in order, but she was nowhere to be found. He detected no scent of cooking or hint of meals eaten. Even the dishrag at the sink was dry. Carrying the oil lamp from the tiny front room to the bedroom, it didn't look as if a struggle had taken place, so he didn't think someone had dragged her off.

Now he opened drawers and the closet door to find her clothes missing, along with a single, battered brown suitcase, which she toted from place to place every time they had to move.

All her belongings were gone.

Amy was gone.

He gripped the doorknob on the closet until he heard his finger joints pop. She had *left* him? How did she dare? He thought he'd deflated her overblown opinion of herself over these four years—she'd barely read a newspaper without his permission, and he'd cured her spendthrift ways by keeping her on a strict budget. He'd even made her turn over the pay she earned washing dishes at a neighborhood café. Now, without even so much as a note, she'd had the nerve to pack up and escape to who knew where—

He froze. Deep in that closet behind the suitcase was a loose floorboard, a perfect hiding place where he kept something important that she knew nothing about. The board wasn't easily noticeable, with a lamp or in broad daylight. With the tip of his penknife, he pried up the board and held the lamp over it. He saw a dark, empty hole.

Panic filled him, and then a fury so great that for a moment his vision was dimmed to a dull, red haze. He dropped flat to his stomach and plunged his hand into the hiding place and groped around, feeling for something, anything that might be what he sought.

He found nothing.

He raged through the tiny house, pulling out more drawers, spilling their contents, and overturning furniture. Then, with a kitchen knife, he cut open the cushions on the settee and tore apart the bed. Stuffing made of coconut shell fibers, feathers, and fabric scraps filled the air. He kicked and plowed through everything that landed on the floor, but he couldn't find what he was looking for.

Winded and sweating, he dropped into a hard hickory chair, the only piece of furniture still upright. Would Amy—cowed, obedient, timid Amy—really have the guts and the gall to leave and take his property with her? How had she even found it? Was there another man? The questions and possibilities flitted around his brain. She couldn't go back to Powell Springs. No one there, not even her sister, would forgive or forget what had happened in those last days of the war. But if she didn't come home by tonight, he'd go about finding her. Then he'd teach her a lesson she would remember for the rest of her life.

Her short life.

• • •

Under a rare blue sky, Whit pulled the Ford out into traffic in front of the Multnomah County courthouse. "I don't remember the last time I had to make two trips into Portland in the same week," he said, dodging an Alpenrose Dairy wagon that rumbled past. "I'm not too partial to the crowds and hubbub of city life."

Bax rode shotgun, happy to let someone else drive the shuddering vehicle for a change. "You know, I would have filed those documents when I was here the other day if you'd told me about them. I'm not that eager to come to Portland, either."

"It doesn't matter. We had to sign them in front of the county clerk. I guess they must think we don't have anything better to do than lose two hours to come down here and drive back."

Bax glanced at the neatly trimmed park that covered several blocks along Fourth Avenue and gestured at it. An ornate octagonal horse trough and fountain, topped with a huge elk, stood in the middle of the intersection. It looked a lot better than the one that stood in Powell Springs with a Statue of Liberty replica in its center. "Even this can't make up for all the cars and delivery wagons and people jammed on the sidewalks."

"I guess we're just country boys at heart," the sheriff said. "If I had to live among all these sky-high buildings—five-six stories— I'd skedaddle back to open, rolling fields where I belong."

They were making progress down Fourth, working their way over to the Morrison Bridge, when traffic came to a dead stop. Up ahead, some traffic mishap between a horse-drawn delivery truck and a taxicab blocked both lanes of the street. Vehicles surrounded them, making escape impossible.

"Damn it, I guess we're just going to have to wait this out. I hope I'm not ready for the poor farm in Fairdale by the time we get loose," Whit said, rubbing the back of his neck.

While they sat there with nothing to do but watch for signs of improvement ahead and take in the sights around them, Whit's sharp gaze riveted on a well-dressed couple coming out of a luggage store.

Bax noticed Whit's keen attention to the pair. The woman was wearing a fur-trimmed coat with a fancy hat, and the man guiding her by the elbow wore an expensive-looking suit and a diamond stickpin that even from where Bax sat seemed as big as an aggie marble. "Must be nice, huh?" he commented, assuming Whit was fascinated by the high-toned pair.

As they passed, Whit twisted in the seat, craning his neck to watch them. "I swear I know that man. Not the woman, but he reminds me of—naw, it's not him. It can't be."

Bax turned, too. "Who, Mr. High Society over there?"

Just then, traffic began moving again and the objects of their scrutiny fell behind their view and disappeared into the flow of pedestrians on the sidewalk.

"Yeah." Whit waved off his own comment, and as they picked up speed he shifted the car into second gear. "Lately I've come to realize that if a man lives long enough, everyone starts to look familiar, whether he knows them or not."

"You're not ready for the rocking chair yet."

"*Yet.* Maybe I could get a job like Wyatt Earp, offering my expert opinion on the West for the moving-picture business."

They both laughed at that idea, then Bax said, "But you'd have to move to California."

"Yeah. That's not happening. Hell, I don't even like coming to Portland." After a pause he added, "I sure wish I'd gotten a better look at that fancy dude, though. There was something about him . . ."

• • •

The next morning Amy closed the front door behind her and set off for Dilworth's Women's Furnishings & Dry Goods. The weather had cleared and the mellow sun made a valiant attempt to dry out the sodden ground, but it would take several days of blue skies to accomplish that. The hydrangea bushes along the sidewalk had begun to leaf out. Birds that had hidden in the shelter of trees yesterday during the downpour flitted across the sky, carrying tiny twigs and pieces of fluff to build their nests, and she could hear them calling to each other. Spring was here at last.

Last night, she'd lain in bed and felt comfortable and safe for the first time in years. For those few hours, no one would bother her; she didn't have to listen to high-pitched arguments or screaming children in some rundown rooming house or shifty neighborhood. Adam wouldn't bother her, although she didn't feel free of him—and she certainly was not free. For the time being, though, she had a reprieve. That would give her time to decide what to do next.

When she turned the corner onto Main Street, she looked at the tidy storefronts with swept sidewalks and attractive window displays. She sighed and allowed herself a private smile. It was good to see it all again.

But when she walked into Dilworth's, she remembered that not everyone would be glad to see *her*. A couple of other women shopping in the store whose faces were vaguely familiar saw her and put their heads together to begin whispering.

She knew this would be a test of strength she might no longer possess.

Sylvia Dilworth herself eyed Amy from behind the counter where the shelves were lined with all sorts of goods—buttons, hairbrushes, cans of beeswax polish, bolts of fabric, and trims. A woman in her fifties, she was bound up in a corset that made her look like an overstuffed sausage that bulged at both ends, and her mouse-colored hair had been tortured into curls that matched the look, one that was about twenty years out of style. She didn't seem surprised to see her, so as Amy supposed, news of her arrival had spread quickly. "Mrs. Jacobsen. I didn't expect you to come back to this town again. And not to this store."

Amy swallowed and forced herself to rise to her full height. "I used to come in often. I spent a lot of money here when I last lived in Powell Springs. And if I remember correctly, my sister took care of you and your husband during the influenza epidemic."

Behind her, Amy heard the door open but she didn't look up to see who else was going to witness her humiliation.

"Yes, she did. A fine woman, your sister, and Cole Braddock is a good *husband* to her." Sylvia narrowed her eyes. "I'm glad they discovered the dirty trick that was pulled on them to separate them from each other."

Amy paused, unable to think of an answer to the charge. Had Cole and Jessica told *everyone* what had happened? She supposed they hadn't needed to. At last, in a low voice, she said, "If you feel that strongly, perhaps I should take my business somewhere else. Based on what I've seen, you have a lot of competition from similar establishments now." The other two women watched the proceedings like avid spectators at a public hanging.

"Well, since you're here, you might as well get what you came for. Money is money, even if it's yours."

Amy Layton would not have tolerated this rudeness for two seconds. But that confident person was gone, and now Amy Jacobsen handed her list to the old hag, able only to wonder why she didn't turn on her heel and leave this place. She realized it was because she feared she would only suffer the same treatment everywhere else. It was her fault. Everything was her fault and she deserved what she got. Hadn't Adam impressed that upon her often enough? In his anger, which showed itself more and more frequently, even he threw her disloyalty in her face. His own offenses—spying on his innocent neighbors and reporting them as traitors to the government during the war, frequenting the local prostitute, working to ruin Jessica's reputation—faded to minor transgressions. Her memory raked through every unkind word he'd uttered, every viselike grip on her arms or wrists, every derisive insult about her hair, her intelligence, her body, her appearance, her behavior. Just when the change had come about, she wasn't certain. Gradually he'd turned into a different man than the one who had courted her so fervently in Mrs. Donaldson's living room. When he'd changed, he'd remade her as well.

"Did you bring a marketing basket?" Sylvia demanded, after she'd gathered everything on the counter.

"No, you always wrapped up my purchases with paper and twine before." She tipped her head toward the big roll of brown paper in a holder next to her order. She'd selected a number of small items such as spools of thread and cards of buttons that would get lost and be impossible to balance with everything else she had to carry if they were loose.

"We have a new policy. I'll have to charge you an extra dollar for that."

"A dollar! But—"

"Wrap up her stuff, Mrs. Dilworth. You don't charge extra for that and you know it. And I'll take a bottle of ink when you're finished."

The audience cast eager eyes at this new player in the drama. Sylvia looked past Amy's shoulder and gave the man a gray-toothed smile. "Nice to see you, Bax."

Amy glanced back, surprised to see him standing there and even more surprised that he had intervened. Thank the stars she hadn't bought underwear here, too. He didn't return Sylvia's smile, and hers faded. Grumbling under her breath, she wrapped up Amy's purchase and tied it with twine.

Amy paid her, and with only a quick look at Bax, she scuttled out of Dilworth's, trying to hold up her head but feeling like a whipped dog. Outside, she drew a deep breath to steady her nerves and hurried down the street, vowing never to return to that horrible place again.

Bax watched her leave and frowned at Old Lady Dilworth. He got his ink and emerged from the store in time to see Amy about a half block away, heading toward the house. He needed to get back to work, but something made him call her name. "Mrs. Jacobsen—*Amy!*"

She turned and paused, showing him only a three-quarter profile and looking around like a trapped bird. He trotted up to her before she could get away. "I wish that hadn't happened back there. Most of the time that old bitch—um, battle-ax—is rude to me, too." As he listened to himself, he couldn't help but wonder what had gotten into him to even bother with this.

She wouldn't look directly at him, but he could see the tears edging her eyes. He also noticed that furious-looking bruise near her throat that her collar didn't quite hide. Clearing her throat, she managed a crisp, "Thank you, Mr. Duncan."

"Bax."

"Yes, well, Bax. Thank you. If you'll excuse me, I have to be on my way."

As he watched her walk away, she tried to square her shoulders and straighten her back. He let her go without another word, still wondering why he'd stuck his nose into that scene. He supposed it was because he thought he knew how she felt. The outcast, the one everybody shunned, including his own family, even the woman he'd planned to marry. It was lonely, and sometimes solace could be found only with complete strangers. Or with people in the same circumstances.

The spring-sparse tree branches cast slim shadows across her small frame as she passed. Whatever she had done to get to this point in her life, she didn't look as if she'd prospered from it.

Aw, what the hell—he shrugged and with his bottle of ink turned toward the sheriff's office. It was none of his business. They had finally released Winks Lamont this morning, and he hoped the place was aired out by now.

• • •

"Do you think you can find her?" Adam Jacobsen asked a man who looked as if he'd crawled out of the gutter. He handed him a photograph of Amy that had been taken shortly after they left Powell Springs. She looked better kept in the picture, but it would have to do. She'd let herself go over time, turning scrawny and tired-looking all the time.

He had arranged to meet Milo Breninger here at Porter's Café, a working man's lunch joint down the street from the café where Amy worked. Or had worked. No one there had seen her in days and they were surprised that he hadn't either. Amy was as dependable as a railroad watch. He'd left with their concerned good-luck wishes ringing in his ears and a hot ember of rage burning in his gut.

They sat at a table in a dark corner with a rough-sawn plank floor, sipping gin hidden in coffee thanks to Prohibition. A few well-placed inquiries around the neighborhood had led him to Milo. He had a huge, ragged mustache and the diary of a hard life on his weathered face. He might have been in his early or midthirties, but it was hard to tell by the look of him. His nose appeared to have been broken a few times, and beneath the black scruff of a two- or three-day beard, old scars crosshatched his rough features. With his cheap, rumpled suit, he looked like someone who would kill a man for the gold in his teeth. But what could he expect? Adam asked himself. He wasn't talking to the Federal Bureau of Investigation. This was a shady, under-the-table arrangement.

The man studied the photograph. "Yeah, I might be able to track her down. But why ask me? Why don't you go to the police?"

"I'd rather keep them out of it if I can. For my wife's sake."

"What if someone kidnapped her? Wouldn't you want the law on the bastard who did it?"

"Of course, I'd want that . . . or maybe something else done about him. I thought you might handle it if that's the case."

Milo sat back in his chair and looked at him from beneath brows almost as bushy as his mustache. "What's really going on here, mister? Did she run off with some other fella and you just want revenge? I don't have a problem with that, but I need to know the straight goods or I won't touch it. I don't like surprises or walking into something unprepared."

Adam put on the expression of a wronged husband and sighed. "Yes, it's very possible there's another man involved." He doubted it but it sounded better. "But she also took something very valuable to me. That isn't part of the deal. If you find *her*, I'll find what she took."

"So what you really want isn't your wife. It's your property."

Adam signaled a waiter to bring two more cups of "coffee."

"I want both. After all, she's my property as well. You only need to send me a wire care of Porter's to let me know where she is. I'll take care of the rest. Of course, depending on the circumstances, I might have other work for you. But trust me, you'll be well compensated for your time and expenses." The cups were set before them. "Well," Adam continued, "are you interested in the job?"

Milo took a long swallow of the gin coffee, leaving a fringe of droplets on his tobacco-stained mustache. He wiped his mouth on the back of his hand and let out a rumbling belch. "How well compensated?"

"One thousand dollars. One-third down right now, in cash, if you agree."

Milo nearly choked, and put down the cup. "By God, you're not fooling around here."

"No, I'm not."

"And you say I wouldn't have to do anything but learn where she's hiding out?"

"Ideally. If you encounter obstacles, I'd expect you to take care of them. But otherwise no, unless I find that I need more help, for which I will pay extra. And you must be discreet about your business. If she discovers you and she's scared off, you'll forfeit the rest of the money."

"Don't worry about me. I'm pretty good at dodging trouble."
The man sucked on his lower front teeth—the upper ones were
missing—until he found whatever was stuck in them. He gestured
with a spoon he picked up from the table. "When the law got too
close to my trail a few years back, I just ducked into the army and
went to war. It was a risk, but a better one than life in prison."

Adam replied, "I would have made sure there was no one left
who could tie a crime to me to begin with."

Milo gazed at him with obvious amazement. "I never would've
figured you for such a cutthroat. You look more like a school-
master or a preacher or something in your plain, prim clothes
and with that baby-smooth face." He shook his head once. "Well,
you'd better give me what details you have so I'll know where to
start."

With the agreement made, Adam volunteered just enough
information to get Milo headed in the right direction. He kept his
tone direct and unsentimental.

Milo fingered the three hundred thirty dollars that Adam had
given him in an envelope, then looked up. "I sure as hell wouldn't
want to be your wife or her fancy man when you catch up with
them. Nope, I surely wouldn't."

Adam drained his cup. "I imagine not."

CHAPTER FOUR

"Harlan, all you do is work. You put in so many late nights, and now you're leaving again," Tabitha Pratt Monroe complained.

Harlan Monroe stood in front of a full-length mirror and knotted his tie. "Now, Tabbie, you know I'm a busy man. I have details to attend to. I'm paid well but Robert Burton demands a lot for his money. It's hard to believe he's retired—I can only imagine what he was like before he started running his lumber business from his office at home," Harlan replied, buttoning his vest. Moving to the marble-topped dresser, he picked up a pair of silver-backed hairbrushes and buffed his dark hair into place. Then he fastened a sterling stickpin in his necktie. He had dressed in his own bedroom but saw to the fine details here so he could reinforce his expectation that she spend her day with effective purpose.

He glanced at Tabitha's reflection in the mirror. They had been married for just over a year and she was still getting accustomed to acting as the lady of the house. She sat against ornate bed pillows and pouted in her satin-and-lace bed jacket just as the maid, Elsa, brought her breakfast tray of tea, a poached egg, and toast with specially imported rose petal preserves. Tabbie's bobbed blonde hair looked like an abandoned bird's nest after the night they'd spent. At least she was a willing lover, if a rather dull one. He faced her and gestured at the beautifully appointed bed-room, with its tall leaded-glass windows and French hand-carved furniture purchased from Gevurtz Furniture, one of the best stores here in Portland. "You can't say that you're unhappy with your lot. After all, you may have admirable social connections, but you were trapped in that schoolteacher's job until I rescued you." He tipped a smile at her and her pout disappeared.

"I know. I never dreamed I'd live on Park Place, on the same street with the Ledbetters and Washington Park." She sighed. "I just would like to share more time with you in this grand home you've gotten for us."

"You have all that luggage we bought—we'll take a trip later this year. And summer will be here soon. We'll have dinner on the veranda and you'll be cheerful again. Which reminds me, don't forget about that dinner party we're hosting here tomorrow night. I've taken care of the liquor and wine. I hope you've gone over the menu with the cook," he said, taking one last look at his reflection.

"There are a few things left to settle." She adjusted her ostrich-trimmed bed jacket with an impatient huff. "I wish the Burtons would host a dinner once in a while. Their house and grounds are so much more . . . *aristocratic* than ours with that beautiful view of Mt. Hood. And they have more servants."

They hosted many dinners. The Monroes weren't usually invited, a situation Harlan was working hard to change.

"Excuse me, Mr. Monroe." Elsa reappeared at the door. "The car has been brought around." They didn't have a chauffeur, but one of the gardeners did odd jobs like this one.

He reached for his coat. He had just recently taken delivery of a Chandler Metropolitan sedan. It wasn't as imposing as a Cadillac or a Lincoln, but it certainly turned more heads than one of

Ford's proletariat vehicles. "Thank you, Elsa. And try to help Mrs. Monroe find something useful to do today."

"Yes, sir." The maid withdrew.

Tabbie stirred her tea and gave him a stony look. "Harlan, *really*, I wish you wouldn't talk to me like that in front of Elsa. She won't respect me."

"She will as long as she knows that you're her superior and not someone to share gossip with. We'll continue to do well, but your role in this is just as important as mine. You can't lollygag around the house all day, just puttering." He considered an overcoat and then looked toward the window to see if it was raining. The sun had emerged so he abandoned the idea.

"Puttering!" She sat up straight against her pillows. "I have a number of responsibilities and things I tend to. The Rose Society is meeting today, and that alone takes a lot of my time. I'm the recording secretary, and you know we're in the midst of planning the annual Rose Celebration. Putting together the rose show alone is a herculean task, and that doesn't even begin to address the parade. Those women are impossible to deal with. They won't listen to a single suggestion I make even though they know I'm right. I know the correct process for *everything*. After all, I was a teacher—I went to normal school."

Harlan often thought that she had probably been at the bottom of her graduating class. Dogmatic, arrogant, and full of herself, but certainly not academic. Now and then he had to bring her down a notch, and that wasn't an easy thing to accomplish. But then, he hadn't married her for her intellect or for love. She was an old-maid cousin to an established Portland family. They'd been eager to marry off this highly opinionated biddy who'd been living on their charitable sufferance, and they had just enough influence to help him on his way to a life of power and wealth.

That was the dowry that Tabitha had brought with her, although she didn't realize it. Power was important, but wealth, that was the icing on the cake. If one had money, one could easily acquire power. Thus far, she'd proven herself worthy on that note.

"Do you know anything about roses?"

"No, but our gardener does. Besides, that's not the point!"

"Do they know anything about roses?"

"Harlan, I'm talking about proper procedure and—"

"Do they know anything about roses?" he demanded.

She gave him a venomous glare. "Yes, of course the flowers are beautiful."

"I don't care if they're growing flowers or weeds, but isn't that the objective of the society? To help establish and protect new varieties of roses? That was what I heard."

A frown scored her brow. "But those people simply don't follow *procedure*. There are ways of doing things that cannot be ignored." Her mouth thinned to a slit in her face before she continued, and he felt a twinge of sympathy for any child who'd sat in her classroom. "I could make nagging them a full-time job if I thought there was any hope they'd finally admit their ignorance, accept that I'm right, and learn what I've tried to teach them. They barely know the difference between meeting minutes and old business. I don't know why I bother wasting my valuable experience on them. They should be paying me for my knowledge." Her mouth thinned out again.

"It must be so very trying to possess a brilliant mind and have to deal with the rest of the simpleminded rabble."

"You have no idea," she replied with resignation, missing completely the sharp irony of his remark.

What an excruciating bitch she could be, he thought, and she wasn't important enough for people to tolerate it, or forget that he was married to her. She always tried to squeeze in the last word. "Well, for God's sake, don't offend any of them. Most of them have husbands I have to deal with every week, including Mr. Burton. His wife is the president of the society, isn't she?"

"I am the very *soul* of tact."

"Is that *s-o-l-e* or heel? Insulting them won't do us any good."

She made an impatient show of flapping out her napkin. "I am not incompetent, you know. And I can't pretend to be."

He rolled his eyes. "I mean it, Tabitha. Now, I really have to leave." He approached her side of the bed and leaned over to give her cheek what passed, at best, for a dry peck. "When I get home tonight, I want to hear about the final plans for the party."

"*Harlan*," she huffed.

• • •

It's that dream, Bax heard himself say in the dream's setting. This moving-picture show had been playing an exclusive engagement in his head for the last four years. It usually ran at night in his sleep, but once in a while his mind showed a matinee if he took a nap during the day.

The details might vary, but they were always vivid, and the end was always the same.

The stench of rotting corpses, garbage, sewage, and mildew was everywhere under the gray skies of the Western Front. Even when they tried to bury men in shallow graves, the thundering shells and pounding rain blew them out of the ground again. The task was futile.

Sometimes a German officer shouted the command.

"*Lassen Sie ihn nicht entkommen! Schießen Sie!*"

Sometimes it was an American.

"Duncan! Get back here, by God!"

In the end, the result was the same. He was left to die. In the dream, he watched the life flow from him, leaving his body to join the dozens of other corpses in the mud. Blood ran thick with the rain, filling holes and forming puddles. The very earth, scourged and gouged with horrible wounds, seemed to be bleeding.

The cause of his injury never changed and neither did the outcome. In the dream, he did die. And even though he knew it was a nightmare—didn't he tell himself so?—he was always shaken when he woke. But he was also grateful that it *was* only a dream. He was supposed to die but someone had decided to save him. Bax had rejected his commander's heartless stupidity and had paid the price for it. Of course, though the true consequences were miserable, he wasn't sorry for what he'd done. That had really irked everyone he encountered wearing a uniform— his lack of remorse. But insubordination had its price.

The battlefield promotion, the medals, and commendations had been stripped from him without the pomp that often marked the French army's elaborate ritual, but had lacked only a cigarette and a blindfold. In fact, the American Expeditionary Force rarely bothered with as much trouble as they had taken with him.

Several years later, he'd gone back to Cedar Mill. No one in town would have anything to do with him. His family—their reaction had been even worse. His father claimed they couldn't hold up their heads with his deed putting a big black mark on their good name and reputations. But he was alive, for whatever that was worth. He wasn't the same, but alive.

Awake now, he was relieved to find himself in his rented room in Powell Springs.

Slowly he rolled over to his back in the darkness of the quiet room in the quiet house, and felt the crisp sheets brush against his bare skin. He was conscious of Amy Jacobsen lying just on the other side of the wall. Nothing about her personality should draw him to her. He was no angel, but she had done a dishonorable thing, trying to steal her sister's intended. She possessed all the charm of a bottle of castor oil, and he hadn't seen her smile even once yet. Thanks to her, he'd have to take his wash to Wegners, which was damned inconvenient, and that lit a low flame under his patience with her. But there was something . . . something about her that wouldn't let him cross her off the list of images that floated across his mind during the day. Something bad had happened to her, of that he was certain. Whatever it had been, it was enough to change her from what he'd heard was a sparkling, confident, though selfish young woman into someone who looked ten years older than she probably was.

But, hell, everyone had their secrets. Some, like his, were bad enough to destroy lives—it had cost him everything.

So, she had hers. He had his own.

Outside, the rain was back, driven by heavy wind gusts that rustled the trees and shrubs and slammed hard drops against the windows. The sound served to remind him that her life was complicated by a lot of things, including a husband, and that only a fool wouldn't keep his distance.

Bax pulled the covers up to his chest to ward off the chill and waited for sleep—and maybe that damned dream—to claim him again.

• • •

The next morning, the sky was still gray and threatened rain. With her sleeves rolled up and wearing an apron over a black skirt, Amy stood at the Maytag electric washing machine on the back porch. It was only a year old, and Deirdre told her that Mrs. Donaldson had bought it just before she fell ill. To Amy, it was a wonder of technology that bordered on magic. It cut in half the drudgery of washing. In the tub, a load of Bax's shirts and underwear agitated beneath the layer of suds created by curls of laundry soap she had shaved from a bar of Fels-Naptha. She had originally planned to charge him and Tom Sommers for this. But after Bax stepped in to help her with Sylvia Dilworth, she felt she owed him something, even though that help had been uninvited, and it was exasperating. She couldn't very well give him free laundry and expect Tom to pay, so her plan to make money from this drained away with the wash water. It would be just this one time, though. She was determined that a single good deed wouldn't obligate her to a never-ending handout.

She told herself this, even as she remembered seeing him trot toward her on the street yesterday afternoon, the nickel-plated deputy's badge pinned to his vest, gleaming dully under the clear sky. And then hearing him hail her. *Amy!*

As she filled the washer with clean rinse water, it occurred to her that she'd never given much thought to money before she married Adam. She had never had to worry about such things and had supposed that nothing would change with him. It had been a rude awakening to realize that he was a penny-pinching skinflint. She'd had to wheedle money from him for every hairpin or pair of stockings she needed. As time passed, he only became more miserly.

In the kitchen, Deirdre presided over the wood-fired stove, cooking eggs, bacon, potatoes, and toast for breakfast. So far, Amy had seen no evidence of the odd behavior Daniel Parmenter had hinted at. She was a shy woman, and a whiff of sadness seemed to envelop her, but Amy chalked it up to her widowed status.

On the back stairs that led to the kitchen from the second floor, she heard the clomp of men's footsteps. Tom and Bax appeared in the kitchen, where the table had been set for everyone.

"Mrs. Gifford, ma'am?" Tom said.

Deirdre turned and nodded at the young man. "Breakfast is almost ready. I know you're due at the mill—"

He shook his head. "No, ma'am, it's not that, although I do appreciate it. I'm looking for my dirty clothes. I left them where I always do, in that basket in the bathroom. I wondered if you'd seen them, since we're supposed to take care of our own stuff now."

"I have your wash here, Mr. Sommers," Amy said over her shoulder, hearing the question. "And yours, too, Mr. Duncan." She left the machine to do its job, wiping her hands on her apron, and started shaking out things that had already been through the wringer. "Mr. Duncan did a favor for me yesterday, and I thought I'd return it by taking care of his wash. I included yours, too, on the house," she nodded at Tom. "Just this *one* time."

Bax looked at her with raised brows and a baffled expression. Then comprehension seemed to sink in. He walked out to the porch, ducking around wet laundry that hung from the retractable clotheslines. "Thanks, Amy."

His eyes bore an intensity that was ever present, and she wondered what had happened to him to put that look in their gray depths. "You're welcome."

Amy sighed. She had a feeling that "just this one time" was going to become permanent.

● ● ●

49

"How have you been feeling?" Jessica asked Susannah Grenfell. "You look *luminous!*" The two women sat in Jess's examination room.

Susannah grinned and patted her pregnant belly. "I'm starting to feel like one of the mares."

Jess laughed. "Well, at least you'll get a bit of a break—only nine months instead of eleven or twelve. Although toward the end, it will seem like that long, and you've got another two and a half months to go. How is Tanner handling this?"

The other woman shook her head. "I never saw him worry more. And he's the sort who'll sleep in the stall with a mare that's about to foal. He treats me like I'm an invalid and fusses over me so much, I try to find things for him to do to keep him busy. He's missed Wade and Josh since they've gone back to live with their mother. He fostered them for so many years when Em was working and couldn't keep them."

"You're hoping for a boy, then."

"You know women don't care, as long as the baby is healthy. *Tanner* might be hoping for a boy. At least I'll have you for the delivery instead of Granny Mae."

"There weren't a lot of choices. When Margaux was born it was either her or Cole. I didn't think he was up to the task. Actually, she's a pretty good midwife, and yes, I know she used to help farmers around here pull a calf now and then, although she's gotten too old for that. She's become Margaux's substitute grandmother."

Susannah leaned forward. "But what about Amy? Everyone is buzzing about her."

Jessica sighed and rubbed her forehead. "I'm not surprised. It was the shock of *my* life to walk into Laura Donaldson's old place and see her standing in the kitchen. I can't say that I'm holding a grudge—she's my sister, my only blood relative. And Adam isn't with her, thank God, but I'm not sure just what's going on. She claims he'll be along soon." She shook her head. "Really, I think people around here will tar and feather him if he shows his face, and I doubt that anyone would try to stop them, not even the sheriff or Reverend Mumford. As for my sister, she left a lot of hard feelings and burned bridges behind her."

Susannah, who had believed Amy was her best friend, later realized she was just using that friendship to get close to Cole. The shadow of an old hurt fluttered across her face. "I didn't realize how selfish and immature she was." She stood up and gathered her coat.

Jess stood, too. "I don't think anyone else did either. But I guess she's about to find out how they feel about it."

• • •

Amy did find out, almost everywhere she went.

One day she and Deirdre were walking home from Bright's Grocery on Main Street when she saw an old schoolmate, Glynis Landon, approach, holding a little girl by the hand. Amy smiled at her automatically, recognizing an old acquaintance, and not thinking of all that had happened since. Glynis merely glared back. Although the streets were muddy after another rainy spell, the woman pulled on the girl's hand to cross to the opposite side rather than be forced to share the sidewalk with her. Amy lowered her head for a moment, surprised by how much it stung. After all, this certainly wasn't the first time she'd experienced humiliation in the past few years, both public and private.

"You know her, don't you?" Deirdre asked.

Amy swallowed and cleared her throat. "Oh, I used to. I doubt that she remembers me, though."

Deirdre waited a moment before responding. "Your business is none of hers. It's not as if you ruined *her* life." She gazed at Glynis and her child across the street, then turned back to Amy. "Some people don't know what real grief is."

Amy nodded, but didn't trust her voice to speak again at that moment. She appreciated Deirdre's kindness, even if it sounded a bit backhanded. Yes, Amy *had* ruined her own life.

There had been other incidents like that one and her visit to Dilworth's.

She was now forced to accept that the price of refuge in her hometown was rejection.

A rare few did not see her as a pariah. Leroy Fenton, the telegraph operator who had unwittingly sent the telegram she'd signed Cole's name to, telling her sister that he was breaking their engagement, had died. No one working at the railway station knew her now. And at the time of her disgrace, some people were far too busy with their own concerns of death, grief, and war to be bothered with social scandal. Others had shorter memories or didn't care about her doings. Those individuals, when Amy encountered them, were indifferent to her. And that might be the best she could hope for. But she'd made up her mind that if people were rude to her, she didn't owe politeness in return.

She had to remind herself that she could survive the snubs. Her singular goal, to pick up the pieces of her old life—before the war, before the scandal—was more important than any other she'd ever had. But while dread and apprehension had been her constant companions when she'd lived with Adam, sometimes she still felt a weight dragging at her heart. At least she had a couple of new dresses, underwear, and a pair of new shoes. Her old ones, worn through at the soles and water damaged beyond saving, had gone out to the burn pile in the far corner of the backyard.

The days passed as she settled into life at the boardinghouse. She and Tom had arrived at a compromise regarding the laundry, which she now did for less money than she'd originally planned. They were an odd little mix, she and her tenants. But more often than not, she felt her eyes straying to Bax Duncan when he was around.

Worse, her interest and curiosity were increasing about the man she saw. Tom Sommers was beefier—husky, with a barrel chest and big hands that made him look as if he could pick up a felled tree and carry it to a wagon. But Bax . . . he moved with a long-legged, rugged stride that tended to make her follow his movements with her gaze.

Early one afternoon, as she stood at the ironing board in the kitchen, running the iron over the collar of one of his shirts, his image rose in her mind's eye. He was a lot like Cole Braddock and Whit Gannon in that way—tall, slim-hipped men who seemed comfortable in any situation. There was something more about Bax, though. In his eyes she glimpsed a troubled, shuttered look that did not invite questions. She knew nothing about him. He wasn't inclined to talk about himself the way that Tom did, although most of Tom's bashful comments were directed at Deirdre.

Amy was ironing a sleeve when she heard boots thumping up the back porch steps. As if her thoughts about him had conjured his presence, Bax walked in, obviously in a rush.

On the front of the shirt he was wearing, a large brown stain stood out like a cow pie. He unbuttoned the top two or three buttons and pulled it off over his head.

"What in the world hap—?" she began.

He recognized his own shirt on the ironing board and snatched it away from her. "I need that."

"But only one sleeve is ironed!"

"I don't care. I can't wear this," he said, wadding up the dirty garment and throwing it over a chair. "There was a fight at Tilly's between a couple of loggers and I got in the way of someone's flying beefsteak and gravy."

"Oh, my—"

"At least it wasn't a hammer fight."

"A hammer fight!"

"I've seen two or three of those, and they never end well. Anyway, both men are sitting at Whit's office. Since there's just the one cell, we can't put them together. One of them is locked up and the other is shackled to the hitching ring out front. He's a big, liquored-up lummox, and he's boiling mad, braying like a mule. I wouldn't be surprised if he pulled the whole damned thing out of the concrete and escaped. I have to get back."

Plainly unconcerned about a lady's delicate sensibilities, he stood there naked to the waist and wearing no undershirt. He revealed more muscle and sinew than she would have expected him to possess. She tried not to notice, but with him standing so close she could only drop her gaze to the ironing board. He pushed an arm through the unironed sleeve. The other one, flat, crisp, and ironed shut, kept eluding his hand and he turned in a full circle, chasing the opening.

While his back was to her, Amy saw two scars on the left side of his back. One was completely visible. The other disappeared into the waistband of his pants. They were horrific—the color of calf's liver—and she blurted out her question without thinking. "Dear God, what happened to your back?"

He whirled around to face her and gave her a scowl so dark and menacing that she backed up a step. "Mind your own damned business!"

Without uttering another word, he got both arms into the sleeves and started buttoning the shirt. Then he picked up the dirty one from the chair and shoved it into her hands. Charging outside, he slammed the door behind him and pounded down the back stairs, stuffing the shirttails into his jeans as he went.

• • •

Two houses down the street, a man in rumpled clothes, partially screened by a laurel hedge, peered at Bax Duncan as he jumped into a county sheriff's car and drove off. He allowed himself a very satisfied smirk.

"Well, I'll be damned," he murmured. This day was turning out to be even better than he'd expected. Yes, indeed—that thousand dollars might be about to turn into a bigger jackpot.

CHAPTER FIVE

"What do you know about Bax Duncan? Weren't you the one who rented a room to him?" Amy had Deirdre seated at the kitchen table with a cup of coffee. The scent of Amy's dinner rolls baking in the oven filled the air.

Deirdre cringed as Amy stood over her with her hands on her hips. She hadn't touched the coffee. "Yes, it was just after Mrs. Donaldson passed away. He works for Sheriff Gannon. Is something wrong?"

Amy described the earlier episode with Bax and his shirt. "Do you know anything else?"

"No—he doesn't talk about himself much. He doesn't talk much at all." Deirdre pulled out her handkerchief in time to catch a series of sneezes. She'd been sniffling since last night and now it sounded like a cold had a firm grip on her.

"And doesn't that make you wonder why? Have you seen the scars on his back?"

Deirdre frowned and swallowed. "Goodness, how—why would I? He's always been nice to me. You know, respectful. He might have gotten those scars in an accident. Anyway, a lot of men have scars now. We went through a horrible war, Amy. Maybe he was in the army and was wounded."

Amy sat down at the table, and the other woman visibly relaxed a bit. To Amy, it seemed the Great War had occurred in the distant past while she was still living in Powell Springs. After she left, the focus of her life had narrowed to her own basic survival, and so many other things had happened to her in the interim. "Yes, yes, I thought of that. He's been nice to me, too, a couple of times—" And not so nice a few times as well, she thought. "I didn't mean to say anything. But I was so surprised, the words just popped out. If you could have seen the look on his face when I mentioned it . . ." Amy shuddered. She'd seen that kind of furious expression before, the sudden, frightening switch from one mood to another, and knew what it could lead to. "He practically bared his teeth at me like a vicious dog. I thought he might hit me, he looked so angry. Then he had the nerve to throw his dirty shirt at me."

Deirdre's eyes widened, and she put her hand to her throat. "Oh, no, that just can't be! It's so hard to believe it of him. He's always been quiet and polite. He doesn't make any demands or cause trouble. Some men don't like to be reminded of what they went through in the army."

"We don't even know if he was in the army," Amy replied, not really listening to Deirdre's rationale while old memories of her own marched through her mind. "You never know about people. You might think you do, and then you see a whole new side, one you never expected."

"But if there's a-a *problem*, don't you think Whit Gannon would have discovered it by now? He's a good judge of people."

Amy pushed the creamer toward Deirdre. "Maybe." But she was still wary.

Deirdre let the coffee sit. "I have a sore throat—the coffee wouldn't help it. What are you going to do about him?"

Amy took back the cream and drizzled it into her own cup. "Nothing for now, except keep an eye on him."

• • •

Harlan Monroe walked into Robert Burton's office with a manila folder. Like the others in the house, it was an impressive room, lined floor to ceiling with bookshelves that contained valuable first editions and antique volumes. A large Oriental carpet covered the floor, one which a servant tended daily, combing its fringed edges as if it were a pampered cocker spaniel. Paintings and sculptures from around the world decorated the room, and behind Burton's mahogany desk hung a fine, rare tapestry from the court of Louis XIV. A pair of French doors opened onto the red tiled terrace that wrapped around the east side of the magnificent home and provided a broader view of Mt. Hood and the Willamette River. "For your signature, sir."

"And what are these, Monroe?" the man asked.

"Checks for the usual household expenses, the grocery bill from Strohecker's, the utilities, staff pay, and so on."

Robert Burton was in his seventies and still a vital, commanding presence in any room. His hair was Arctic white, although his carefully trimmed Vandyke beard bore a hint of the dark hair he'd once had. He had but two infirmities, which he made an effort to camouflage: arthritis that had put an end to his morning horseback rides around the hilltop property where his house was built, and eyesight that was failing to the point of being a serious disadvantage. He could see well enough to navigate his way through the house—he'd had an elevator installed to avoid the marble grand staircase—and for the most part still recognized faces and could address people at a well-lighted dining table. But in his office, he needed a strong magnifying glass to read even the largest print. All the eye specialists he had visited agreed that his condition, something they called disciform lesions, was stealing his sight. There was no cure.

Now he opened the folder and moved the papers this way and that, trying to read them with the big lens. At last he picked up a pen to sign the first check and his signature ran off the edge of the paper onto the desk blotter. In frustration, he pushed away the folder and its contents. "Damn it, Monroe, this is no good."

Harlan did his best to hide his jittery impatience. The old man was still sharp enough but could be querulous and easily upset over small matters. "Mr. Burton, you could use that rubber signature stamp we ordered for you. It's in your desk."

His white brows rose in an instant of recollection. "Of course, of course. I'd forgotten about that." He unlocked the drawer where it reposed and brought it out. "Thank you, Monroe. You're always thinking and you're resourceful. I value those qualities in a man."

Harlan did his best to put on a humble expression. "Thank you, sir."

"I believe I'll go up for my afternoon siesta when I finish here. You won't be bored, I assume?" the man said.

"No, I have your bank deposit to make and I need to pick up your pocket watch from the jeweler's." Harlan watched as Burton stamped the signature line with more success than he'd had writing out his name with a pen. Then he collected the papers and retreated to his own desk in a tiny office down the hall. It had a narrow view of the garden but at least it wasn't downstairs with the kitchen and the rest of the staff. And it had a door that locked.

With the knob secured, he sat down at his desk, made out another check, pulled out a rubber stamp identical to the one he'd ordered for Burton, and stamped it. Folding the paper, he put it in the inside pocket of his suit jacket.

He checked his watch and saw that he had just enough time to get to the banks before they closed. That was good. He had an important errand tonight that would require a significant amount of cash. It was a high-risk venture, but it paid very well.

• • •

It was late afternoon when Amy opened the door to Granny Mae's café. The smell of freshly brewed coffee and other familiar, savory aromas filled her head and stirred her memories. The restaurant had never had any other name but the word *Café* painted in red letters on the windows. And it took all the courage she could muster to walk into the place, knowing that Mae and Jessica had become friends during those days they'd fought the influenza epidemic, side by side. They had taken care of Amy, too, when she had been so ill she was delirious.

It looked the same as it had when she'd last seen it, right down to the checked tablecloths. She'd heard that Granny Mae and Shaw Braddock, Cole's father, had had a brief romance going until he'd died from a bleeding ulcer in 1920. She found the whole idea a little revolting, especially since Shaw had been more rude and abrasive than anyone she'd ever met. She'd doted on him when Cole had been courting her simply to win him over to her side and away from Jessica's, no difficult task. Jessica had always been the golden child, the apple of their father's eye. Corrosive jealousy and a schoolgirl crush on Cole had fueled her conviction that Jessica was not worthy of him. She didn't dwell on the memory. It was not something she was proud of.

Weary of the treatment she'd received around town, she wasn't expecting anything better from Granny Mae, and only Deirdre's sickbed appeal had made Amy come in. Her cold and barking cough had worsened and kept everyone awake last night. She swore by Mae's sovereign cough remedy. Amy had tried to persuade her to accept something from the druggist's or even Bright's Grocery, but the pale, wan soul looked so pathetic that she'd relented, if only to give peace to the rest of the household.

There were several people in the café, and when they glanced up to see who'd walked in, heads came together and the whispering began. Suppressing a sigh, Amy pretended not to notice and looked around for Mae. Finally the old woman came through the swinging doors that led to the kitchen, her apron as worn as her seamed face.

She looked Amy up and down, with her bony arms crossed. "Well, Mrs. Jacobsen, this is a surprise."

Oh, God, if one more person—just *one* more—said that to her, she'd scream. "I came here because Deirdre Gifford is down with a bad cough and she begged me to buy a batch of your medicine. Otherwise, I wouldn't have troubled you."

If there was one way to sweeten up Mae Rumsteadt, it was to acknowledge or praise her healing skills. Her hard expression softened. "Deirdre is sick?"

"Yes, but she's certain she'll feel better with your help."

Granny Mae sighed. "All right. Come on to the back and I'll mix up something for her."

Amy followed her and saw the chaos usually hidden from the customers' view by the swinging doors. Next to a slab of ribs, a roast she must have been cutting up sat on the worktable like a stabbing victim, the knife still protruding from it. A big cast iron stove crouched against one wall like a black, fire-belching dragon with its eight burners, and each burner bore a simmering pot of *something*. Bunches of drying herbs and flowers hung from a beam above it all. Amy wasn't sure if this was all food for the restaurant or other concoctions Granny Mae was brewing. She could easily imagine the old woman standing over a boiling cauldron, cackling like a witch in *Macbeth*.

Mae grabbed a white soup bowl from the shelf and mixed together honey, ground black pepper, and some mysterious powder, and finished it off with two hefty splashes of liquid that looked like vanilla. Taking a funnel from a side table, she poured the mess into a brown bottle and topped it with a cork.

"Here," she said, handing it to Amy. "In case Deirdre doesn't remember, tell her to take two teaspoons every two or three hours."

"How much do I owe you?"

"Since it's for Deirdre, nothing." The unspoken alternative hung in the air—*If it was for you . . .*

"Thank you." Amy turned to leave.

"Amy," Granny Mae said, stopping her. She looked back at the woman she'd know her entire life. She saw judgment in her eyes but also a hint of compassion. "Why did you come back to Powell Springs?"

She gave her a level look before answering. "Because I had nowhere else to go." Then she walked out.

• • •

"Duncan!"

Bax was headed for home when he heard someone call his name. He turned toward the source and saw a rough-looking bum in an alley between two stores that had closed for the day. It was still light out at this time of year, but the street was quiet. The muscles in his gut tightened and he moved his right hand closer to his sidearm. Something about this lowlife seemed familiar but he couldn't imagine why. He hadn't seen him around town. He kept his distance and stared at him.

"You have my attention. Who the hell are you?"

The man grinned, showing missing front teeth. "You don't remember me, Sarge? Tsk, tsk, tsk. And after everything we went through in France."

Bax frowned and his pulse began to thud in his ears. "No, I don't." He started to turn away.

"Remember that last day of the war? You got yourself into hot water for—"

Faster than he himself would have imagined, Bax rushed the stranger, grabbed his throat, and pushed him deeper into the alley. He thumped the man's head, once, against the brick wall. At this close range, he smelled of tobacco and stale sweat. "Let's try this again. Who the hell are you?"

A flash of fear crossed the stranger's face. "Milo Breninger."

Fog, mud, rain, deafening bombardments, corpses, disembodied limbs, misery, screaming horses, screaming wounded . . . In the time it took a shooting star to cross the sky, all these images whipped through Bax's mind—images that would never leave him, not if he lived to be one hundred. Sure, he remembered him now, a scheming, cowardly bastard who cheated at cards, complained about everything, and was always the last one over the top going into battle. He tightened his grip.

"What are you doing in Powell Springs?"

"Let—let go of—my throat," Milo croaked.

Slowly, Bax released his bristled neck. "Well?"

Milo slid farther along the wall to put some distance between himself and Bax. "I'm just passing through on business."

"Yeah? What kind of business goes on in alleys? Purse-snatching?"

"I just had to take a piss—"

"Powell Springs isn't that kind of town. We don't put up with that stuff. I could arrest you for that alone."

Now Milo smiled again through his ratty mustache. "I don't think so, Duncan. Don't you need a record as clean as a choirboy's to get a job with the county sheriff's office? I'll bet you didn't tell them about those good old days in the army."

Bax clenched his teeth until his jaw ached. "What are you doing in Powell Springs?" he repeated.

"I told you I have business here and it's none of yours." He nodded at the deputy's badge pinned to Bax's shirt. "But I'll bet the sheriff would like to know about his helper's past."

"He already knows I was in the army."

"But does he know the rest of the story?"

"What's it to you, Breninger?" Bax said, growing more tense and angry by the moment.

"It looks like you made a new start here, with a nice job. If you want to keep it, I think we need to strike a bargain, you and me."

Bax suspected where this was heading, but he wanted to hear the rest of Breninger's threat—because he felt certain that's what this was—so he'd know where he stood. "Bargain. You mean blackmail."

"Yeah, call it what you want. For the right price, I keep my mouth shut and you keep your job. Otherwise"—he shrugged—"I'll sing like a canary for the county."

"And get nothing."

"Not money. But sometimes satisfaction is good enough." His voice dropped and his smirking, oily tone turned dark with a lazy contempt. "You thought you were so high and mighty. Sergeant

American Hero. In the end, you were just the same as everyone else. Worse, maybe."

Bax's insides were churning like Amy Jacobsen's washing machine. He'd be damned if he'd pay this scummy son of a bitch a single dime to buy his silence and give Breninger control over him. There would be no end to the harassment if he started paying him. He was willing to take his chances and hope that this was a bluff. After all, the man was no saint, either. But if it wasn't a bluff, well, he'd been to rock bottom before. "If I were you, I'd leave Powell Springs. It wouldn't be hard to find information about you that would interest the law. But sing, canary—sing if you want to." He looked Breninger up and down, from his cheap suit to his greasy sneer. "Who would believe *you*? I'm not giving you one damned cent."

Obviously insulted, and disappointed with the outcome of his brilliant plan, Breninger turned red in the face and actually shook his finger at Bax. "Don't think I won't, you piece of shit! This isn't over!"

Bax waved him off and turned to walk away, hoping he'd successfully hidden his rattled nerves and shown only strength and fury.

"And I can go anywhere I want. This is a free country!" Breninger yelled.

Bax almost laughed at the juvenile absurdity of his declaration.

● ● ●

Amy left Deirdre in her bed with a hot water bottle, Granny Mae's medicine, a cup of tea, and some toast. She looked miserable and sounded worse, like a honking goose. Amy would handle dinner tonight, but she was up to that. Domesticity had always been her chief talent in her youth. Jessica might have had a scientific mind, but she could barely boil water. Amy knew her way around a kitchen and homemaking very well.

The first man in the door was Tom, but he dropped by just long enough for Amy to make him three sandwiches from the pork chops she'd cooked. He was working late at the mill. With Tom gone and Deirdre sick, that meant—

Bax came home, and she heard him on the enclosed back porch, following his usual routine of washing at the sink. She took dinner out of the warmer and put it on a platter. He walked in and nodded at her but wouldn't look at her. He seemed even angrier than he had been when he'd snapped at her yesterday.

She refused to acknowledge his rudeness and directed him to a seat at the table. "Tom is working tonight and Deirdre is still sick with her cold, so we'll be eating in the kitchen," she announced.

He sat down and pushed his food around on the plate but didn't eat much. If he was silly enough to carry a grudge, she wouldn't indulge him. But the silence stretched out until it was awkward, and she found herself poking at her own food. For the life of her, she couldn't think of what to say, and he didn't seem like a man who bothered with small talk. She supposed she owed him an apology, but it came hard to her. It shouldn't—she'd spent the past four years apologizing every single day for something. It had become an automatic response to apologize to Adam since he found fault with her for the most minor things. Now, though, it wasn't as easy.

When Bax wasn't looking, she studied his profile—his lean jawline, the merest cleft in his chin, the strong brow. He was a very nice-looking man, but with many secrets, she suspected. Maybe even more than she had.

"Mr. Duncan—Bax—" she stumbled.

He looked at her.

"I-I'm sorry about what I said yesterday. I didn't mean to blurt out—well, you were right. It was none of my business. I was just surprised to—"

"Never mind, Amy," he muttered, cutting her off. "I'm sure you didn't mean to be nosy."

How could someone sound polite and uncivil at the same time? she wondered, feeling stupid and no better for her effort.

He put his fork down on the plate with a clatter. "I'm not very hungry tonight. Maybe you can give this to Tom when he gets home."

He pushed away from the table and got his jacket where it hung on a coat rack by the back door. "I'll be back later."

Amy watched him go, and found herself sitting at a table with a pile of food and no one to eat it.

• • •

What a shitty, *shitty* couple of days it had been. Bax walked to Tilly's under a clear, star-flung sky, alert as a guard dog for any shadow or other hint of a person lurking around. A few people were on the street, but most were at home, eating dinner. Certainly he'd known worse times, but yesterday Amy had seen his back, and today that encounter with Milo Breninger had taken more out of him than he wanted to admit.

After the last few lousy years, he believed he'd finally found a place among the people in Powell Springs. He worked at a respectable job, no one knew about his past, and he'd even allowed himself to begin thinking about the future. Maybe a wife, kids, a place of his own.

He'd imagined that once with Polly, had it all planned, until everything had gone to hell. Sometimes he'd regretted not marrying her before he left for the war, as she'd wanted. She wouldn't have been able to shed herself of him so easily if he had. Then he'd think, what would he have been left with—an angry woman who despised him? Or maybe she would have divorced him before he got back and married Jack Bradshaw anyway.

So he abandoned that dream, along with a lot of the others he'd once had.

But now, when he pictured it, the image of that wife had begun to wear Amy's face. Amy, a married woman. He wasn't sure why. Maybe it was the combination of vulnerability and iron-willed strength that he detected in her. Or the sense that she could fill the emptiness in him that he'd known for so long. But at least he'd had a flicker of hope. Now that tiny spark might be doused by a man who had dodged the law by enlisting in the army—Bax had overheard him bragging about it in the trenches one night. He'd been a fool to think things could really get better.

He reached Tilly's, and when he looked through the windows, he was glad to see it was fairly quiet in there tonight. This damned Prohibition had really put a knot in everyone's knickers. Thanks to the governor, Oswald West, Oregon had even imposed a dry-state order three years ahead of the Eighteenth Amendment. It was an incredibly stupid law that was causing more trouble than it stopped. Bootleggers and rum-runners were making a fortune on alcohol smuggled over the border from Canada, and moonshiners operating their own stills were killing people with the brews they cooked up. Human nature being what it was, even people who usually didn't drink wanted to now. He was grateful that Whit Gannon didn't enforce the law around here, but this saloon was the only one he permitted to operate in Powell Springs. All

Whit demanded was that Virgil Tilly sell true bottled whiskey. If Virgil bought homemade hooch from anyone, or worse, set up his own still, Whit had promised he'd personally deliver Tilly into the hands of the Prohibition agents. There were a few men living up in the hills to the east who cooked up wood alcohol—Dr. Jessica had been called to treat a couple of their customers in the past few years. But there was no saving them.

Virgil Tilly was reluctant to sell a whole bottle to someone because deliveries were unreliable and risky, but tonight, Bax was willing to pay the premium he asked for.

He pulled open the screen door, and although there were only a few customers standing at the bar, a layer of what might be permanent tobacco smoke hung over them. They were some of Tilly's regulars. They bought the swill that Virgil made up in his back room for people who didn't want to pay for straight whiskey or gin. Some swore the saloon owner used horse liniment, Worcestershire sauce, Listerine, or plain water to cut a bottle of Canadian alcohol. He wouldn't own up to anything, apparently very closed-mouthed about his secret recipe, which tasted like poison.

It was a colorful place, Bax had to admit. Stuffed trophy heads observed the proceedings from their places high on the walls, which still bore posters left over from the war, a calendar, and other signs that reminded customers that no minors were allowed and credit was not offered.

"I tell you truly," Tilly testified to his audience. He had a piece of paper and a pencil in his hands. He gestured at the counter behind him, where he kept his glassware. "You'd think those loggers would be good for business. They can drink like it's their last day on earth, and they'll even pay for the good stuff. But if they get into a fight, all the profits go right out the door. Yesterday, those two lamebrain oafs broke ten dollars' worth of stuff. Ten dollars!"

He whacked his inventory list with the pencil for emphasis. "They even managed to knock down my four-point buck. Here, Bax." While he handed Bax his purchase, everyone else looked up at the empty space on the wall.

Tilly was still worked up about the fight and complaining to anyone who would listen. No one paid much attention to Bax as he bought the bottle and walked out. People had gotten used to seeing him around town and had begun to accept him as one of their own.

And now—now it could all be wrenched away from him, thanks to that greasy scum, Breninger.

Bax walked back to the boardinghouse and flopped on a back-yard bench. Maybe he'd brought this on himself. He'd started to make plans and the fates decided to slap him down.

Opening the bottle, he looked at the stars, as cool and distant as they had been in any sky he'd ever seen. If he could, he'd pull that blanket of stars over himself to hide from the yearning. All the things he'd once thought would be his—they never would be as long as someone knew his story, no matter how far he ran or where he tried to hide. He lifted the bottle in a weary salute to those ghosts in his past and took a drink.

• • •

It was late when Amy went to the porch to retrieve a nightgown she'd brought in earlier from the clothesline. It needed ironing but she was just tired enough to talk herself out of the task. Any-way, the sun and a stiff east wind had pretty much worked out the creases made by the wringer.

The darkened room allowed her to see into the backyard, and she froze when she noticed a dark figure sitting on the bench out there. Who—Adam—was it him? Could it be? Her heart seized in her chest and then took off like Cole Braddock's thoroughbred stallion.

A half-moon was just climbing over the roof line and still hid the bench in its shadow. Everyone was home, she thought, running a head count through her mind. But then she remembered that Bax had gone out and not returned. She leaned closer to the glass and peered, trying to tell if it was him. When he lifted his head to look at the sky, she recognized his dark profile and released her breath. What on earth was he doing out there at this hour? It was almost midnight. He took a drink from what looked like a bottle.

She stepped over to the door and gripped the knob. It was cool and round under her touch, with a raised design that impressed itself into her palm, and she hesitated. She felt drawn to Bax but had yet to understand why. He was taciturn, sometimes to the point of rudeness, and he did not invite questions. Her own behavior at their first meeting still embarrassed her, and probably hadn't helped the situation. Then there was the matter of Adam, who always lurked in the corner of her mind regardless of what she was doing or what time it was. At least he wasn't lurking in the yard. Not right now anyway.

Finally she released her grip and took a last backward glance. Bax's head and shoulders were now in the moonlight, and he looked as if the misery of the world lay upon him. A sharp pang of empathy twisted her heart before she turned and went upstairs.

CHAPTER SIX

Beneath the dark girders of the Hawthorne Bridge, Harlan Monroe waited for a large rowboat to make its way to the west bank of the Willamette River. A shaded lantern bobbed in and out of sight, marking the boat's progress.

He'd brought along Ralph Boyer and Paul Church, the men who maintained the grounds around his house. He'd used them before, paying them the princely sum of one hundred dollars each, more money for a few hours than either of them saw in two months' wages. Only Harlan was armed, but he'd never fired a weapon in his life. This was nerve-wracking, dangerous work, but it also paid handsomely, far more so than what he made working for Robert Burton, and that was considerable. Especially if Harlan included the perquisites that had helped to fund his personal ventures, such as this one. Some men might be tortured by guilt and a conscience that harped at them relentlessly. Fortunately, he was not one of those men. He slept unencumbered by such annoyances.

Harlan had learned many useful lessons, but the most valuable of all taught him that money was the power and the glory. Right now, Prohibition could bring that to him.

The water shimmered like black oil when the occasional headlamps of an auto passed overhead on the bridge. At this hour, two in the morning, not many people were out and about, particularly under the bridges. It was cold down here beside the river. At last the boat approached the shore and two rough-looking men in black clothes threw out lines to tie up. Although he'd bought smuggled alcohol before, these two were strangers to him. Behind them, Harlan could see wooden cases of Canadian scotch stacked two and three high on the bottom.

"We've got a delivery here," the smaller of the two said. He eyed Harlan in his suit, although it was difficult to tell *which* eye was looking at him since they didn't line up. "Are you the one who ordered it?"

"Yes, ten cases. Where are Engels and Flett?"

"Busy with another job. Let's see the money."

"Just a minute," Harlan replied. "I want to open one of the cases first. I'll choose it, and if everything is fine, then you'll see the money." He didn't know these two thugs, and he wasn't about to pay good money for turpentine or worse, plain water.

He walked over to the river's edge where the boat gently bumped against a piling. He nodded at his men. Boyer held a lantern, and Church waded into the shallow water to select a random box and brought it to Harlan. The bigger man pried it open with a crowbar and Harlan pulled out a bottle to look at in the lantern light. Opening it, he took a taste. The sharp but mellowed flavor filled his head.

He nodded and extracted an envelope from inside his coat. It contained two thousand dollars. "All right." He looked at his men and said, "Put it in the car."

Odd Eye took the envelope and counted every bill. "This is two thousand dollars. I need twenty-five hundred. The price is twenty-five hundred."

Harlan knew that, but he also knew he could do better. "That isn't what I was quoted," he bluffed. He wasn't born yesterday and he'd watched Burton haggle prices often enough to know how to dicker, although he'd never tried it himself. And Burton had been buying lumber, not smuggled goods. Still, if he could save the five hundred, it was worth the effort. "I was told two thousand and not a dollar more."

"Mister, this isn't bargain day at that Fred Meyer grocery store on Fifth Avenue. Either pay the going rate or we'll take this booze back upriver."

"*Not a dollar more.*" He knew he had to stand firm.

"You two," Odd Eye said to Harlan's gardeners, "put those cases back in the boat."

They looked at Harlan for confirmation but he shook his head, still certain he could win this negotiation. "No. You've got a fair price in that envelope, and that's all you're getting."

Chaos erupted when Odd Eye pulled out a revolver. A flash exploded from the muzzle and the sound of gunfire echoed off the bridge piers and the deck above. Paul Church screamed and clutched his belly, and even in this low light, Harlan saw blood pouring from the smoking wound. He stared at the sight in slack-jawed horror, barely able to comprehend what had happened. He reached for his own weapon inside his jacket and fired a wild shot.

"Get those damned cases back!" Odd Eye barked at his companion. The man moved fast while Boyer, Harlan's remaining assistant, scurried up the bank and took off running toward Front Avenue.

"My God—" He backed up from the barrel of Odd Eye's gun, which was now pointed at him. His heart felt as if it were lodged in his throat like a pulsating duck egg.

"Next time, you'll remember not to try to cheat the people you do business with. This isn't some bullshit game, Mr. Muck-a-muck. This is serious," Odd Eye growled.

The wounded man lay on the ground, writhing and moaning. Shocked and in fear for his own life, Harlan's false courage dried up like a raindrop on a hot rock. He ran to the driver's side of the car, jumped in, and sped off, abandoning his mortally injured gardener in the mud beside the Willamette River.

With his ears still ringing from the noise of the gunshot and the sound of his own blood pumping through his head, he left without his money and with only a single case of scotch. The Chandler sedan's wheels spun as he jammed his foot on the accelerator, but after what seemed like an eternity, they gained traction and he reached the street. The tires squealed as he made the turn onto the cobblestones.

To his left he saw a witness, a man who stared at him and his car with an open mouth. *Damn it!* Did the man look familiar or was it only Harlan's feverish imagination? Sweat poured down his face and soaked through his clothes. His whole body shook so badly he could barely keep the car in a straight line on the deserted late-night street. On top of that, he kept looking back over his shoulder to see if he was being followed. He knew it was irrational. No rowboat could pursue him, nor a man on foot, but his feverish imagination galloped on. Maybe the bootleggers had lookouts posted in case of an event like this one. *Someone* else had seen what happened. Every shadow on the sidewalk was sinister; every stray drunk on the street was a potential killer.

How could things have gone so wrong, he wondered, swiping at his forehead. What was he going to do now? He drove up Pine Street, down Oak, over to Broadway, zigzagging his way through the lower streets. When he felt certain that no one was behind him, he made his way up the hill to Park Place, past the majestic homes, now dark as their occupants slept peacefully. The grisly scene he'd just been through played through his mind over and over. Leaving Church in the weeds to die was far down the list of his worries. His greater concerns were if he had been recognized by anyone and whether Boyer would blab everything that had happened. He could only hope that the man was frightened enough to keep his mouth shut and would never come to the house again.

Right now his goal was to return to birdbrained Tabbie, who would believe any remotely plausible story, before he decided his next move.

He pulled into the driveway and parked in the back, certain the car couldn't be seen from the street. Somewhere on the block a dog barked several times, then gave up with a halfhearted grunt. Harlan entered the house through the kitchen door. Looking down the hallway, he saw that his wife had left a lamp on for him in the foyer. She always that did when he came in late. As irritating, spoiled, and self-satisfied as she could be, he knew she was a loyal spouse, and right now he wanted nothing more than to be safely lodged in her bed.

He tiptoed up the stairs and into their adjoining bedrooms, which overlooked the street and the park. Stripping off his expensive suit, he left the jacket, vest, and trousers where they landed and made his way to Tabitha's side.

"Harlan?" she mumbled, rolling over toward him and touching his shoulder. "What time is it?" A faint breath of an exclusive new French perfume, Chanel No. 5, escaped the folds of the sheets. One of Tabitha's cousins had brought it back to her from Paris, and she now wore it day and night.

"Time for us be asleep."

"Did your meeting go well?"

He put a dry peck on her forehead, actually glad to see her. "Tomorrow. We'll talk about it tomorrow."

She drifted off again but all Harlan could do was lie awake, staring through the darkness at the plaster acanthus medallion above the bed, reliving the events down at the river. After twenty minutes of this, he noticed the glow of headlights creeping across the ceiling from the street below. The lights came to a stop in front of the house, where a car idled for a moment.

He bolted upright and went to the window, hiding behind the damask drapes, his blood pumping hard enough to sound in his ears.

"Harlan? What is it?" Tabitha called from the bed. She slid out and padded over to him. Peering around his shoulder she asked, "Who is that?"

"Go back to bed and stay there," he ordered quietly, never taking his eyes from the vehicle.

She didn't move, but the dark coupe slowly pulled away from the curb and disappeared into the night.

• • •

"That's what Amy said, Jess. 'I had nowhere else to go.'"

Jessica and Granny Mae were sitting over coffee at the café. A few customers sat at tables by the windows but the morning breakfast rush hadn't started yet. Jessica and Mae lingered at a back table.

Jessica gripped her temples between thumb and middle finger. "God, what does that mean? Did she leave Adam? Did he throw her out? Where has she been living?"

"I don't know. That's all she told me and I didn't think I should ask anything more. But you could."

Jess was surprised. Granny Mae never hesitated to speak her mind or voice an opinion, which was one of the reasons they had butted heads in the past, and still did once in a while. In fact, she could be quite blunt and tactless. But the soft heart beneath her tough exterior made her a worthy and loyal friend.

Jessica sighed. "I could, but why should I have to be the one to extend an olive branch? Cole and I were the injured parties, and Adam Jacobsen tried to run me out of town after I turned down his marriage proposal. He *did* chase me off for a while, with his vile accusation of my 'low moral character.' You can't have forgotten that town council meeting when he tried to turn everyone against me—you were there. And all he'd seen was Cole and me kissing on the front stoop of my office one morning." With greater indignation she added, "He approached us in front of the building, like he'd been waiting out there for us, and called me a fornicator and an educated tramp!"

Granny Mae gave her cold coffee a stir. "I know. But in the end, didn't you come out way ahead?"

"Yes, I did," Jess admitted. "I have Cole and Margaux, and my practice here. But it was a close call."

"Well, remember that saying, what doesn't kill you makes you stronger."

She sat up straighter and looked at the older woman. "Mae! I never took you for the philosophical type. What do you know about Nietzsche?"

"Knee—what? What's that?"

"Friedrich Nietzsche—he was an eccentric German philosopher. At least *I* think he was eccentric. He's the one who wrote that."

Granny flapped a dismissive hand. "Oh—I don't know anything about Germans except they fought in the war, and Mrs. Schulze makes a wonderful apple strudel that wins a blue ribbon every year at the county fair. I know a couple of German swear words, too."

Jess laughed, but then her smile dimmed again. "What am I going to do about Amy? Pretend that nothing happened? I won't do that. I can't." She lowered her gaze to the table. "And she said horrible things to me."

"Still . . . you might give her a chance to mend fences. Maybe she's not brave enough to come to you first. I think she's in trouble and has probably paid for what she did."

Jessica pursed her lips. "She was in trouble when her shenanigans were revealed and she ran away with Adam to avoid the consequences. Now she's run away from *him*, and how convenient to have an inherited house to come back to. I don't think she knows what real trouble is." Her memory flew back to the time she worked in the New York tenements, where she saw true misery as a public health physician. Women dying in childbirth; scores of children dying before their fifth birthdays; people crammed into tiny, windowless, airless flats, sometimes ten to a room. Beaten wives, drunken husbands, trapped in an endless cycle of poverty and ignorance, rats and cockroaches. Ultimately, her dedication to humanity's poorest was tested, and she'd failed, broken and disillusioned. She had run away, too. But all the while, she was sending money home to support Amy, and her sister had repaid her by lying about Jessica and trying to steal Cole's heart.

"You don't hate her—"

Jess looked up suddenly. "No, of course not. But I'm not rushing to her with bouquets of flowers, either! And Cole isn't too happy about all this."

Alexis Harrington

"Jessica, Jessica." Granny shook her head. "You're still young enough to see everything as either black or white. Sometimes things are gray."

Mae must have mellowed, as well, Jess thought. When she'd first come back to Powell Springs, the old woman had been suspicious and resentful of her, a college-educated physician she eyed as an uppity smart aleck determined to make her look foolish. A lot had happened since those early days.

"I've heard talk around town—others are blackballing her, too." Granny related the episode at Dilworth's, as told to her by Sylvia. "Since I didn't see it myself, I can't swear to the truth of it. But that should give you some idea of how things are going for her. Sylvia was just *gloating*."

"No one has said a word about Amy to me."

"I don't suppose they would."

Jess toyed with the sugar dispenser. "I guess I could invite her to lunch . . ."

Granny Mae pushed out her chair as more customers began to file in. "Dinner would give you more time to talk."

Jessica looked at the watch pinned to the bib of her apron. "All right, I'll *think* about it. I've got clinic in fifteen minutes so I'd better go. Thanks, Granny."

As she crossed the street to her office, Jessica tried to imagine how she would word such an invitation.

Hello, Amy. I see you've landed on your feet. Again.

• • •

Adam sat at the window and looked down at the street from his second-floor room in the recently constructed New Cascades Hotel. He had a perfect view of Main Street, but so far he hadn't seen anyone he recognized since he'd arrived in Powell Springs late last night, except for Milo Breninger. Adam had not imagined it would take the man almost a month to find Amy. He'd all but given him a step-by-step map—her photograph, instructions on where to find her, and money. He realized that paying him so much up front had been a mistake, one that stalled the search while Breninger swaggered from one bar to another, buying women and drinks for his lowlife pals.

Early this morning, Adam had taken the train from Portland to meet Breninger in Twelve Mile, the next town over, to get better details. Breninger had expected to be paid the other six hundred seventy dollars and go his merry way, but Adam decided he might require the man's help to accomplish his goal. He convinced him to string along for a while and act as his spy. He needed a person no one would recognize to keep tabs on Amy's comings and goings. Breninger had been furious, but Adam persuaded him with flattery, vague hints of a bonus, and a veiled but cold-blooded threat. Milo was a tough bum, but Adam fancied that the man was afraid of him. That gave him great satisfaction—and an advantage.

The town had grown so much since he'd last been here, he could scarcely believe it. New stores, offices, and restaurants lined the adjacent streets, and more autos and foot traffic made the once-quiet village more lively and vibrant. There was even a new moving-picture theater on Powell Springs Road, the main east-west thoroughfare in town.

Despite the increased population and busyness, he knew he dared not stay here long and risk the chance of being seen before he found Amy. He'd come as soon as he could after receiving Breninger's telegram at Porter's Café. The wire told him she was back here, as he'd suspected, living at the same boardinghouse where he'd visited her during the last days of the war.

Letting the curtain fall into place, he sat at the small desk in the room, pondering his next move. He'd learned a lot from the desk clerk by asking some casual questions and pretending to be a stranger to this place. With very little coaxing, the clerk, a chatty man with no discretion—something Adam noted for his own protection—had told him a number of helpful details about the past couple of years in Powell Springs. Marriages, births, deaths, arrests, even killings.

He'd get Amy back. He'd get his property back. After all, they both belonged to him.

CHAPTER SEVEN

Amy had looked out the porch windows often enough to decide that she couldn't ignore the state of the large backyard any longer. She took advantage of a stretch of clear weather to tend the roses growing in ragged, weed-filled beds. Wearing her last old dress, an apron, and a pair of gloves, she went outside with a couple of garden tools, a can of coffee grounds mixed with broken eggshells, and a watering can filled with a sulfur mixture for the roses. She wore her hair in a braid and it hung over her shoulder with a ribbon tied at the end. She'd hired one of the neighbor boys to pull the weeds out here, but he'd missed more than half of them. Still, it almost made her feel young again to kneel on a pad of old newspapers and dig in the soil with her trowel under the warmth of the mild spring sun. It was easy to forget, just for a while, the troubles she'd known for so long. Now there wasn't much she couldn't do. She didn't have to like it, but she'd been forced to learn such basics to survive.

She was busy snipping off rose leaves withered from black spot when she heard someone at the gate. Alarmed, her back stiffened, she gripped the sharp-pointed shears and looked up, always expecting to see Adam. She feared that he would show up eventually . . . the how and when were what drove her to distraction. But it wasn't him this time. She saw Bax come in and let the spring-loaded gate slam behind him.

He nodded and walked toward her.

"Hi, Amy."

She shaded her eyes. From this angle, his legs looked as long as telephone poles. Everything about him called to the woman in her, even though she resisted the feeling. His dark hair and lean torso. He crouched beside her, one elbow on his knee, and the small, raw flame she saw in his eyes almost took her breath away. It was a feeling she'd never known before, not even with Cole. Was he just a mysterious attraction because she knew so little about him? Still, she couldn't forget that scene over the ironing board, and it made her wary.

"Hello, Bax."

He nodded at the flower bed she'd been weeding, where her cleared area plainly ended with an abrupt edge. "This looks like a Winks Lamont job."

"No, I paid the Newton boy to do it, and to chop wood for the stove." Then she waved a dismissive hand and shook her head. "Either it didn't hold his interest or he gave up."

He gave her a wry smile. "The result is about the same. Tilly usually asks where the money comes from when Winks can afford to buy a drink. It's free entertainment for the rest of his customers to hear the stories."

Amy snipped another yellowed rose leaf. "*Entertainment?* Did you hear about him working with another man during the influenza epidemic? Fred Hustad—he's got the furniture store and the undertaking business in the back of his place—he hired them to dig graves and bury the people who died. There were so many, he couldn't keep up and they were stacked in coffins behind the high school." She stopped for a moment, remembering those horrible, dark days. Her memory spun backward to her own experience of drifting in and out delirium while she lay in one of the beds of the makeshift infirmary Jessica had managed to set up in the school gymnasium. She sighed. "Bert Bauer, the other man, was married to Em Gannon before he abandoned her a few years before. He saw himself as the smart one of the two." Idly, she pulled out a weed and shook the soil from its roots, then threw it on the pile she'd gathered. "Winks followed along, and before those people were buried, they'd been stripped of anything valuable they were supposed to take to their graves—jewelry, watches, family keepsakes. God, I think even gold teeth. *He* bought drinks at Tilly's." Of all the wrongs she had seen committed, and committed herself, robbing dead people was the worst.

Bax plucked a blade of grass and spun it between his fingers. "Whit told me. It sounds like all kinds of things were going on back then. Bauer was shot and killed a couple of years ago."

She stared at him. Deirdre hadn't mentioned it. "I didn't know that. This used to be a quiet, out-of-the-way place. But between the influenza outbreak and the war—" She paused to cast him a sidelong glance to see if the latter provoked a reaction, but his expression didn't change. "Powell Springs has turned into a busy town. Was that you I saw sitting on the bench out here the other night?"

He looked off into the distance at the lushly timbered butte and hills south of town. "What if it was?"

Amy tugged hard on a dandelion that seemed to have a taproot that went down twenty feet. "I was just wondering. At first I thought maybe—I thought it might be a stranger or—or someone else."

He sighed. "I didn't think you'd want me drinking in the house. Besides, sometimes I'm not very good company and I just want to be alone."

She nodded and let his answer stand, but only because she couldn't bring herself to pry. A dozen questions bumped around in her mind. Then she pulled so hard on the stubborn weed that she lost her balance and fell backward when the thing finally gave way.

Bax sprang forward and grabbed her left wrist to pull her upright. She winced at the pain that lingered from a year-old fracture. Although it had been splinted by a doctor who asked no specific questions as to how she'd broken her arm, the bones hadn't set properly. Adam had grabbed it so many times before and since, it throbbed with a dull ache most of the time. Her wrist bone jutted out at an odd angle, and she felt self-conscious about its appearance. Bax still held it in his hand. She looked up first and saw that he was studying her arm.

"Did *he* do this?" he asked, his voice low. There was no doubt about whom Bax referred to.

"Oh, no—I was careless and I-I—" She tried to pull away but he kept a gentle grip on it. She saw a faint pulse throbbing in his throat, pushing his blood through his veins and heating her own.

"He did, didn't he?" Lightly, he rubbed his thumb over the prominent bump.

She swallowed and drew a deep breath but didn't answer.

For an instant his expression darkened with the same fury she'd seen that day he'd come home for a clean shirt. Then he did a most unexpected thing. He pressed a kiss to her maimed wrist. His touch was careful, hardly more than the brush of a moth's wing, and her heart jumped inside its bony cage.

When their eyes met, she noticed his dark lashes, and the faint weathering of horizontal lines that crossed his wide brow. He seemed to be studying her, trying to figure out what she was hiding. In his face, she saw shadows and salvation, troubles and tenderness. Finally, she realized she was staring back and tore her gaze away, her face hot with embarrassment. Goose bumps crawled over the rest of her body.

All the romantic gestures and trappings of courtship—candy, bouquets of flowers pilfered from neighbors' yards, the promises of happiness and a bright future together, all the sugared words that Adam had heaped upon her—she had believed them. She had not loved him, but she'd envisioned a life of companionship and evenings spent twirling around the floor of their eventual home while a Victrola played scratchy Strauss waltzes. His promises had evaporated shortly after he married her and never emerged again. They were gone for good, and when that happened, Amy began to dislike him. Eventually, she came to despise him.

Now, here was Bax, a man like neither of the others in her past, with a vague history, slow-burning moods, and an undercurrent of compassion, and she didn't know what to think of him.

He released her arm and rose to his feet. "Well, I didn't mean to take up your time. I just wanted to give you this. I saw it on the front porch when I passed it just now." He extended a letter to her. "It was tucked under a corner of the doormat."

She glanced at it and felt a catch in her chest. "Th-thank you. Dinner will be ready soon."

He nodded at her again. "Oh, and in exchange for my laundry, I'll chop the wood for the stove from now on." He walked toward the back porch, careful to scrape the dirt off the soles of his boots at the bottom of the stairs.

• • •

Married. She's *married*, Bax reminded himself as he watched Amy from his bedroom window, his forehead pressed to the frame just below the lock. Her husband was a no-good, sadistic bastard—but she was legally bound to him. To top it off, she came with a load of other problems, more than Bax supposed he even knew about. Despite all that, something drew him to her, something so strong he resented her for it and tried to keep his distance. The sight of her small wrist, though, like a sparrow's cruelly broken wing, had sliced through his heart. And there was a light in her clear, green eyes, beyond the fear and weariness, that made him believe, against his will, she could save him from himself and the empty shell of a man he had become. A man could fall into those eyes. Whenever he thought about her, desire and yearning for a better life pulled at him. Even though it might be foolish on his part, he realized that she gave him hope, and he sure didn't know why. Her history was enough to scare off any man. But his was no better, only different.

In the yard below, she gathered up her tools and walked toward the back door. Her slight figure cast a long shadow in the grass, and the ribbon tied at the end of her braid had come loose. Its tails fluttered in the breeze stirred up by the last of the afternoon sun.

The door slammed downstairs in the kitchen and shook him from his reverie. If like attracted like, maybe that's what pulled him to her—she was wounded and an outcast, just like him.

Just before he turned away from the window, his attention snagged on a lone figure standing at the far edge of the back fence. He gripped the window frame, instantly alert. Was it Breninger? Someone else? Bax wasn't sure. He didn't recognize the man from here—there was just enough distance between them to distort his features, and daylight was fading. A dark, wooded space behind him blurred the definition of his outline—but the stranger made him uncomfortable. And damn it, he realized the lousy creep had been watching Amy. She seemed not to notice.

Bax didn't envision himself as a guardian angel. Now he'd have to keep an eye out for this stranger. He had a strong hunch that he had something to do with the man who'd broken Amy's arm. Bax didn't know what he was up to, but it couldn't be good.

• • •

After dinner, Amy moved around the kitchen, putting dishes in the cupboard, drying the silverware with a tea towel, always circling the kitchen table and letting her eyes stray to the letter.

She'd put it there, leaving it unopened. It was addressed to her in Jessica's hand, a beautiful Spenserian script that, as far as Amy knew, was her only artistic accomplishment. Her sister's interests had always leaned toward the scientific. She'd loved peering into their father's microscope and grubbing around under rocks, looking for specimens and following other unfeminine pursuits. But she had elegant handwriting.

Finally, when all the dishes had been washed, all the flat surfaces scrubbed, and the towel folded precisely, she knew there was no more avoiding it. Deirdre, recovered from her cold, was in the living room with some mending. Tom was in there too, watching while she stitched a couple of buttons back onto one of his shirts. Their conversation reached her in low murmurs but she couldn't understand what they were saying. Bax was upstairs. Amy knew she wouldn't be disturbed for a few minutes. She pulled out a chair and sat, then opened the envelope. Smoothing out the sharply creased paper, she read the brief letter.

Dear Amy,

Although we did not part well, four years have passed and we are still family. I am concerned for your welfare and I'm hoping we can at least reach a meeting of the minds. If you long for this as well, please come to the New Cascades Hotel for dinner Wednesday evening at six o'clock. I'll wait for you in the dining room.

Your sister,
Jessica

On the defensive since Bax had given her this letter, Amy had expected a bitter, scathing diatribe, full of anger and accusations. She'd found something else. She took a deep breath and rested her head in her hands.

She had no friends here, or anywhere else, for that matter. Adam had systematically blocked her from creating friendships with other people, even women. Fear and relief warred within her—she knew Jessica had swallowed her pride to make this offer. But the prospect of facing her sister across a dinner table was daunting. Under the best of circumstances it would be awkward. And dear God, what if she brought Cole with her? She couldn't face them both.

She picked up the letter and reread it.

I'll wait for you in the dining room.

It didn't mention him. Maybe . . . maybe it would be just Jessica and her.

Wednesday evening. That was tomorrow. She could do this, she resolved, clutching the paper. She was strong enough to face her sister. She had something decent to wear now and no good excuse to avoid her.

Pushing away from the table, she made her way up the back stairs to the second floor. She kept her eyes on the letter as she walked down the hall toward her room. When she passed the bathroom she noticed that the light was on. Since the door was open, she assumed no one was in there. She had to stay on top of these things—the power company wasn't giving them electricity for free. With her concentration on her sister's letter, she didn't look up, but walked in, unseeing, and pushed the button switch.

"Hey!"

Amy jumped and fumbled with the switch, mortified. "Oh! Bax! I—I'm sorry! I didn't know anyone was in here."

He stood at the sink holding a long razor, a towel slung over one shoulder, and his face half-covered with shaving soap. This time he wore a white sleeveless undershirt with the neck unbuttoned to the center of his chest. She'd seen Adam shave countless times, but the sight had never once stirred her, certainly not as Bax did now.

He gestured at his soapy face and held out the hand clutching the razor, as if to reinforce the obvious evidence of his presence and task. Then he turned back to the mirror and continued scraping his face with the blade. The sound of the light rasping noise sent pleasant chills rushing over her scalp and down her arms. This was the second time today he'd roused that feeling in her. His backside was slim, and his jeans fit his legs as if they'd been tailored just for him.

Embarrassment competed with fascination within her. How much more forward could she be? She straightened and focused on getting out of the room. "Perhaps if you had closed the door— please excuse me, I'll just—I wasn't paying attention."

"Is there trouble in that letter you got there?" He nodded at the page in her hands.

He was just full of nosy questions. First that business about her wrist, now this. "Excuse me," she repeated, more firmly this time, and turned to walk away, grasping the doorknob behind her as she went.

"Do you know why someone would be watching you?" He looked at her reflection in the mirror over the sink.

The question all but nailed Amy's feet to the floor. "W-watching *me*?" She spun around. "Someone is watching me?"

"Yeah, I'm pretty sure of it."

"Where? How do you know? What makes you think that?"

He leaned closer to the mirror and the razor flashed again. The muscles in his right arm flexed. *Whssk.* "I saw a man standing at the far west end of the yard, just outside the fence after I came in from giving you that letter."

"But why?" Of course, she already knew the answer to that.

"I asked first—why?" He wiped the blade on the towel. "Is it Jacobsen?"

His directness flustered her. "I don't—well . . . would my own husband spy on me? That's silly. He knows I was coming here. I told him," she lied. "He could just knock on the door and talk to me."

Raised brows and a skeptical expression served as his answer.

"There have been all sorts of people wandering through Powell Springs since the war ended." She continued, "You should know that yourself. After all, even you didn't live here when I was in town before."

She saw the muscles in his back stiffen, and he faced her.

"Everyone has a past, Amy. *Everyone.* Including you."

Diverted momentarily, she gave him an even look. "And what's yours? You know far more about me than I do about you."

Whssk.

He ignored her question. "I just thought you'd want to know about this so you'll pay attention to who's behind you, who might be hanging around outside, or following you. I'm telling you what any lawman would. You don't have anyone else to give you cover."

"I do, too. My husband—"

"Oh, bullshit," Bax said, frowning. "Just give up on that lame-horse story." He had to interrupt her. He couldn't listen to her defend that lousy Jacobsen, and he hadn't even met him. Amy might not be an angel, but from what Bax had heard, while that good-for-nothing had lived here, he'd intimidated people around town during the war with his threats to report them to the government as unpatriotic, preached brimstone and bleak retribution, and then was caught with his pants down visiting a prostitute. "Some husband. He broke your arm, left bruises on your neck, and you're terrified of him." He sucked in a hiss of breath when he nicked his chin with the razor. He pressed his thumb to the dot of blood and then turned to face her. "He's not protecting you. And he could very well be the one keeping an eye on you." It could also be Breninger, he realized, but he didn't want to complicate things. As long as she stayed sharp, and he did too, that would help.

Amy stared at him, aghast. How could he know all that? She searched for words to refute everything he'd said, *anything*, then realized she had nothing to fight back with. Everything he said was uncomfortably true. She was surprised that he'd noticed the bruising but she knew he was right. His comment hit her like a slap with a cold washcloth. A lump the size of a peach pit formed in her throat. He'd reminded her again that she was friendless, and except for her sister, she was alone in the world. That was better than being some man's doormat and slave. But surely there must be some middle ground, some happy in-between. Susannah had found it twice. Jess had it—despite Amy's maneuverings.

Without another word, she walked out and went to her own room.

CHAPTER EIGHT

Tabitha Monroe sat at her dressing table with a hand mirror, trying to subdue both her nerves and her blonde bob. The short haircut was oh so chic, at the very crest of fashion these days. But her own hair, permanently waved, had suffered from the drying, ammonia-smelling chemicals used to wind her arrow-straight mane into tendrils. It was difficult to manage, and the memory of longer hair was bittersweet. Still, it was all the rage and she liked keeping up with the latest looks. Oh, how her charity committee had squirmed with jealousy upon learning of her Chanel No. 5. When she told them it was sold only in exclusive Paris boutiques, ah, what joy that had brought her. She knew that envy was eating them alive. Her marriage to Harlan had elevated her from the lowly, barren status of old-maid schoolteacher surviving on relatives' charity, to this wonderland of social and material wealth.

But she was not in the mood to host the arts league luncheon today. It had been scheduled for two weeks and only her own death would be an acceptable excuse for canceling at this last moment. In any event, it was now one o'clock and the cook was busy in the kitchen with chilled poached salmon for twenty guests, who had already begun to arrive.

She turned this way and that, trying to see the back of her head while maneuvering the mirror. At least with her hands occupied she couldn't chew her cuticles, a dreadful habit that emerged when she worried. Right now, those cuticles were torn and ragged.

She had not seen or heard from Harlan since the morning after his late-night "business meeting," and it simply was not like him. She barely slept, listening for him to come home. Elsa turned off the lamp in the foyer every morning, the sedan wasn't in the garage, and the help was beginning to talk. She'd made up her mind—if he wasn't here by dinner, she would call the police. The impulse had struck her immediately, but she'd hesitated. If nothing was wrong, he'd be furious with her for making a big fuss and involving the law. After the night that car had idled at their curb, she'd asked a lot questions, but he'd dismissed her demands for answers. Now, of course, she was suspicious again. Who had been in that car? And why were they interested in the Monroes?

Dear God, maybe he was lying in a ditch somewhere, or drowned in the river . . . any number of things could have happened. This was simply not the kind of trouble that Tabitha Pratt Monroe allowed in her well-ordered life. If Harlan wasn't hurt, he'd better have an excellent excuse for making her worry so.

On top of everything else, the gardeners had not come to work either. Her roses were suffering and the grounds were beginning to look shaggy. And to think that Harlan said she did not make good use of her time. The responsibilities were never ending.

"Miss Tabitha?"

Tabitha heard the maid's quiet voice along with a light tapping on her bedroom door. "What is it, Elsa?"

Elsa slipped into the room and closed the door behind her with a quiet *click*. "There are two gentlemen here to see you, ma'am."

She frowned slightly. There were no men on the guest list. "Gentlemen? Who are they?"

Elsa held out a small silver tray bearing a white calling card. *Donald F. Rinehart.* Tabbie examined both sides, one of which was blank. The name meant nothing to her. "You said there's more than one?"

"He didn't introduce himself. First they asked for Mr. Monroe, but when I told them he's not here, they asked for you."

"For heaven's sake, didn't they say what they want?"

Elsa shook her head. "I tried to find out but they wouldn't tell me."

Tabitha took one last look in the mirror, then put it down and did her best to remain calm and keep her hands still. Inwardly, she felt as if birds were flapping in her chest. "All right, I'm coming. Put them in the library."

"Shall I serve tea?"

"Certainly not. They can't arrive without notice and expect more than five minutes of my time. I'll call you if I need anything. And tell the ladies I'll be with them shortly."

The maid withdrew, but Tabitha's anxiety continued to climb, and her index finger found its way to her teeth. Something was wrong, she just knew it. Her mind would not proceed further to imagine what that could possibly be.

With a final poke at her hair with a comb, she stood and smoothed out any wrinkles in her skirt, then went downstairs.

Her taupe silk dress swished lightly against her stockings as she descended the steps. Along the wall on the stairway, she passed oil paintings of people neither she nor Harlan knew, but which they fobbed off as pictures of his distant relatives. In truth, the portraits had been purchased through a buyer in New York. Their biggest challenge was keeping straight the names and family connections each painting was supposed to represent. In the Monroes' social circle, if one had no family pedigree, one had to invent something. In some ways it was almost better than the real thing because they could make up anything they wanted, within credible reason. Of course, some care must be taken to avoid shining too bright a light on any one family member; the story had to be one that couldn't be verified or denied by someone wise to society.

She reached the bottom of the marble staircase and heard the light chatter of feminine voices coming from the parlor. Before anyone could see her, she made her way to the library where two men stood in quiet conference while they waited for her. Immediately defensive, she lifted her chin and put on her haughtiest schoolteacher expression.

"Good afternoon. I'm Mrs. Tabitha Monroe. Perhaps you can explain to me what brings you here."

The older of the two, well dressed in an expensive suit, stepped forward and extended his hand. "I'm Donald Rinehart, Mrs. Monroe. We met once at one of Robert Burton's dinner parties. I am Mr. Burton's attorney."

"Oh, of course." She was still certain she'd never seen him before or heard his name. "And that man rearranging my chinoiserie figurines?" She nodded toward his companion, who stood at the mantle fingering the artifacts.

"*Blackburn!*" he whispered harshly, and the man promptly put down the carved ivory dragon he'd been studying. "Please excuse my assistant, William Blackburn, Mrs. Monroe." He bent a brief, severe look on the man. "Assistant for the time being, anyway."

The young man reddened and stepped forward to shake her hand. She said nothing to him.

"I still don't know why you're here, Mr. Rinehart, and it cannot have escaped your notice that I have luncheon guests arriving."

The attorney cleared his throat. "Yes, I apologize for the interruption, and I wouldn't have troubled you if this were not important. We were wondering if Mr. Monroe is at home."

"No, he isn't."

"Do you know where he is?"

"I imagine he's at work in Mr. Burton's office," she hedged. Maybe you should look for him there."

"Mr. Burton hasn't seen him in several weeks. Naturally, he is concerned." He gave her a look that implied she should be as well.

Faced with this news, Tabitha worked to maintain a calm exterior, but growing panic swelled in her. "My husband has many interests and responsibilities."

Rinehart considered the comfortable room, tastefully decorated with fine furniture, potted ferns, and elegant lamps. "You have a grand home, Mrs. Monroe. Do those interests extend beyond the scope of his job with Mr. Burton?"

She frowned at the suspicious tone of his questioning. "No wife concerns herself with the details of her husband's occupation." Truthfully, she had no idea what kind of work Harlan did, for Robert Burton or anyone else. The few times she'd bothered to ask, he had given her only a vague response. She suspected he would never tell her anything specific. That wasn't surprising— her female friends and acquaintances didn't know the details of what their husbands did for a living, either. But Harlan was an important man. He told her so, and because they lived well, she believed him.

"When did you last see him?" Rinehart asked.

Her fear continued to escalate. "Well, I-I—Mr. Rinehart, has something happened to him?"

"That's what I'm trying to find out."

Oh, this was worse than she'd originally thought. She twisted her diamond wedding ring on her finger. "The police—we should call the police."

"Not just yet. Mr. Burton would like to avoid a scandal if possible."

Tabitha, never at a loss for a rejoinder, now found herself groping for words. "Scandal! What are you talking about?"

"Unfortunately, there are some irregularities in Mr. Burton's accounts that point to Mr. Monroe's area of responsibility, and he would like to get them sorted out. It involves a considerable amount of money."

Irregularities.

Money.

Dear God, what had Harlan done?

"Tabbie, dear!" she heard Greta Van Weider trumpet behind her, "There you are! We were wondering—oh, good afternoon, Mr. Rinehart. Tabbie, are you part of the scandal you two are discussing? There's nothing quite so deliciously naughty!"

While the two acquaintances made small talk, Tabitha felt as if the room were spinning. It dimmed to a gray mist and then turned black.

• • •

"Are you sure you'll be able to manage while I'm gone?" Amy stood in the kitchen, wearing a new dress and shoes and a nice spring coat that had seemed like an unforgivable indulgence when she bought it. Owning a wrap that was designated for only part of the year was such a departure from having two dresses and a single drab coat that must serve for any season and any weather. To compensate, she decided to manage with the hat she already owned.

At the stove, Deirdre gave her a sidelong glance while she made gravy from the chicken she'd roasted. "Before you got here, I took care of Mrs. Donaldson and did this, too."

Amy smiled. "Of course."

"That teal color suits your complexion."

"Thank you." She glanced at the clock above the sink. "I'd better go. I don't want to be late." Amy smiled again, but inside her nerves quivered like a strand of spider's web, and she wanted to hide in her bedroom. She was annoyed with Bax for telling her about some man watching her, even though it was something she should know—if it was true. Now she felt trapped in the house and hadn't ventured beyond the back porch since last night after that indelicate scene in the bathroom. For all she knew, he'd been wrong or—or made it up. *Why* he would do that, well, she had no idea.

Then there was her apprehension about facing Jessica. Originally she'd thought she would ignore her sister's invitation to dinner. But . . . she was lonely. As a child she had been shy and close to her mother, disinclined to follow Jess on some of her close-call escapades. When Jess went away to school, and with their mother gone, Amy had come into her own. She'd developed friendships and become involved in local activities and charities. Over the course of a single autumn, that had changed. She thought again about her sister's letter and her own fragile hope that they could close the gaping wound Amy had opened between them. The events of those days past were not ones she visited often—their memories were painful and only served to remind her of the disastrous marriage she had entered into as a result of her actions.

When she opened the front door she looked up and down Springwater Street and at the vacant lot across the way. She didn't see anyone except a neighbor four doors down who'd come out to get the mail from his mailbox. She adjusted her handbag on her arm, straightened, and headed down the sidewalk toward the New Cascades Hotel.

The day's busy street traffic was dwindling on Main, and a cool, clear dusk settled over the town. Shops had already closed or were in the process of doing so. She passed Jessica's office and saw that she'd locked up for the evening. Of course—she was meeting Amy for dinner at the hotel.

As she walked, her new shoes pinched but her attention was consumed with staying alert to any suspicious-looking man who might seem to be shadowing her movements. She saw no one until she reached Granny Mae's café. Through the large front windows, she saw a few diners sitting at tables. She barely recognized the mayor, Horace Cookson, sitting alone with a roast beef dinner in front of him. His son, home on leave from Camp Lewis during the war, had brought the first case of influenza to Powell Springs. It had spread like a kerosene fire, and both his son and Mrs. Cookson died during the epidemic. The rumpled old dairy farmer looked as if he'd aged twenty years instead of four.

As if waiting for her to come along, Granny pushed open her side door and hailed her. "Hello, there, Amy. My, but you're looking smart and dressy." The old woman wore her standard practical dress and dirty apron, and a strangely self-satisfied expression.

Amy groaned to herself. She hadn't talked to Granny since the day she'd gone to her for Deirdre's cough remedy. "Thank you." She didn't stop, though.

Ahead, the hotel's facade came into view. It wasn't as grand as the Benson Hotel or the Portland Hotel downtown, but it had two stories and covered half a block. It was constructed with brick, and green awnings hung over the lace-curtained windows. Potted blooming roses were stationed on either side of the entrance, adding a touch of elegance to the place. She stood in the lobby and looked around. It was fairly quiet, although a pair of obvious newlyweds sat forward in facing chairs with their heads together, exchanging the private whispers that lovers share.

Feeling like an eavesdropper, Amy searched the lobby for some clue as to where the dining room might be located, but all she could see were the front desk and the staircase leading to the upper floors. To her right was a hallway with a ladies' room at one end.

A desk clerk emerged from a side office and she took a step forward to ask about the dining room when she saw another guest approach first. He carried a suitcase and an arrogant set to his head that she recognized before he spoke. Amy stood riveted in place, her throat as dry as burned toast, while sickening waves of terror flooded her.

"Mr. Jacobsen, how nice to see you again. What can we do for you?" she heard the clerk ask him over the rush of blood through her head.

"I'm hoping you can give me some information—"

She didn't wait for the rest. Overcome with a panicky urge to run, she turned and hurried to the doors and escaped into the street.

Oh, God!

Oh, dear God!

Had he seen her? Was he behind her? Glancing over her shoulder, Amy pounded down Main at a trot, barely aware of her surroundings. She ran as if the devil himself had appeared at that front desk, and her heart thundered in her chest. At the end of the block she ducked into the deep doorway of a closed shop and pressed her back against the wall. She peeked around the edge of her hiding place and saw Adam emerge from the hotel. He turned the corner, disappearing from view. The breath she'd been holding whooshed out in an exhale that made her shoulders droop.

Then, just as she was about to step out of the doorway, she saw Jessica leave the hotel, too. Her sister looked around furtively and dashed down the other side of the street to a car parked in front of Cole's blacksmith shop. Getting into the driver's seat, she started the vehicle and it lurched forward like a startled horse, issuing a loud backfire as it went.

Amy's thoughts churned and raced. Her sister and Adam in the same hotel—coincidence? Coconspirators? Had this invitation just been some kind of scheme they'd cooked up? No, no, that wasn't possible. Jessica hated Adam.

Didn't she?

Suddenly she felt exposed and vulnerable on the dusk-shaded street. She turned and darted from the doorway, dodging a couple of people along the way. She looked back to see if she was being followed, and felt herself caught by the shoulders. With a shriek, she whipped her head around and saw Bax in front of her.

"Whoa, what's going on?"

She knew she should be glad to see him, but right now her panic overruled everything else. Gasping for breath, she tried to free herself, but he held her fast. "I have to go home. I have to go home *right now!*"

He looked down the street over her head. "What happened? Were you insulted or bothered by someone?"

She gestured in the direction of the hotel, then tried to shrug out of his grip. "I don't want to talk about it. Let me go. I'm going home!"

He gave her a short, gentle shake, trying to calm her down enough to pry a story out of her. "Amy, is there anything the law should know about?"

"No, no, let me leave!" She managed to squirm out of his grip and ran toward home.

. . .

Jessica wanted nothing more than the peace and safety of her husband and child. She left the hotel and rushed back to her office, where her car was parked in front of Cole's blacksmith shop, next door. He had already picked up Margaux from Susannah and gone home.

The trip home seemed to take forever, and although she was tempted to drive faster, full darkness had fallen and there was no illumination along the road except her own headlamps. When she finally turned onto the rutted path leading to her house, the warm glow of light in the windows welcomed her. Roscoe, Cole's black-and-white sheepdog, barked a greeting at her from the porch.

"I'm glad to see you too," she said, rubbing the dog's head.

The door opened and Cole held the screen door for her. "You're home already?"

The sight of him still made her catch her breath. Tall and ruggedly blond with chin-length hair, he wore his thirty-four years very well. Though now a married man with a baby, there remained a touch of wild independence in him that had always drawn her to him. Horses, women, and the elements—he handled them all with an easy sureness she loved.

"You were right. Amy didn't come to dinner." She set her doctor's bag on the entry table and sank into the chair beside it.

He gave her an arch look. "I could say 'I told you so'—"

"But you're a smart man, so you won't. There's something else. Adam is in town."

He scowled. "Shit. I should have known it would happen. So they've made up."

"Really, I don't know if they split up to begin with. If they did and reconciled, why would he be staying at the hotel?" She shrugged. "Since I didn't talk to her tonight, I really don't know anything. Personally, I have trouble with the idea of living in the same town with him."

Cole walked to a cabinet in the dining room and pulled a bottle and two glasses from the china cabinet. "Come on in here. I'll buy you a drink."

She pulled herself to her feet and followed him to the table. "Where's the baby?"

"Asleep. I had dinner with Susannah and Tanner, and she fed Margaux at the same time. I think she wants the practice." He poured her enough whiskey to cover the bottom of her glass, then poured an inch for himself. "Drink that and I'll fix you a fried egg and bacon sandwich."

She sat at the table and wrinkled her nose. "Fried eggs and whiskey."

He went into the kitchen and pulled a cast-iron skillet to the front burner. "Hey, it's what I know how to do. You were supposed to eat in town."

She nodded and sipped at the liquid fire. "I know. You're a wonderful husband."

"Don't I know it." He gave her an impudent smile that made her laugh, then shaved three thick strips of bacon from a slab and put them in the frying pan. The smile faded, replaced by a frown. "What about Jacobsen and your sister?"

"I hardly know what to think. I guess I'll just have to wait and see what happens. I don't think anyone is going to bother you. Neither Adam nor Amy will be jumping at a chance to see you, you know. Have you even caught a glimpse of her?"

"Yeah, once so far—from a distance." He poked at the bacon and cracked two eggs in beside it. "At least I'm pretty sure it was her. She looks so different, I had to check twice."

"I was hoping to find out why tonight."

"Maybe I'll drop by Whit's office tomorrow and let him know one of his old buddies is in town. He made a lot of trouble for Whit, what with him on his witch hunt for everyone he thought wasn't patriotic during the war. He and Bax ought to know."

She sighed. "Yes, I suppose. If they don't already. Bax lives at the boardinghouse." A cranky wail came from the baby's room. "Okay, Margaux, I'm coming."

"I'll have your dinner on the table," Cole said.

Climbing the stairs, Jessica wished with all her heart that they could go back in time to the day before Amy came back to Powell Springs.

CHAPTER NINE

"What are you doing here? I told you we'd meet only in Twelve Mile, and when *I* contact you." Adam peered at Milo Breninger through a narrow crack of his hotel room door.

"I got damn tired of waiting for you. We've got some business to take care of, you and me, right now. I found your wife for you two weeks ago. It's time to pay up, Jacobsen."

Adam opened the door just enough to grab the man's arm and pull him inside, hoping that no one had seen him lurking in the hall. He scanned the empty corridor and shut the door. "What the hell is wrong with you?" he demanded in a low voice. "Do you want everyone to know what you're doing?"

Breninger shrugged. "I'm not the one who cares about what your wife does. Or did. You hired me—I didn't volunteer for this."

Exasperated, and with his temper threatening to escape his control, Adam directed Breninger to a chair.

He shifted from one buttock to the other on the rigid, unupholstered desk chair, looking oafish and out of place in the pleasant surroundings. Adam was annoyed that the man had chosen to seek him out here, in an all-too-public place where they might be seen together.

"Our 'business' isn't finished yet. I told you when we met at Porter's that I might have other things for you to do."

"It's finished. You said you'd pay extra for anything more. All I had to do was find your wife and you'd handle the rest. I did my part."

Adam lifted a brow and looked over Breninger's cheap suit. It was a different one than he'd seen before, but of no better quality. "You spent the three hundred dollars already?" He'd suspected as much. "Anyway, I don't have that kind of money with me. I'd be an idiot to carry so much cash."

The corner of Milo's mustache dropped with his scowl and he leaned forward. "Y'know, there's ways of dealing with a man who welches on his debts."

Adam gave him an even, icy glare. "You don't want to forget just which man you're dealing with now. You're not in a position to make threats. Your past isn't a secret—it would be very interesting to certain people." He was bluffing. He didn't know much of anything about Breninger beyond what he'd mentioned at their first meeting, but it didn't take a genius to figure out that he had a closet full of skeletons.

Breninger didn't back down. "You're no choirboy yourself, Jacobsen. In Portland I heard talk about the wolf in minister's clothes with debts and shady dealings attached to you. People here remember you, too—and Amy."

Adam clenched his jaw briefly. "She's Mrs. Jacobsen to you, Breninger. Don't forget it."

The man stood and uttered a sly chuckle, revealing his mostly toothless gums. "Maybe you should tell *her* that."

"What's that supposed to mean?"

He headed toward the door. "It'll cost you six hundred and seventy bucks and then some to find out." With his hand on the knob he turned and added, "Isn't that what you thought, anyway? That she has a fancy man?"

Adam worked to keep a firm grip on his anger. Yes, he'd said it to Breninger, but he hadn't meant it. Amy would never, ever— *"What's that supposed to mean?"*

Now the grubby fool was laughing outright, and Adam felt his blood begin to boil. "I told you she's living at that boarding-house with two other men. That's all I bothered to find out. You figure out the rest yourself or go talk to her. I could ask around too, but I'm not doing a damn thing more unless you pay up. I'm glad you're not the only iron in my fire."

Eager to be rid of him, Adam disregarded his bragging and said, "I'll meet you in Twelve Mile tomorrow noon. Across the street from the tractor store." He had no intention of meeting him or paying him until he had the facts and his property—all of it— in his possession.

Apparently satisfied with his day's work, Breninger nodded and touched his brow in a smart-alecky two-finger salute before leaving.

Adam barely noticed him going. His mind was now turning on two problems: Amy still had that damning evidence against him and now she'd possibly gotten herself involved with another man. *Another man.* The very idea made him want to put his fist through the wall, since he couldn't hit anyone else at the moment. He briefly considered the idea that Breninger was just egging him on to pry money out of him.

But if it was true—if she believed she could two-time him— she was in for a big surprise. As comfortable as it was, he'd have to move out of this hotel. To put all of his plans into action, he realized that he needed to be someplace less conspicuous, close enough to town for convenience, but far out enough to maintain his cover.

And he knew just where to find it.

• • •

Bax leveled his gaze on Amy. He had cornered her in the living room after dinner. They had eaten, but Amy stayed hidden in her bedroom during the meal until Deirdre went upstairs and asked to use the sewing machine. Tom was working a night shift at the mill. The faint, rhythmic sound of the pumping treadle drifted down from the floor above.

"I don't know what made you decide to come back to Powell Springs, but from what I've seen, I'd say it's a fair bet that you're running from that man. Even though you don't want to admit it."

Her back stiffened. "What? You have no right to go stirring up trouble and poking around in my personal business!"

"You'd expected to see him again, hadn't you? That's what you've told people."

Bax sat her down on the sofa and dropped into place on the other end.

"Yes, but deep down, I dreaded the thought that he'd come here. I hoped he wouldn't."

"Tell me what happened out there on the street this evening."

Her gaze wandered to the flowered wallpaper, and suddenly she looked very tired and frail, even though he suspected there was a lion's heart beating beneath that exterior. After all, she'd scraped together the nerve to leave Adam Jacobsen to begin with. Some women became so browbeaten and defeated, they were terrified to even try to get away from an abusive marriage. The subject was only whispered about—if it was discussed at all—but Bax had seen enough in mill towns to recognize it.

"I was on my way to meet my sister for dinner at the New Cascades Hotel. That's what was in that letter you gave me—a dinner invitation. I thought it was supposed to be a reconciliation for us. I was hoping for that, anyway." She sat with her hands tightly folded in lap. "But when I got there, I saw my husband talking to the clerk at the front desk."

Bax put his elbow on the sofa arm. "And you have good reason to be afraid of him." He waited for her to acknowledge this. "Right?"

"Yes," she muttered. "You know I do."

"But didn't you tell me just the other night that he knows you're here in town?"

She dropped her chin and her knuckles whitened. "That wasn't exactly true. At least I didn't think it was. I left in the middle of the night while he was out of the house."

"You ran away."

She looked at him and her brows rushed together. "I didn't steal the silver, if that's what you're implying. As if we had any silver. If you're going to insult me—"

He shook his head and waved off her protest. "No, no, settle down. That's not what I meant. I mean you escaped."

Some of the indignant sizzle left her. "Yes, I did. I had to. I'd been waiting a long time for the chance." She pleated the fabric over her knee. "And the courage . . ."

"Do you think your life is in danger? Maybe this is something I need to tell Whit about."

Her head came up again. "No!"

"Because . . ."

"Adam didn't see me and I don't want to make trouble." She leaned forward, her expression adamant. "You don't know why he's—well, you don't know."

"Make trouble! Lady, you've already got that, in spades." He eyed her with a searching look. "What's really going on, Amy? It's more than him breaking your arm and leaving bruises on you, although God knows that's plenty. And it's not just that he's a bully who wants to drag his wife home so he can keep telling himself that he's king of the world and all he surveys. I think you're hiding something. You said I don't know why. Well, tell me."

Amy wanted to trust Bax. But life had taught her that people were often not what they seemed to be. She'd crossed paths with liars, poseurs, schemers, and swindlers at almost every turn on the road she had traveled with Adam.

Worst of all, the most damning, shaming fact of all—she had been one of those people before she set one foot on that road.

Bax, though . . . there was something about him, something in his eyes, that made her want to finally lay down the burden of all she'd carried with her over the years. She didn't want to tell him anything, but he pulled scraps of information out of her that she never intended to give him.

"Adam gets . . . angry. Easily. If he learns that I inherited this house, he'll try to claim it for his own since we're married. He'll force me to go back to Portland." Fury and her tiresome companion, fear, rose in her. "And I won't go. I can't." She'd gotten a taste of peace, even though it had come at a high price, and she wasn't going to give it up.

"You need to talk to Dan Parmenter about that, and right away." He crossed his ankle over his knee and pulled at a loose thread on the hem of his jeans. "I keep hearing about Jacobsen being a minister here. What has he been doing all this time since you left? It's hard to imagine that he could have a church and a flock of parishioners."

"He idolized Billy Sunday. The man has made a fortune with his traveling revival meetings. Adam got it into his head that he wanted the same thing. Not so much the religion part of it, I came to realize. He wanted the adoration, the money, the influence. When we left here, that was the path he took us on."

There weren't too many people who hadn't heard of Sunday, the flamboyant, melodramatic evangelist who drew large crowds wherever he appeared. Preaching rigid, grim doctrines, his meetings were a combination of unrelenting hellfire, P.T. Barnum showmanship, and baseball analogies. His followers ate it up with a knife and fork and paid him handsomely when the collection baskets came around.

"I'm guessing he didn't find it."

"We went from town to town for two years, living like gypsies with no real home. Just rented rooms. His grand plan to pull in big donations was only a pipe dream."

"It sounds tough. Especially for a woman."

She looked at him straight on. "I hated it." She surprised herself with her low, bitter vehemence. It was the first time she'd admitted it, even in her own mind.

"And he's still doing that?"

"No. A couple of years ago, he decided to settle in Portland and see what he could find there. What he found was a job for me."

"What the hell does *he* do?"

"I'm not sure, and I learned not to ask. I believe there was some gambling involved." Without thinking, she cradled her wrist, and her mind returned to that mysterious book she'd found in the closet in Portland, now hidden in her chest of drawers.

The muscle in his jaw flexed. "If Jacobsen threatens you— anytime—I'll see to him."

She gave him a jaded look. "No one cares about what happens to women behind closed doors. Least of all the police." It was a harsh truth that she'd learned early on in her marriage. What a sheltered life she'd lived here. "They treat the situation like it's none of their business, unless the woman is finally killed. Then they'll get involved."

He unhooked his ankle and leaned toward her. "It's my job to keep the peace among the people of Powell Springs. That includes you."

She glanced at her lap. Maybe that was true. But from a hushed, timid corner of her heart, she wished his dedication stemmed from more than a sense of duty to his occupation. In that instant, she wished for so many things that she hadn't known for so long. She wanted to laugh again, for old hurts to finally stop; she wanted to be happy again, even if just for a while.

He stood up and held out his hand to help her from the sofa. His was so much warmer than her own. "I've got to go back to the office and finish some things."

She rose and looked up into his face. "Oh. Of course." She wasn't eager to be left here with just Deirdre. Two women alone . . .

"Are you afraid here, by yourself?"

"No, of course not," she lied. "Anyway, Deirdre is just upstairs."

"I won't be away long. What time is Tom due home?"

"He's working the night shift. Did you get your dinner?"

"Yeah. But you didn't. You never talked to your sister, either?"

She didn't want to tell him what notions that had run through her mind about Jess conspiring with Adam. It was just so . . . far-fetched. "I didn't. I-I can fix you something more to eat, though."

"I'll pick up something at Mae's if I get hungry."

"No, no, meals are part of your room and board. I'll make you a meatloaf sandwich to take with you. It's not fancy, but it's ready, left over from lunch."

He smiled. "If you knew about some of the disgusting things I've eaten, you'd know that meatloaf *is* fancy to me."

She headed from the living room into the kitchen, still faintly fragrant of roast chicken and apples, with him following close behind. She pulled a loaf pan from the icebox and began cutting slices, thin, to bring out their flavor. He studied her movements with seemingly great fascination, as if she were repairing a watch.

"Those interesting things you ate—was it during the war?" she asked with no little trepidation, not knowing how he'd react. And really, she didn't mean to sound like she was prying, but he knew so much more about her personal life than she did about his. An exchange of information only seemed fair.

He sighed. "Yeah, a few of them. If you're hungry enough, you'll eat almost anything."

The silence opened between them while she worked, and she thought of those two angry-looking pink scars on his back. "Of course, here at home we heard about some of the odd canned things like monkey meat—we all tried to imagine what that could possibly be."

"We were *told* it was corned beef, but it wasn't like anything we'd ever tasted before. Sometimes in France we'd get a chicken or a pig from a farmer, although they didn't have much to share. A dozen eggs was a real prize."

She spread mayonnaise on homemade bread, then piled on the slim slices. From a colander on the counter, she grabbed a washed leaf of early spring lettuce, then put it all together and sliced the sandwich diagonally.

"See, pretty fancy," he said, watching as she wrapped it all up in waxed paper.

"I learned to cook when I was a girl, but I was only allowed to find work as a dishwasher. Still, sometimes I'd get a glimpse of what the cooks were putting together. That diagonal cut makes even toast look dressy."

"Who said you had be a dishwasher?"

"My hus—Adam."

He accepted the sandwich without another question. "Thanks, Amy. Keep all the doors locked."

She followed him to the back door, which he always used, even when leaving. "You could use the front door, you know." She smiled at him.

He twisted the knob and pulled it open. The night breeze eddied around them, bringing to her his scent of laundry soap and freshly cut wood. "No—I can't."

She was about to ask why, but he stopped her when he wrapped an arm around her and tipped his head to put a soft kiss on her mouth. Briefly, she leaned forward, her breasts brushing his shirt front, and made a small, anguished noise in her throat. Then he was down the stairs and gone into the darkness.

She was too surprised by the feel of his lips and the thrilling shiver that flowed through her to say anything more.

• • •

What the hell had he been thinking, anyway, kissing Amy like that? Bax wondered. Instead of disentangling himself from the woman and her problems, as a sane, smart man would, he was just digging in deeper. He didn't know why, he had no reason to believe it, but she represented home to him, a safe haven where his case-hardened heart would learn to beat again, well and truly washed of the raw grief of war, both on the battlefields of France and upon his return to America.

He sat at his desk in the office—they'd finally managed to find a real one for him—shuffling papers around, but his mind wasn't on the task. For all of Amy's fragility, he detected strength. Despite her past disgrace, he suspected honor.

They each had pasts that dragged at them. Hers was not a secret. His was, but in Amy he might find understanding. The single biggest problem was that part of her past was still her present. Like it or not, she was bound to Adam Jacobsen.

And he anticipated the day that his path and Jacobsen's would cross. That day was coming soon.

• • •

Two days later, Jessica was standing in the back room of her office when she heard someone come into her waiting area. The overhead bell on the door clanged furiously. "Dr. Jessica! Dr. Jess, are you here?"

Despite the urgency in the words, she recognized Sheriff Whit Gannon's low, rumbling voice. She hurried through the hall to meet him. He was a tall, rangy man with the most luxurious silver hair and mustache she'd ever seen. "Whit, what's wrong?"

"It's Winks—I think he's finally pushed himself over the edge. We've got him behind the office with Bax watching him." He glanced out the window. "At least it's not raining, since he's pretty much running from both ends and we didn't want to bring him inside if we could help it. I think he must have gotten some bad moonshine. He says he's blind, but sees things that aren't there, he's twitching, having fits—hell, he's a mess."

"Oh, God," Jess sighed. "Tilly isn't involved in this, is he?"

"No. Virgil knows I'd close him down pronto if he sold that shit—I mean junk."

"You don't think Winks decided to try to make his own . . ."

"He said he got this stuff yesterday, so cheap he couldn't pass it up. But it was from someone he didn't know."

She thought for a moment. "Did Cole tell you that I saw Adam Jacobsen at the hotel the other night?"

"He did, but—you don't think he has anything to do with this, do you? Whiskey making doesn't sound like something he'd be involved in."

"Why, because he's so moral?" she couldn't help but snipe.

"No, because it's grubby work and he was never the sort who liked to get dirty."

She had to give him that. Even as a child, Adam had been as stuffy and finicky as an elderly bachelor. "You're right. But we have Winks to worry about right now. Of course, I'll come." She put a hand on Whit's arm. "But you must know he's probably not going to survive this. I saw some cases in New York. Wood alcohol poisoning is fatal, and it's a pretty gruesome way to die."

"Yeah. I know." He looked morose. "I hate to see him go this way, though. It's like giving a kid cookies baked with rat poison. And I'm going to find out who's selling that moonshine, I hope before someone else drinks it. Damn this Prohibition. People are drinking more now than they did when it was legal." Winks Lamont was a Powell Springs fixture. He was a pain in the neck for Whit and a few others around town, and rarely drew a sober breath. But people were used to him, and although he was no smarter than a sack of doorknobs and had long ago pickled his sensibilities, he was pretty harmless, and he had a long history in this town.

Jess grabbed her bag and coat, then scribbled a hasty note and thumbtacked it on the door, telling any visitor where she could be found. She locked up the office behind her and got into Whit's Model T.

When they arrived at his office, there was a small group behind the building, standing around two benches that had been pushed together, upon which Winks lay under a moth-eaten blanket.

The buzz among the onlookers hummed. "Well, if that don't beat all. I sure didn't expect Winks to end up like this."

"It was bound to happen one day—"

"Let the doc through," Whit boomed upon getting out of the driver's seat. "Give her some room."

"I don't think she's going to be able to do much about this," one of Tilly's regulars speculated.

"He don't look too good—"

"Did he ever look good? He drank himself right into the grave."

As soon as Jessica drew near, the first odor that slapped her in the face, beyond her patient's serious lack of hygiene, was vomit. It reminded her of the grim days of the influenza epidemic and the makeshift hospital she'd set up in the school. Over that, she caught a strong whiff of formaldehyde, the byproduct of a chemical reaction that occurred in a person poisoned with methyl alcohol.

"Gentlemen, *please* let me through!" she snapped, elbowing her way to Winks's side.

"Everybody, out of here!" Bax Duncan commanded. "This isn't a carnival sideshow. Go find something else to do."

The rubberneckers only backed up and with perceptible reluctance, muttering among themselves.

Cyanosis was obvious in Winks's slack, blue-gray face and dirt-embedded fingers. She reached into her bag for her stethoscope and hooked it into her ears. Bending over his still form, she listened hard to his lungs and heart, hoping for some sign of life. She shook her head.

"I'm sorry, Whit," she said gently. "He's gone." She gazed down at the wreck of a man in his stained, mismatched clothes, who was, by everyone's best guess, about forty years old. His hair had already lost most of its color, and even in death he looked twenty years older.

Whit's fury collided with regret. "Damn it. I want to get to the bottom of this. We've been doing fine working around this crackbrained law. Those fools in Washington want to legislate morality and it won't work. People are *going* to drink. This is bad. We can't have those fools in the backwoods cooking up poison to sell."

"No, but it might get worse," Jess prophesied.

With a pensive expression, Bax studied the dead man's scarecrow form and sighed before he pulled the blanket up to cover his face. The moment was not lost on Jess. "Did you know Winks?"

Bax glanced up at her, and she was struck by how handsome he was. "Not really. He's spent a few nights here sleeping off a drunk. I've just seen a lot of death in my time. It never gets easier."

He wore the same look as a lot of men who'd been in the war. She knew he boarded at Amy's, and for a fleeting moment, she considered asking him about her. Then she thought better of it. She had no idea how much, if anything, he knew about her sister, and it wouldn't be appropriate to discuss family matters with him.

"I think some people around town should be persuaded to take up a collection to pay for his burial," Bax continued.

Whit nodded. "I'll have Fred Hustad come and pick him up. He should forgive a dead man for what happened years ago now."

"Do you mean that grave-robbing business during the influenza epidemic?" Bax asked, tucking the blanket around Winks to keep the breeze from lifting it away. The gesture touched Jess.

"Yeah, but Winks was just the brawn, not the brain behind that."

The onlookers drifted away in ones and twos, ready to report the event.

Jessica tucked her stethoscope back into her bag. "Sometimes death is kind of like baptism. Past wrongs are forgiven, or forgotten completely. I'll go back to the office and write up the death certificate and send it over to Fred."

"Thanks, Dr. Jess. I'll give you a lift."

"No, thanks, Whit." She glanced up at the dark-green hills that backed up to Powell Springs. "I believe I'll walk."

Jess had seen a lot of death, too. Bax was right.

It never got easier.

• • •

News of Winks's death flew through town. Whit Gannon delivered it to Virgil Tilly himself. He walked in and saw that no customers were around, so he strode through the sawdust and peanut shells on the floor and sat at the corner table everyone coveted.

"What'll it be, Whit?"

He sighed and stretched out his long legs. "I wanted to let you know that Winks died."

While Tilly's jaw was hanging open, Whit gave him the details. "Fred came and got him just a few minutes ago."

The saloon owner sat down on the nearest chair, his face chalky, his expression stunned. "Well, good God," he intoned. "Good God."

Whit straightened up. "He got that moonshine from somewhere. You don't know anything about it, do you, Virgil?"

His head came up. "Me? Whit, I don't buy that stuff! And don't think they haven't tried to sell it to me."

"Who's 'they'?"

"Nobody I knew. But I've had two-three shifty-looking types come through here, practically giving it away. I won't take it. You and I have a deal. Besides, look what happened"—he dug around in his back pocket for his red bandana and blew his nose with a honk—"to—to Winks, that poor old rummy." His voice broke.

"You know he didn't have anyone left alive in town or a penny to his name. His mother died ten years ago. We thought maybe you'd help take up a collection to bury him. I don't think Fred is going to do it for free. We're not going to give him a twenty-one gun salute and a war hero's funeral, but he shouldn't get put in an unmarked hole, either."

Tilly nodded, staring at the floor. "Sure, sure. Whatever he needs."

Whit left him to ponder the mysteries of life and death.

Prodded by conscience, Tilly took up a collection among his customers late that afternoon. "Let that be a lesson to you boys," he said, passing around an empty pickle jar. "I might have to charge more than a bootlegger, but I'll never sell you poison."

"Winks wasn't a bad sort," Jack Willard said. "He just couldn't give up the drink, and no government was going to make him." He added this just before downing a shot of whiskey. He signaled to Tilly for another and pushed his money across the bar.

"Well, then, here's to Winks, the poor bastard," Cud Portman added. "I hope he goes to the land of milk and honey, where you can paddle a boat in a lake of whiskey and another one of stew, like they talk about in that song."

"What song?" someone else asked.

"Some old song, 'Big Rock Candy Mountain,' I think it's called. It's a hobo paradise with cigarette trees, and you never have to work. But I wouldn't want 'To be buggered sore like a hobo's whore.'"

"I don't think Winks will have to worry about that," Jack said, then looked him up and down. "Neither do you, Cud."

"Hell, none of you have to," threw in Tom Sommers, still wearing his cork boots from a day spent at the mill.

"They don't do that in a paradise!"

By the time this subject had been exhausted, the pickle jar was filled and Tilly chipped in the rest to give town drunk Winks Lamont a decent send-off.

CHAPTER TEN

Tabitha Monroe woke to the suffocating feeling of a man's hand clamped over her mouth. Her startled cry was muffled by more pressure.

"Don't scream!" A dark, shadowy figure hovered above her. "If I let go, will you be quiet?"

A bit sleep addled but awake enough to agree, she nodded. "Harlan!" she exclaimed when he released her. "What are you doing? Where have you been?"

In the dim glow of streetlights streaming through the windows, she saw him hold a finger to his lips. "Shhh!"

She reached out to turn on the lamp.

"No!"

The low bedside light glowed around them. "Harlan, it doesn't matter. No one is here except me."

"Where's Elsa?"

"She quit. I couldn't pay her and she wouldn't wait. I can barely pay the grocery bill. The yard is turning into a jungle because the gardeners stopped coming for some reason, and that was before I ran out of money. My roses are covered with black spot. Where have you been?" she demanded again. "And why are you dressed like a second-story man?" He wore a dark jacket and a black billed cap.

"I've been away on top secret business for another client. Someone who wants to remain anonymous."

She pulled herself upright and fluffed the pillows behind her back with angry thumps. "Another client—you've never had any clients. You work for Robert Burton. Didn't you think to tell me *something*? That I might be worried? I even thought you could be—might be, well, dead." Her voice quivered on the word. "You've been gone for a month, and I haven't heard a single word from you! Really, Harlan, this is simply indefensible! Mr. Burton's lawyer has been here looking for you and they are on the verge of involving the police. They claim you're responsible for some sort of financial 'irregularities.'"

She told him about the day that Donald Rinehart made a surprise appearance at her luncheon. "And he's been here twice since."

Harlan sighed. "Nothing else?"

"Nothing else! Isn't that bad enough? I can barely hold up my head among our friends—they all smell blood and scandal. Right now I'm invited to functions just for my gossip appeal. They think I don't know, but I hear people whispering. Soon, though, the invitations will dry up and they'll just shun me. I try to pretend that everything is fine, and feign confidence when I'm asked awkward questions that I can't answer."

"Truly, Tabitha, it's best that way. The less you know, the better."

She punched an uncooperative pillow again. "How could you do this to me? I can't pay the bills since I'm not a signatory on the bank accounts. I don't even know what we have. Vendors just keep calling on the telephone and coming to the door. I have to pay Strohecker's from the cash I keep in my jewelry chest just to eat, and that's almost gone. What have you done?"

"I told you, I'm doing confidential work for a client who must remain anonymous."

She scowled. "Is that what I'm supposed to tell people? That discretion prevents me from explaining that my husband is not really a criminal—that it only looks like he is? When are you coming home? That is if we still have a home to come back to. This is frightening and unacceptable, Harlan. How could you do this to me?" she repeated.

He reached into the breast pocket of his coat and gave her an envelope. "Here, take this. It's a thousand dollars, and should see you through for a while. Try to get Elsa to come back. If she won't, find another maid."

She looked inside and leafed through ten one-hundred-dollar bills. "Where did this come from?"

"I'm a man of many interests. You knew that when you married me. I still have other matters to see to. I really believe that when this is over, we'll be set and all of the misunderstandings here will be easily sorted out. Trust me, Tabitha, the less you know, the safer you are. But everything will be set to rights. You believe me, don't you?"

She did believe him. Even though every alarm in her mind rang, she chose to disregard them. Early in their marriage she had learned to ignore her misgivings about many of the things he told her. Life was so much smoother that way. "Yes, of course, but what should I tell—"

"It's better this way, but it's only temporary." He put his hand on her thigh beneath the blanket and his gaze wandered to the décolletage of her silk nightgown. "I've missed you."

"I've missed you too! I've been so worried. Couldn't you have called or even sent me a wire?"

"No, I have to be extremely circumspect in all of my actions. I'll explain it to you someday. But for now, you're better off knowing nothing."

"Is it illegal, what you're doing?" She clutched the soft linen sheet to her bosom.

"No, no, not really. It would just look odd at this stage of the proceedings. I swear it will all be ironed out pretty soon." His hand crept higher up her leg, and his eyes darkened. "How much have you missed me?"

She didn't resist when he leaned forward and kissed her passionately, perhaps more so than he ever had before. "A lot," she whispered. He flipped aside her blankets and tore off her nightgown.

He left an hour later and Tabbie watched from her window as he faded back into the night, with no idea of where he was going or when he would return.

• • •

Amy sat at the desk in the living room, going over the monthly finances. Everyone had just paid their room and board, and she hadn't yet taken the money to the bank. For the time being, she locked it in a drawer. She tried to make herself concentrate on her task but her mind kept straying to Bax, the conversation they'd had two nights earlier, and everything else about him. That kiss, that wonderful, frightening kiss. She'd felt herself respond to it like a drought-withered plant blessed with a sudden shower.

Since then, every time he came and went she found a reason to be nearby, and she didn't think she was imagining that he was nearby more than ever before.

It was a dangerous, foolish daydream to entertain. She was beginning to catch herself listening for him coming in the back door, for the sound of his voice. While her imagination wandered over his height and his promise to defend her, she gazed out the side window, lost in thought. So when someone knocked on the front door she froze, her fountain pen stilled in her hand. She heard Deirdre's soft footfalls as she walked to the entry hall. The two women were alone, although they had stopped leaving the doors unlocked. She heard the murmur of voices, one male, but it wasn't familiar. Not like that terrible evening in the hotel lobby.

Soon Deirdre approached her in the living room, her stubborn cough and chest congestion preceding her. She couldn't seem to recover from that cold she'd had, and Amy thought her creamy redhead's complexion looked almost translucent now. She could see fine, pale-blue veins in the woman's temples and in the backs of her hands.

"Who is it?" Amy whispered, wishing Tom or preferably Bax were home.

"He says he wants to talk with you," she whispered back.

"Do you know him? Does he look familiar?"

"No, but he asked for you by name. He says he knows Mr. Duncan."

It sounded strange to Amy. She didn't want more boarders than she had, but if he knew Bax, she supposed she should at least talk to him. She pushed herself away from the desk. "All right. I'm coming."

She followed Deirdre back to the entry hall and found an unshaven, rough-looking man standing there in rather shabby clothes. Her guard went up immediately. "I'm Amy Jacobsen. I'm sorry but I have no rooms available."

He eyed her up and down in a way that gave her chills. It wasn't lust she saw, it was a baffling contempt. "I'm not here for a room. I'd like to talk a little business with you, though."

"Business. Mrs. Gifford told me that you know Deputy Duncan. Perhaps he's the one you want to see. He should be along soon."

"No, ma'am. I do know Duncan, but you're sure enough the person I want to talk with."

She didn't want to let him any farther into the house. "What is this about, Mr.—who? You haven't told me your name."

He scraped off his grease-stained hat and gave her an ingratiating smile of mostly gums. She took an involuntary step back.

"For now, just think of me as Milo. It's kind of personal, Mrs. Jacobsen." He didn't break eye contact with her but tilted his head in Deirdre's direction.

"Oh—well, I have some mending to get back to," Deirdre said. Even though Amy shot her a desperate, purposeful look, she added, "I'll be upstairs."

When her footsteps faded, Amy put on a false front of bravery, but her heart began pounding so hard she had trouble breathing. "All right, *Milo*, what is this about?"

He looked around at the walls and beyond to the living room and dining room. "This is a nice place. Yes, ma'am, real nice. Adam Jacobsen, your mister, he knows you're here."

Her stomach felt as if it sank to her knees, but she said nothing. She wanted to know if this was a threat or a warning or something else.

"What he doesn't know is that you've got a little romance going with Baxter Duncan."

"I what!" The exclamation whooshed out of her. "I have no such thing going on with anyone! You can tell Bax what you've said to me. He's due home for lunch any minute," she lied.

"Nope, he isn't. The sheriff and him went on an errand over to Fairdale. He'll be gone for a while."

"You don't know that!" Panic began to eat at the edges of her bravado.

"There you're wrong. I do know. I keep my eyes and ears open. I saw Duncan and that sheriff drive off in the county's car myself. Now, I don't care what people do. That's their business. But I've seen those little kisses between the two of you. In the backyard, at the door before he left the other night—who knows what else. I'm guessing you wouldn't want your husband to hear about that."

She realized that his man, this—this *barbarian*, was the one Bax had seen watching her. The one he'd warned her about. "How dare you suggest such a thing!"

"Like I said, people's doings are their business, but you're in a hard spot here. When I suggested to your mister that you might have a fancy man, he hinted that he'd kill you both. And you aren't just fooling around on your husband, someone with a pretty bad temper as far as I can tell. You've got an ex-convict under your roof."

Amy locked her knees to keep them from folding beneath her. "Ex-convict—"

"I guess Bax hasn't told you about that." He chuckled. "Well, I can see why. But he spent some time in prison, and even the sheriff doesn't know about it. Bax told me that himself."

"In prison for what?"

"I'll let you ask him about that. But by God, I guess news like that would put a real charley horse in the man's life. He'd get booted out of his job for certain. Who knows what else might happen if it got around?"

Amy felt as if she'd been punched in the midsection, and she did know what that was like. Trying to maintain her outward composure while everything in her mind was running in circles and screaming, she said, "Just what is your purpose in telling me all of this?"

"Well, I'm a fair man and I'd hate to see everyone's lives torn up. So I'm willing to make you a good offer. You pay me a hundred dollars to keep your secrets and it'll be smooth going."

"If I refuse and demand that you take your disgusting proposal, filthy insinuations, and get out right now?"

His expression and tone turned menacing. "Okay, I tried being polite and nice about this but I guess you aren't going to be reasonable. I'll go, but one hell of a lot of trouble will come to you instead. Don't think it won't."

"I'm sure Baxter Duncan would like to hear about you as well," she bluffed, keeping an iron grip on her fear.

He chuckled. "Ho, I doubt that, lady, and you seem to have missed the point. He doesn't want anyone to know about his past, including you. So if word gets around, I'll make sure you're the one who gets blamed."

From a shallow, evaporating reserve of pent-up fury and steel she didn't know she possessed, she clenched her jaw and stared at him, eye to eye. "Fifty dollars."

He gave the appearance of thinking it over. "Sixty—cash only, by the way—and we'll call it good."

She huffed out a breath and went to the living room. Fortunately, he stayed in the hall and couldn't see all the way to the locked desk drawer where she kept money. Her hands shook as she tried to get the key in the lock and missed three times. At last she took out the sixty dollars, leaving her only five to get through the rest of the month, which still had twenty-five days left in it.

She returned and put the cash in his dirty, outstretched hand. He stuffed it into an inside pocket in his jacket. "There's your money. Now take it and get out."

He put his hat back on and tipped it. "Nice doing business with you, ma'am." He'd opened the front door and stepped outside. She was about to slam it behind when he said something that sucked away her last reserves of courage. "I'll see you again next month."

"What do you mean?"

He sneered at her. "People don't always understand the finer points of buying someone's silence. But it usually involves an ongoing payment. And since the point of buying silence is to keep a secret, you won't want to be telling anyone about this."

"Don't you *ever* come back here!" she uttered in a menacing tone, and this time did slam the door, making sure to lock it.

God, what had just happened? she wondered, trembling like an old fencepost in a strong wind. Both frightened and furious, she leaned her back against the door and sank to the mat under her feet. The feeling sizzling through her reminded her of the time she'd pulled an electric plug from its outlet and the prongs touched her fingers. The jolt had run through her hand and up her arm to her shoulder.

This man Milo knew Adam? Knew Bax? And Bax—his mysterious past involved prison. Was it all true? None of it? Some of it had to be. Did it having something to do with Bax's comment that he couldn't use the front door? That grimy stranger knew things that only a spy or a Peeping Tom could know. Both were possible, both made her so uneasy she wanted to jump up and close all the curtains, but she was trembling so much she couldn't quite take command of her arms and legs to hoist herself from the floor.

With her elbows on her upraised knees, she rested her head in her hands, trying to decide how much more trouble she was in now. Her plan had been to get away from Adam and, with luck, reestablish her life in Powell Springs. But not much had gone well since she'd arrived with the exception of inheriting this house, and now even that was in peril. She felt as if she'd traded one set of bad problems for another. She had more freedom here, but she felt as much a prisoner as she had in Portland.

How would she feed everyone for the rest of the month with five dollars? There was no doubt that living with Adam had forced her to learn creative ways to stretch money, but even her ingenuity had its limits. If that blackmailer came back again in June, as he'd said he would, they wouldn't survive unless she refused to pay him. She wished she could share this with someone, but it wasn't possible. She didn't think she could trust anyone now. The information involved was too sensitive. Once more, Amy felt alone in the world.

From the staircase she heard Deirdre's cough. She came into view, still pressing her handkerchief to her mouth. When she caught sight of Amy, she hurried across the braided hall runner.

"Oh, dear heavens! Amy! Are you all right? I'm so sorry I left you alone—I didn't think anything was wrong." She crouched next to her and brushed frantically at straggling strands of Amy's hair so she could see her face.

"I was hoping you wouldn't."

Deirdre wore a stricken, guilty expression as she examined her face and neck for signs of abuse. "Are you hurt? Did that man hurt you?"

"No. Not physically."

"What then?"

"Never mind, he's gone. I got rid of him." She took Deirdre's outstretched hand to regain her feet. As she brushed off her skirt, she added, "But some strange things are happening in Powell Springs. People who never would have bothered with this town are coming here now. From now on, we can't let in anyone we don't recognize. No one. I don't care who they claim to know."

Deirdre turned toward the kitchen. "Come sit down and I'll make you some tea."

"No, thank you." From that angle, Amy could see that Deirdre's dress, which had fit before, was now beginning to hang on her, but it was only a fleeting thought. Right now, her mind was fixed on securing her privacy.

Only the windows on the west side of the house had roller blinds because in the summer it got so hot. The rest of windows had curtains, some made of lace that didn't provide much cover, but they were better than nothing. She closed them all.

• • •

That afternoon, nervous but determined, Amy tidied her hair and put on a spring hat that she'd finally splurged on—now to her regret—and went to see Daniel Parmenter. All this time, all these years, Adam had made her believe that everything that went wrong in their marriage was her fault. But after this morning, she'd begun to realize that it wasn't true. She'd have no true peace until she was not legally bound to him any longer.

His clerk had her take a seat in front and Dan came out to join her. His shirtsleeves were rolled up his forearms and his tie was askew.

"Please forgive me, Mrs. Jacobsen. I'm afraid you've caught me in the middle of a research project."

"Would you rather that I came back another time?"

"No, no, as long as you don't mind sitting among some books."

She released a little sigh of relief and nodded. "That's perfectly fine. I appreciate you interrupting your work to speak with me."

He led her to his office and directed her to a chair, brushing a clean handkerchief over the seat. He hadn't been exaggerating about the books. "I'm researching some property ownership laws and I'm afraid I've managed to get sidetracked. Research can be like that. One interesting fact leads to another. Please—sit." He settled across from her. "Now, how can I help you?"

She looked around to make certain she would not be overheard, but his door was closed. Inhaling deeply, she knew what she must do and should have done her first day here. "I'm not sure how to go about this, or how to approach—I've never known anyone who did this—"

"Just say it quickly. That will help."

She dropped her gaze to a book sitting on the desk in front of her. "I want to divorce my husband."

If he was surprised, he didn't show it. "It's not all that common, but it happens far more often than you'd think. You are not the first married woman looking to escape from, shall we say, an unhappy union."

"Is it difficult?"

"No, it can take some time. But really, there are just two requirements. You have to show cause. You know, give a reason."

Her head came up. "Reason?" She imagined the intimate details of her life recorded in some legal document and filed in the county records for anyone and everyone to see.

"An example would be abandonment. A man goes out for a newspaper and simply disappears. Or decides he's had enough and packs up and walks out, leaving the wife and possibly children with no means of support. Then there's infidelity, although that can be more challenging if the law requires proof. Another reason is mental or physical cruelty. I imagine you might be more familiar with that."

Amy felt her face heat up like a cast iron skillet on the stove and she closed her eyes briefly. Did she have a scarlet *B* for *Beaten* sewn to her dress front? "And the other requirement?"

"In order to get the ball rolling, after we work out the details on our side, we must serve divorce papers to the spouse. That means we need to know where to find him. If he's nowhere to be found, the announcement must be published in newspapers."

She cringed at the thought. "I hope that won't be necessary. I-I believe I know where Mr. Jacobsen is."

He went on to explain some other fine points when she asked, "What about this house I've inherited? Do I get to keep that? It was left only to me, but I can easily imagine that if Adam finds out about it, he'll expect to confiscate it."

He nodded. "In some states, he could take it outright. Oregon is more equitable when it comes to division of assets."

"You mean I have to share it with him? *I'm* not looking for anything from him—we never had anything. I just want to be left alone."

He studied her with a mild, comforting expression. "All right." He searched through the stacks on his desk until he found a ruled yellow pad and his pen. "Let's get things started. Tell me what's going on."

So Amy did.

• • •

"I suppose it was bound to come to this, but I'm not looking forward to it." While Bax sat in the passenger seat holding their weapons, Whit Gannon piloted the Model T over rutted back roads that led to the hills behind Fairdale. It had been dry for a few days, so at least the mud had solidified a bit. "Some of these boys know and care about what they're doing. They make decent stuff. Others don't and it's hard to tell the difference until someone like Winks dies."

"Isn't that a smoke plume up there?" Bax asked, pointing to a forested hillside.

"Hmm, yeah, that looks like the right place. They must be just getting started. Once a good fire is going, it doesn't smoke."

"How did you hear about this?"

Whit resettled his hat and gripped the steering wheel with his right hand. "I talked to Luke Becker—he's an old guy who's lived around here with his wife for over forty years. I used to help out in the summers on his farm when I was a kid. He was a nice man, a young widower, and his wife was a mail-order bride from Chicago. He brought her out here to help him raise his daughter. They had four more children after that. Anyway, he said he sees wagons hauling barrels and cases of Mason jars past his place on a pretty regular basis. And he knows who they are. I just don't want him and his wife, Emily, getting harassed for reporting it. They're in their seventies now. Their kids and grandkids visit all the time, and I don't want anyone getting hurt."

Bax gripped the two shotguns between his knees, and both men were armed with pistols. "I wish we knew how much of this is going on around here. We might be trying to fight a forest fire with a watering can." He felt a little jumpy about it—he hadn't even pointed a weapon at anyone since the war. But then, why would he?

Under a dull, gray sky, they made their way up through the woods and came upon a setup of a medium size still camouflaged by trees. A stream of clear, cold water flowed nearby, a necessity for the task, but there was no evidence of anyone living here. In another couple of weeks, the trees would be completely leafed out and this metal contraption of boiler and coiled tubing would be almost impossible to spot.

"Not the fanciest operation," Bax commented, getting out. Whit joined him, and he handed the sheriff a shotgun.

"No, it doesn't take much. I don't see anyone but keep your eyes open." Whit glanced around and pointed at a tarp-covered pile shrouded by fir limbs. "Go see."

Bax gave him a wry look that implied *thanks so much.* Anything could be under there. He shifted his weapon to his shoulder and waded through the spring ground cover to lift the corner of the tarp. "Sawdust." He added with a touch of irony, "Premium grade."

"Okay. Let's knock this thing down. I know it'll just pop up somewhere else, but we can't leave it. And if we do a decent job, we'll put them out of business for a while."

Bax scanned the surrounding area, looking for any sign that they were being watched. But it wouldn't be hard to hide here, and it sure as hell wasn't hard to imagine getting shot from some blind up the hill. They went to the back of the car and pulled out an axe and a sledgehammer. With the first swing of the tools clanging on the still, startled birds fled the nearby trees, squawking and giving shrill cries of complaint. The underbrush rustled with two or three unseen creatures and the whole forest seemed to shudder with the noise.

Steam rose from the hot sawdust mash, which flowed downhill like boiling oatmeal to scald everything in its path. The men didn't stop until the cylindrical tank was as flattened as an old tin can, the coil was crushed beyond salvage, the sawdust pile was scattered everywhere, and both of them had sweated through their shirts.

"Hooo!" Bax exclaimed, dragging a forearm across his brow. "I haven't done work like that in a while!"

They put all the tools back and Whit brought out a printed sign that featured a skull and crossbones with the text, WARN-ING! *Moonshiners Will Be Prosecuted to the Full Extent of State and Federal Law.* He nailed the sign to a tree.

"Do you really think that will work? There's sure no shortage of raw materials around here. All the sawdust in the logging camps and the mill could keep someone in business till the end of time," Bax asked, taking a drink of water from a canteen he'd brought along. He passed it to Whit.

Whit laughed and took a long swallow. "Hell, no, it won't work! But at least they'll remember that we're watching them."

"We can't take on all of them—there aren't enough of us to go around."

"I won't bring in the feds. They make more trouble than they solve. Besides, I don't want them to shut down Tilly, or give me grief for not doing it myself. I know he sometimes cuts good whiskey with water or bad-tasting stuff like Worcestershire sauce or angostura bitters he gets from the druggist. If a customer is giving him a hard time, he has a special bottle dosed with cod liver oil that will give the man a chance to ponder his rude behavior later in the outhouse." Bax laughed at that. "But he's never hurt anyone, and now after Winks, he's got the fear of God in him. He's not buying from anyone he doesn't know, or taking any bottles that aren't sealed. Tilly isn't our problem."

CHAPTER ELEVEN

When Bax unlocked the back door and walked into the kitchen the next evening he smelled dinner, and Amy was standing at the stove stirring a pot of something. She'd filled out a bit since she'd first arrived, and her small frame bore more fully rounded curves. The picture, like a still life painting, made him imagine a mellow evening and coming in from a day's hard work to find the precious gift of a woman who loved him, despite his past. Despite everything.

But she jumped when she saw him and gave him an odd look. The frightened, wary face she'd worn when she arrived was back. And this time it seemed to be directed at him. "We'll be eating in a few minutes." The food smelled great—he hoped it was more than she'd served last night. She'd split a chicken four ways and everyone got one piece. He'd seen a few dog scraps left over in the roasting pan, but they disappeared right after dinner.

As if the announcement summoned him, Tom came bounding down the back stairs to the kitchen. "Is Deirdre—I mean Mrs. Gifford going to eat with us?"

Amy smiled at him. "It's all right, Tom. You can call her Deirdre. We've become pretty informal around here." Her gaze cut to Bax and back again. "She's lying down right now. She can't seem to get over her chest cold. I'll take her something myself." She gave Bax another strange glance, not smiling now.

Bax sat in his chair in the dining room, baffled by her shifting moods—distracted and nervous, suspicious and worried. She'd begun treating him like a leper yesterday. If it was because of that kiss . . . it was *just* a kiss he'd given her and she hadn't protested. In fact, he'd felt her respond. Could he have been wrong? He dragged himself away from the memory of it to concentrate on the day's problem.

"Tom, have you noticed anything going on near the mill operation that seems funny?" He went on to explain the sawdust still he and Whit had knocked down that day. "Sometimes bootleggers follow logging camps and set up their operations near mills because they can scavenge the sawdust."

"I haven't seen anyone, but I can ask around. I heard about poor old Winks. Tilly was practically bawling into his bar towel."

Bax nodded. "I didn't really know him but I get the impression he was kind of like furniture around town. Always there." He hitched and lowered his brow. "Now he's not."

Amy put a soup tureen on the table and a plate piled with slices of homemade bread, then took her place. "I can't remember a time when Winks wasn't hanging around someone's porch or scrounging up odd jobs."

Bax looked at the thin, pale broth in his soup bowl with its grains of barley, remaining bits of yesterday's chicken, and a few vegetables, and hoped something more substantial was coming next. But when the soup was gone and the bread eaten, she began clearing the dishes. He and Tom exchanged puzzled looks, but she would not meet either man's eyes. This was a big change from the meals they'd grown accustomed to—roast, chicken and dumplings, pork chops, served with butter- and cream-rich mashed potatoes, candied yams, spring peas, and big desserts. This put Bax in mind of hospital food—or worse. And for Tom, who worked harder than a rented mule at the sawmill, this was no meal at all.

But if Deirdre was sick, he thought, maybe this was the most Amy'd had time for. In the awkward silence that followed, the men pushed out their chairs. He picked up a soup dish and carried it to the kitchen. He found her putting together a tray for Deirdre with the same soup, tea, and toast.

"Are things all right?" he asked, keeping his voice down.

Amy whirled to face him. "Yes, of course," she said with a quick brightness that sounded forced even to her own ears. What could possibly be wrong? she asked herself, feeling a hysterical laugh trying to work its way up her throat. She was being blackmailed, she had barely enough money to feed them all for one week let alone three more after that (and the men had already noticed the lack), bills that needed to be paid, a vengeful husband in town tracking her every move with a hired thug who had come to her door and would probably come back, and an ex-convict living under her roof. Things were positively *grand*.

"You'd tell me if something has happened, wouldn't you?" he asked. He stood so close to her she felt the heat from his body. Or it seemed like she did.

"Of course. Certainly." She smiled at him, a broad grin that stretched her cheeks so much they hurt. "Everything is just fine."

He looked down, searching her face with a close scrutiny that almost paralyzed her. The corner of his mouth dropped and he shook his head. "Nope. I don't believe that."

She felt her own lower lip tremble and she clenched her jaw, terrified that she'd begin crying. "Really, Bax, I have to take this tray to Deirdre before it's cold." She had to escape from him before he pried anything out of her. She picked it up and slipped around him to hurry up the stairs.

In the hallway, she heard the sound of Deirdre's cough through her closed door. She took a deep, steadying breath. Then, carefully balancing the tray against her waist, Amy knocked before turning the knob. She found Deirdre propped on pillows and in her nightgown, looking pale and sweaty. Her red hair contrasted sharply with her ashen face, which seemed to fade into the pillowcase.

"I've brought you some chicken broth with barley," she said. This bedroom on the north side of the house was dim, despite the two hours of daylight remaining. It smelled like a sick room, stuffy, the air heavy with vain hope.

"I'm so sorry to make you wait on me like this, Amy. I should be better anytime now."

"I think you'd better go see Jessica. This has dragged on long enough and you need a doctor." She put the tray on the night table next to Deirdre and helped her fluff her pillows to put her in a sitting position. Then she opened one of the windows a couple of inches to let in fresh air.

"But I know I'll be better soon. I've just been overdoing it, I guess. If the cough would only let up, I could get some rest." As if to emphasize the point, her now-gurgling cough set off again. It took her a moment to regain her breath. "That's part of the problem. It wakes me up."

Amy set the tray on Deirdre's lap. "What about the cough medicine you got from Granny Mae?"

"It's gone."

"Then we'll have to get more for you. Did it really work?"

"Pretty well."

Amy couldn't imagine why since it was just a mishmash of black pepper, honey, and some kind of powder, with a whole clove and a scrape of nutmeg thrown in for flavor.

"All right. I'll see to it tomorrow."

Deirdre took a sip of broth and put down the spoon. "I could get it myself. I don't want you to bother."

"That's all right. You need to get your strength back." Amy sat in the chair beside her bed. At one time, she would have had no patience for sitting in a sickroom with a rabbity martyr. But since those days, she'd taken care of women recovering from childbirth and miscarriages, botched abortions, beatings, and illnesses. Jessica had once tried to tell her what her life had been like in New York, working in the tenements for the public health department. To Amy, it had all sounded melodramatic and highly exaggerated. She knew better now. "Have more soup," she urged Deirdre. "You won't get well if you don't eat."

Her patient dutifully finished the broth and half a piece of toast, then sagged back against her pillows.

"Tom was asking about you," Amy said, giving her a teasing smile, hoping to win one back. She stood and took the tray.

"Oh, um, that's nice." She offered a faint smile in return and touched a hand to her hair. "I'm glad he can't see me right now."

"He seems like a nice man."

"I think so too," Deirdre agreed, but the conversation was cut short by her thick, ropy cough. She put her handkerchief to her mouth and it was dotted with rust-colored stains.

Amy turned away. Deirdre needed the medicine *and* a doctor. Tomorrow she'd get both.

• • •

That night, Amy tossed and turned so much in her bed that she untucked all the sheets. They'd wadded themselves up into such a small bundle, she lay huddling at a bottom corner of the mattress hugging her pillows. Finally with a huff she got up. In the dim glow of a veiled half-moon that shone through the window, she remade the bed and sank back into its depths.

For the past two days and nights she'd asked herself the same question. What on earth had compelled her to give away good money to protect Bax? It was bad enough to have to pay that thug, Milo, to keep him from telling Adam his vulgar lies about an invented relationship between her and Bax. But to keep Bax's past a secret, too? A past, she realized, that could have been an invention of Milo's as well. And if it was true—God, what kind of man was he, what had he done to be sentenced to prison? Strangely, she had the feeling that he wouldn't be happy about the sacrifice she'd made, but would instead be angry. There was no one else in the house who would inspire that much loyalty in her. Maybe not even another person in her life at this point. She'd not heard from Jessica again after the dinner invitation, and she wasn't sure where to lay the blame for that—on Jess, herself, or Adam. She might learn tomorrow when she went to Jessica's office to bring her home for Deirdre.

Where *was* Adam, anyway? She'd seen him that one time, and now he had an accomplice, an evil toady, spying on her.

Amy sighed and pulled the covers up to her chin with both fists. Despite what she thought Milo might know or could be making up, she knew there was no question that he was watching her. Bax had seen him from a distance, and he knew things he could have learned only by watching them.

And how long was she going to be able to get away with charging her current rate of room and board when the quality of the food had already begun to deteriorate? She had to find a way out of this—somehow. She'd hoped she'd at last escaped Adam's tyranny, and had come all the way back to Powell Springs, endured the whispering and sidelong glances of her former neighbors, and taken over this boardinghouse for what? Only to live in terror too? To be run off from here again? Some secrets were necessary to keep. Others needed to be quelled by being shared.

On the other side of the wall, she sensed Bax sleeping, struggling with none of the troubles that plagued her.

It must be nice, she thought, to be able rest without carrying the weight of so many problems. She punched her pillow and tried to find that place.

• • •

The sun has just cleared the eastern horizon the next morning when Bax came downstairs. Tom followed right behind him. Amy was at the stove again—or still—as if she'd never left it. She didn't speak to either of them. Dawn sunlight streamed through the window over the sink.

He couldn't smell anything that resembled a decent breakfast, and wondered what mouthwatering delight was waiting for them this time. He came up behind Amy to look over her shoulder. He saw a big pot of oatmeal. No eggs cooking, no bacon, no ham or even potatoes. Just coffee perking and biscuits heaped on a plate in the warmer. He glanced at the kitchen table and saw the cream pitcher and the table set for three.

"Take your seat, Bax. Breakfast is ready." She hadn't even looked at him. It was as if she had eyes in the back of her head, and she sounded like a schoolteacher.

He did as he was told, and she flopped scoops of mush into everyone's bowl, then poured coffee and brought the biscuits to the table. They ate in silence, but Bax got a good look at her face. Violet smudges underlined her eyes, and faint diagonal lines led away from them to make her look as if she hadn't slept in a week. Her hair hung over one shoulder, pulled back with a piece of wrinkled ribbon, and she wore the same dress she'd had on the day before.

Obviously sensing the tension, Tom glanced back and forth between them, but remained quiet and left as soon as he could. Bax stayed at the table and as Amy was about to get up to begin clearing the dishes, he stopped her.

"How is Deirdre?"

"I'm letting her sleep in this morning. She's not doing very well."

He nodded. "Did you stay up all night taking care of her?"

She gave him a puzzled look. "No—well, I checked on her once. Why?"

"You look like you haven't slept."

Her brows slammed together over the bridge of her nose, and he sat back, realizing too late that he'd lit the fuse on a stick of dynamite instead of a candle. "This isn't a beauty pageant I'm running here, Baxter Duncan. I've got a sick woman upstairs, wash piling up, and more worries than finding moonshiners up in the hills! I'm sorry I don't measure up to your notion of an ideal female. If you want something better, get a wife, one who meets your standards."

She pushed herself away from the table and prepared to stand. Bax shut his mouth with a *clack* of his teeth. He never would have dreamed that such a fiery hellcat was buried beneath all the apologies and mousy humility he'd seen in her.

He jumped out of his chair and pushed her back down. "All right, all right, I'm sorry, I was just—I wasn't insulting you."

"Oh, no? I'm not dressed well enough, I look tired, my cooking is bad—"

"I didn't say any of—"

"—things around here aren't *perfect* or even good enough, I'm not careful with money or—"

He realized the vitriol pouring out of her had very little to do with what he'd said. Well, maybe he'd uttered what amounted to the last straw, but this was the result of her past, and now all that pent-up resentment boiled over.

He leaned forward again and put his hand on her forearm. "Amy, Amy, take a breath."

She was like a runaway horse. "Well, let me tell you something. I didn't invite an ex-convict into this house and it seems to me that you're in no position to criticize, considering *my* sins don't include spending time in prison!"

His breath left him in a rush, as if he'd been kicked in the chest, and a quiet fury began percolating in him. "I don't know what the hell you're going on about."

Amy stared at his angry, still face, drained of color, and she realized what she'd done. She put her elbows on the table and pressed her forehead in her hands. "Oh, God." She glanced at him and he was as fixed as a statue.

"You'd better tell me what you mean." It was a quiet command, but more frightening than shouting.

With a sense of dreary resignation, she said, "A man came to the door two days ago. A man who said he knows you. I thought he wanted to rent a room."

Bax said nothing but drummed his index finger on the table and kept his smoky gaze on her, waiting for her to continue.

"H-he wouldn't tell me his name but referred to himself as Milo."

The drumming sped up.

She hurried on to tell Bax what else the man had said. "He threatened to reveal everything if I didn't pay him. He wanted a hundred dollars. All I had to give him was sixty."

"You believed him?"

She babbled her explanation. "Some of it was almost right, and afterward I realized he must be the one who's been watching me—us. He even knew you weren't home and where you'd gone. Fairdale, he said. I wasn't sure about the rest, but how could I know? I just heard that he knows Adam and you, and he said he'd tell Whit Gannon about your past, then blame me." She closed her hands into one tight fist in her lap to keep from wringing them.

"God*damn* it!" he barked.

Amy cringed in her chair, worried about what would come next. In her experience, a slap or a punch could very well follow an angry outburst like that.

"I'm sorry," she whispered, hating the timid, fainthearted sound of her voice. Even hating the fact that she'd apologized. But she did it again. "I'm so sorry. There's not much money left to feed us all."

Bax looked at the effect his remark had on her. He sighed then and his shoulders sagged. "It's not your fault, Amy. Stop apologizing, for chrissakes. I'm the one who's sorry. You have troubles of your own and I brought you more. I never thought Breninger would blackmail you."

Her jaw dropped. "You know him?"

"Yeah. It's our bad luck that he met your—*husband*—" He said the word as if it were the most foul of epithets. "And involved you too." He gave her a rueful smile. "We're two sorry lots, you and I. He tried to blackmail me about a month ago, when he first got to town. I told him to go ahead and tell Whit what he knows, because I don't think he will. He doesn't want the law's attention."

"*How* do you know him?"

"We were in the same outfit in France. We were both from Oregon."

"He said you were in prison—"

"That's not why I know him."

"Then how—"

"But he was no war hero, that's for sure. We all knew he joined the army because the law was after him in Portland." He neatly deflected her questions. "He's still living up to his lousy reputation, and now he's involved with Jacobsen."

"I think he's working for Adam. And if I know Adam, he hasn't paid him."

"Oh-ho, so that's it. It makes more sense now." He got up and went to the stove to get the coffeepot. He poured them both warm-ups and put the pot on a folded dishtowel. "You know he won't stop coming around now, don't you? Paying him was like feeding a raccoon."

She drizzled so much cream in the coffee it looked like beige milk. "He already said he'd be back." She gazed up at him with a pleading expression that begged for understanding. "But I didn't know what else to do."

He was out of his chair again, pacing, and she saw his jaw muscle flex. "Great. Look, I have some savings put away. I'll give you the sixty dollars so we can start having decent food again." He took the creamer from her. "Then next time, I'll be here."

"But—"

He waved off her protest. "If I'd handled Breninger better from the beginning, he wouldn't have had a chance to bother you."

"How will you know when he's coming back, though?"

"You let me worry about that." He stopped in front of her and sat down again. "Amy, listen, I've been thinking about this. A lot. We need to get past our messes and salvage something of our lives for ourselves. We've both had a hard time over the years." He reached for her hand. "Things are bad right now. But they won't always be, and maybe you and I need to start thinking ahead instead of always looking over our shoulders at the past. We deserve that, don't you think?"

That pulled her up short. "You and I?"

He released her hand and color crept up his neck to his forehead. "You want out from under this, don't you? I mean we ought to get our lives sorted out."

Weariness, old hurts, and current circumstances brought out a cynical side of her. "Hah—wouldn't that be something." It was all she could offer because she couldn't see anything right now except problems.

After a repeated admonition to keep the doors locked and to stay aware of her surroundings when she went out, he put on his jacket, polished his deputy's nickel badge with his sleeve, and left for work.

It wasn't until he was gone that Amy realized she still didn't know if he'd spent time in prison. If he had, she didn't know why.

• • •

With a hedge cutter in one hand and a machete and crowbar in the other, Adam stood in spot in the woods along Butler Road, assessing the cabin that time and blackberries had tried to consume. Moss coated the roof like a bright-green carpet. Ivy, fir needles, wild rose brambles, and undergrowth wove a dense, tangled net over everything else. Against one side of the structure, a woodpile remained, just as mossy as the roof, but it should be all right.

Just off the road was an old wreck of a car he'd bought from a berry farmer outside of Twelve Mile. The man's son got it before he left for France and he had not survived the war. So the thing had sat in a field through five years of weather. Chickens had even roosted in it at one point. But the farmer let it go for thirty-five dollars. Once Adam was able to get it started, he drove it up here to look around. Then he'd gone back to the farm and bought some tools the old man had lying around to tackle this excavation. No one would notice, he didn't think. The car was hidden by some brush that grew wild, and the cabin sat back far enough to escape all but the most careful scrutiny.

He was no stranger to this place, but he was surprised it still stood. At one time, Emmaline Gannon—then Em Bauer—had lived up here and offered her services to men who knew how to find her. That bitch had been his downfall after her long-gone, half-witted husband reappeared while Adam was here. Bert Bauer had dragged the sheriff with him to have her arrested for moral turpitude, which he refused to do. The sheriff's live-and-let-live liberality was an example of what was wrong with society. If he'd done his job and removed the temptation in the first place, Adam's life would have taken a much different path. Instead, he had been revealed as one of her customers at a town council meeting, and then reviled by his parishioners as a sinner, the pack of hypocrites.

At the same time, Amy's plan to steal her sister's fiancé had been discovered. So they had run away together.

Revealed and reviled, the both of them.

And now Amy had run away from *him*.

When he heard that Whit Gannon had actually married Em, well, he supposed there was no end to some men's idiocy. At least Em's change of circumstances worked to his advantage now.

It was a significant decline in accommodations to move from the New Cascades to this dingy shack that was hardly more than a lean-to. God knew he'd lived in enough of them with Amy, although none of them had been this bad. From what he could see, the windows and the door had been boarded up, but he believed he could still use the place. He just had to hack through the brambles to pull off the boards. It wouldn't be a huge job, but unfortunately he'd have to do the work himself. He couldn't depend on someone else to keep this location secret or his presence in it. And Breninger was proving to be almost more trouble than he was worth. But Adam couldn't be in more than one place at a time so he still needed the man. He'd been able to string him along with another three hundred dollars, and it was much easier than he'd expected. Apparently Breninger had figured out that Adam Jacobsen was an important man, one to be reckoned with. He'd thought Breninger already knew that, but now it was firmly established.

So he pulled on a pair of work gloves, took the razor-sharp machete in hand, and began chopping his way through to the door with clumsy, unpracticed swings that could very well slice off a finger or a hand along with the berry vines. Brush flew in every direction, and in no time he was sweating and gasping like an old man.

"*Damn* Amy," he cursed under his breath. This was her fault. He wouldn't be out here working like a field hand if she hadn't defied him. But he'd fix that. By the time the spring shadows grew long and evening chill settled over the woods, he'd managed to uncover the windows and had pried off the last board blocking the entrance.

Leaning against the weather-swollen door, he turned the knob and pushed hard. It barely budged. He put his full weight behind his shoulder and slammed into it three more times. Finally it scraped open grudgingly, and released a gust of dank, moldy breath.

Inside, the iron bedstead was as he remembered it, the mattress rumpled and stained. The quilt and once-grayed sheets, now taupe with dust and time, had been pulled off, torn into strips, and thrown around. Two chairs were overturned and it looked as if Em had left in a hurry. A couple of jars of canned fruit stood on the shelves of a small pantry, their contents murky and inedible. Overhead, there was no ceiling, just bare rafters and dense clouds of cobwebs.

He'd have to bring in some basic provisions and necessities until this job was finished. And that couldn't happen soon enough.

• • •

"You caught me just in time," Granny Mae told Amy. Although it was just after four o'clock, she had already turned over the sign in her glass front door to read *Closed*. Her early dinner patrons, including widowers Mayor Cookson and Nathan Friedman, the jeweler, went back to their respective occupations. Fragrant aromas of roasting meat and baking bread still hung in the air, contrasting sharply with Amy's menus of late. "I'm closing up to go give Jessica a hand. Susannah Grenfell is in labor and we're going out to the farm to deliver her baby." All the tables and chairs in the café were neatly cleared. Beside the door stood a wicker basket that held a clean apron and some odds and ends that Amy couldn't immediately identify.

"Oh—" The last time Amy had seen Susannah, she'd just been widowed and her last name was still Braddock. Amy didn't like to think about when she and Susannah had been friends. It made her remember everything about those old days and added more weight to the load she carried on her heart. "I'm glad I got here before you left. Deirdre is out of that cough remedy you made for her and she swears by it." She produced the empty bottle.

"She should be well by now. Is she still coughing?" Granny asked, heading back to the kitchen. It still looked chaotic to Amy, with baskets of onions and potatoes on the floor, a garlic braid hanging from the ceiling, and the huge, ever-stoked black stove crouching against a brick wall like some chained, living beast. But despite the overstuffed cupboards and shelves, Granny Mae seemed to know where everything was.

"Yes, and I'm beginning to worry about her. She seemed to get better for just a bit, then relapsed. She's losing weight and her skin looks, well, almost transparent. That goopy cough plagues her night and day. And it wakes up the rest of the house. I think it's pneumonia."

Granny frowned as she plucked the recipe ingredients from her shelves, considering some and avoiding others. "I don't like the sound of that. Does she have a fever?"

"I'm not sure. She *looks* feverish sometimes. I was going to have Jessica examine her, but I guess not today."

"I'll tell her about it. Maybe that baby will be in a hurry to get here and she'll have some time tonight." She rummaged through one shelf, muttering to herself, "Where on earth is that grain? Oh, here—"

She followed the same procedure as before, crushing spices, herbs, and for all Amy knew, dragonfly wings and dried mouse tails, under her pestle. "What's in that stuff, anyway?"

"Just a bit of this and that," she replied, as if it were some secret potion that Amy might steal. She glanced up. "You haven't talked to your sister again, have you? She mentioned you didn't come to dinner."

Damn it all. Amy felt the heat rise in her face. The old woman was known for her bald-faced, uncomfortable candor. The last thing she needed was this opinionated busybody painting her into a corner. "No, I haven't."

Granny Mae added honey, a drizzle of some liquid, a big dose of the stuff she called grain into the batch, and kept mixing. "She was disappointed. I told her you probably had a good reason."

"I did."

"Well?"

Amy's temper, which she had suppressed for years, had been pushed to its limits in the past few days. "Mae, you're not my mother. You're not my sister. I don't owe you an explanation for anything I've done."

"Nope, you don't. But maybe you owe one to her. It might give you the chance to stop punishing yourself for what you did to her and Cole."

"I doubt it." Amy didn't know where that had come from, but suddenly, she realized the truth of it. Not only did she feel the constant isolation of a shunned outcast, guilt weighed on her with a heavy hand.

"It's worth a try."

"I was going to meet her that night," she blurted. "You talked to me when I was on my way to the hotel. But when I got there,

I saw Adam at the front desk. I ran before he had a chance to see *me*. You don't know—he and Jessica might have—I had to get away!" She looked down and realized she was wringing her purse as if it were a wet towel.

Granny Mae studied her for a moment. "Amy," she said quietly, "do you really think that Jessica would conspire against you with *Adam*? She hates him."

"I saw her leave the hotel right after he did!"

"Yes, she saw him, too. Have you forgotten what he did to her? He almost ran her out of town for good. Only her love for Cole was strong enough to bring her back. But you, her own flesh and blood, you failed her."

She couldn't meet the old lady's sharp gaze. "I know," she whispered finally. "I did a horrible thing. So many lives were nearly ruined. But I paid for it. I'm still paying for it."

Granny Mae squeezed her shoulder. "It will all get sorted out eventually. It would be good, though, if you helped things along."

Amy nodded, not trusting herself to speak. Her self-defensiveness, an ugly remnant of her careless youth, crept back to its corner and she shut the door on it again.

Mae funneled the cough medicine into the bottle Amy had brought. Then she pounded the cork into the neck with the heel of her hand and gave it to her. "You're really going out of your way to take care of Deirdre, Amy. I wouldn't have expected it."

Amy cleared the knot in her throat and lifted a brow. She handed her a quarter. "Surprised or disappointed?"

Granny gave her an even look from beneath her sparse white brows and took the money. "Surprised. But pleased."

Fair enough, Amy thought. "Thank you for this," she said, nodding at the bottle in her hand. "I hope everything works out for Susannah. Give her my—if you would . . . could you tell Jessica about Deirdre?"

Granny walked them toward the door and picked up her wicker basket. "I will, and if she can't make it over tonight, I'll come."

Both women were smiling when they parted.

CHAPTER TWELVE

Whit sat back in his swivel chair on the other side of his desk. "Bax, I really like you. I think you're an honest man with a decent sense of right and wrong. Plus you've got a knack for this job, and you're sincere about finding that balance between the letter and the spirit of the law. But I need to know what this is about." He pushed a poorly spelled, ink-splotched letter across the desk blotter.

Bax had never seen it before.

Sheriff—

You shud know that you have a X-convict working for you namly by the name of Baxter Duncen. He was sent to Ft. Leavenworth for dessertion on the last day of the War, Nov. 11, 1918. Im shure he did not tell you about that part did he.

Signed,
A Concernd Citizen

He read it and sighed.

"What's the rest of the story?" Whit asked. "I need to know."

Bax sat in silence for a moment and stared at the cold potbellied stove in the corner of the office. It was as if he were watching his future go up in flames its window. "That was the bare bones version."

"Is there another one?"

"Yes, but I'm curious. Is it so easy to believe this?" He nodded at the note. "An anonymous letter, written by someone who looks like he can barely hold a pen. But you assumed it was reliable information."

Whit tipped his head and peered at him from beneath his silver brows. "I think you know me better than that. I found that shoved under the door this morning. And I don't believe it. But *I'm* curious, too. I grew up with most of the people around here. I met you only a few months ago. Because the public puts a special trust in the men who work here, I have to check it out. They would expect that of me. Wouldn't you do the same?"

Bax nodded, grudgingly. "Yeah. I would."

"Then let's hear your side of it. Then I'm going to contact the War Department and get to the bottom of this. In the meantime, you still work here."

Bax knew that Whit was being fair, but he also knew he was on borrowed time now. Who'd want him working here after the sheriff learned the truth? Word would get around, and everyone—man, woman, and children who lost a male relative in the war—would be ready to tar and feather him. He'd encountered it the couple of times that even a breath of his war record got out.

"Thanks, Whit."

Whit leaned back in his chair. "I'm just hoping it turns out all right. But don't thank me yet."

• • •

Much to her surprise, Amy found that talking to Granny Mae had made her feel a little better. The woman could be as overbearing and tiresome as the world's worst neighbor—nosy, dogmatic, and full of unsolicited advice. Now, walking home with the cough remedy in her bag, staying alert to anyone nearby, she decided that she'd received a small gift. Granny had made her recognize that seeking Jessica's forgiveness would also lift her heart. Forgiveness wouldn't erase Amy's deed, but her sister needed to know that she wasn't the same selfish, feckless girl she'd once been. Jess deserved to hear so much more than a lame apology.

She came through the back gate when she got home and she saw Bax splitting firewood in the side yard, working with a vengeance. The afternoon was mild, and although a breeze made the trees rustle, the labor was hot and strenuous. He didn't see her standing behind him, fascinated by the graceful, machinelike precision of his work. Sweat glued his shirt to his back, and with every powerful, arcing swing of the axe his muscles stretched and contracted. The pieces of wood exploded in two under his blade. The late afternoon sun picked up deep burgundy tones in his dark hair, which lay wet on his collar. She didn't know if he was an ex-convict, but despite her problems, she knew one thing—she had trouble looking away.

At last she forced herself to go inside. Stopping in the kitchen to grab a tablespoon and a glass of water, she slipped up the back stairs and carried the medicine straight up to Deirdre's bedroom. She tapped on her door. "Deirdre?"

The patient's response was garbled by more coughing.

Amy walked in and found her where she'd left her, lying beneath the nubby colonial bedspread, looking pasty and feverish. Even her hair looked lifeless. "I've brought Granny's medicine. She said either she or Jessica will try to stop by tonight. They've gone out to the Grenfells' farm to deliver Susannah's baby. Isn't that wonderful?" she chirped with false cheer.

Deirdre swallowed two spoonfuls of the medicine and shuddered.

"Awful stuff, huh?"

"It tastes bad, but I know it will help. It makes the pain in my chest and back ease up, too." She took a sip of water from the glass Amy offered. "How wonderful for Susannah and Tanner. I'd always hoped to have children."

Amy tidied up her night table and set the water and cough medicine on it. "You're a young woman. You could meet a wonderful man and raise a family." If she recovered, she thought to herself. She looked worse by the day, and Amy blamed herself for not insisting that she get medical help sooner. "Rest now, and I'll bring dinner up in a while."

She nodded, and Amy knew if this batch was anything like the last one Granny Mae put together, Deirdre would be asleep soon. She sat at her bedside, waiting for her to settle down. Being sick and alone in a bedroom could make a person feel abandoned, and Deirdre was spending hours up here.

Down the hall, Amy heard the bathroom door close and water running in the tub. She knew that Bax was probably washing for dinner.

After fifteen minutes, Deirdre's cough had not calmed. "Please, Amy, can I have a bit more?"

"Shouldn't we wait just a little longer to give it a chance?" she asked, hesitant to give in. "I don't know what's in that medicine. Granny won't tell me."

"Please—I'm so tired."

Deirdre looked and sounded so pitiful, she decided that perhaps one more dose wouldn't hurt and might help. It seemed to. In another five minutes, she was finally asleep.

Satisfied that Deirdre was resting now, she left, closing the door quietly, and went to her own room to finish sorting through some material she'd found in the closet.

As she shifted things around in her chest of drawers, she came across Adam's lined book, the one she'd brought with her from Portland—the only weapon she had that stood between her and her husband. It had a brown leather cover. She looked at its pages and studied the peculiar dates, incomprehensible abbreviations, and notations he'd made. She recognized his handwriting but the information meant nothing to her. It must be important, though, if he'd gone to so much trouble to hide it from her. She put it back in the bottom of the drawer and put a fold of gingham over it, then returned to the closet.

"I need to talk to you." Bax stood in the doorway of her bedroom, his fist braced against the jamb. She jumped, her arms full of white cambric, a floral print, and lavender sachets. She hadn't even heard his footsteps in the hall. His expression was grim and pale, as if he'd just been gut-kicked by a horse.

Foreboding turned her hands icy. Oh, dear God, he'd heard something bad about Adam, about her—

"Whit Gannon got an 'anonymous' letter this morning. I'm sure Breninger sent it to him. It has to do with my hitch in the army."

Relieved but mystified, she jammed the fabric into the drawer and shut it. "The war has been over for almost four years. It's history."

He leaned back a bit and looked up and down the hallway, then walked in.

She motioned him toward a small settee that stood under the windows overlooking the rose-lined backyard. "Tom hasn't come home and Deirdre is sleeping, finally."

He crossed the room and stood before her, close enough for her to see dark flecks in his gray eyes. Suddenly, briefly, he put his hands on her waist and rested his forehead on her shoulder as if he bore a weight he could not carry alone. Surprised, she automatically touched the back of his head, damp and clean from a dunk in the bathtub.

"What?" she whispered. "What's wrong?"

He sat on the edge of the settee and patted the space next to him. After she joined him, he put his elbows on his knees and let his hands dangle between them.

"You know about the scars on my back," he said, staring at the floor.

How could she forget? He'd barked at her and given her a murderous glare when she'd mentioned them. "I thought maybe they were from the war."

"There's more to it." He seemed to be studying the grain of the hardwood floor at his feet. He looked up at her. "A lot more."

She nodded to keep him talking, but her foreboding turned into dread, not for herself, but for him.

He released a deep sigh and began. "I was like every new-made patriot when America joined the war in Europe. I didn't wait to be drafted. I joined the army to beat back the Huns, just like the recruiting posters demanded."

Amy said, "I remember some of that. I got involved myself, selling Liberty Bonds, organizing parades, and scrap drives— oh, all kinds of things." She pleated a fold in her skirt. "That was before I—well, before."

He let out a bitter chuckle. "I couldn't wait to get there. I was going to send the kaiser's helmet home to my folks. I was going to help win the war. Be a big hero. Oh, I had all kinds of plans. You'd have thought I was twelve instead of twenty-five, playing cowboys and Indians in the front yard, for all the bragging I did. I thought it was going to be all glory and glamour that would make my family proud, and my girl, too. Polly wanted to marry me before I left. But I told her I'd be home before she knew it and we'd do it up right." He sat back and put one clenched fist on the arm of the chair, but he didn't meet her eyes. "Huh, was I wrong." He began thumping the chair arm with that clenched fist, slowly, quietly.

"I got to France and saw the Western Front. The battlefields, the combat—*nothing* was like I thought it would be. The American Expeditionary Force was in a lot better shape than those poor bastards who'd been there from the beginning, the French and the British. But it was hell on earth. I'd heard the expression in my life, but it wasn't until I saw the trenches that I really understood what it meant.

"We fought in that bloody mess for two miserable years. I killed men I didn't know, men I might even have been friends with under different circumstances. And I saw soldiers standing right next to me drop with a bullet in their foreheads, or blown off their feet with severed limbs flying in every direction. I was wounded myself, patched up, and sent back to the front." He sighed. "Finally, early on the morning of November 11, 1918, word came down that the Germans were pretty much worn out. Their own civilians were starving, and an armistice had been negotiated and declared a few days earlier. The war was *over*. It was signed at five o'clock that morning and announced to the world. At eleven o'clock it would be official. Even though it had been signed, General Pershing and other officers in high command had ordered that we were to keep fighting until eleven. By now, I'd been promoted to sergeant and I reported to a lieutenant who was willing to put his men through that meat grinder no matter what the cost. He'd made the army his career and he wasn't about to disobey. In fact, we knew that he saw a real chance for promotion by sending his men out to die. And all around us, near and far, I heard shells and guns still firing. It was business as usual."

Amy stared at him. "Dear God . . ." She'd never talked to anyone who had given her a firsthand account of being in battle.

"It was freezing cold and foggy. Around nine thirty, we were ordered to cross the Meuse River. Over half of the men in two divisions had already gone over and were shivering on the other side, as dull-eyed as cattle. I started over, and then—" He looked at her for the first time since he'd begun his story. "I said *no*. I wasn't going. The war was over, in ninety minutes—the eleventh hour of the eleventh day of the eleventh month—it would be official. I'd had enough. I'd done my duty, scraped through with my life, and I was not going to sacrifice it or anyone else's to make some glory-hungry officer look good."

"What happened?"

He raked his fingers through his hair. "That lieutenant, his face was almost purple from screaming at me. He said if I didn't cross the river he'd shoot me himself for desertion and dereliction of duty. I turned around and started walking away. He was following me and kept yelling at me."

"And he shot you?" she demanded, outraged at the disregard for human life. "*In the back?*"

"One bullet from him, and one from a German sniper on the other side. He must have seen his opportunity and taken it. Then the sniper shot the lieutenant, clean and neat, right through the head." He shrugged and held his hands open on his knees, as if still trying to believe it himself. "I knew I was bleeding but it took me a while to realize that not all of the blood was mine. I had brains sprayed all over me."

Horrified, she gaped at him. "Oh, Bax! That—that's terrible! How did you know who did it if your back was turned?" Her eyes stung with tears.

"Others saw it happen. I guess some of the men took pity on me because they carried me through the trenches to the back and got me into one of the aid stations." He shrugged. "They weren't eager to die either for a war that had already ended, and it was a good opportunity for them to get away from the fighting."

"Were you discharged?"

"I ended up in a hospital for a long time—the wounds got infected. But the story of how I got shot followed me. After I recovered enough to be transported, I was court-martialed and sentenced to ten years of hard labor at the military prison at Fort Leavenworth."

Amy stared at him. "Ten years . . . prison . . ." Her heart twisted at the thought. So that was what Breninger had been talking about.

"Sometimes I think that if there was anything good left in me . . ." He closed his eyes for a moment and sighed deeply. "After everything else, killing men I bore no grudge against, getting shot, court-martialed . . . I worry all those things took the goodness out of me."

"No, I don't think so." She wouldn't accept that. Not about him. "Did—did you escape?" she whispered.

"No. I was lucky—they took the circumstances into consideration, and a year later there was an inquiry in Washington, DC, about that day. Some congressmen were pretty mad. So were the families of men killed. I was released."

He got up and began pacing in front of her, his hands jammed into his back pockets. "I made my way back to Cedar Mill and to my folks. I couldn't bring myself to write to them from prison so they had no idea what had happened to me. At least, *I* didn't realize they did. I was an outcast before I even got there."

Amy's head came up sharply. "Outcast." She knew something about that.

"Oh, yeah. My father came right out and said he wished I'd been killed in battle. It would have given him something to brag about. But I'd brought shame down on the family, he said. Not like he hadn't, beating the tar out of all of us over the years, including my mother."

Amy felt the blood drain from her face at the mention of the abuse. "Ohh . . ."

He nodded. "Yeah, I know something about that, too. My mother wanted to bring me into the house, but he ordered me off the front porch and wouldn't let her talk to me. Cedar Mill isn't very big and the whole town seemed to agree with him. I couldn't get my job back at the sawmill or work anywhere else there. And Polly—she was already married to another man."

"But what does this have to do with Whit Gannon?"

"It was Breninger. You know he tried to blackmail me. After I refused to pay him, he sent Whit the letter. And probably told some other people. If you can't make money on something like this, revenge is next on the list. Breninger called it satisfaction."

She stared at him. All that money she'd paid to that greasy Breninger—"But *I* paid him. He made money."

"I think he'd already set this motion by the time he involved you. Besides, he wanted money to keep your secret too. He saw an opportunity and he took it."

"There *are* no secrets!"

He shrugged. "But the threat worked, didn't it? I should have told Whit my own story the day I met him, but I didn't know how he'd take it. I sure as hell didn't expect him to find out this way."

"Now what?"

"Whit is writing to the War Department to check the facts for himself. But he wanted to hear my side of it first. At least that was fair of him."

"But what will happen?"

"I don't know. He said I still have a job there until he gets information from Washington." He shook his head. "I'll probably have to move on again, depending on how everyone reacts when they find out about it. They're not going to want a deserter working in the sheriff's office." He flopped back onto the settee.

Without thinking, Amy put a hand on his arm. "But that's not deserting! That's—that's just common sense! And you were exonerated. Why would they make all those men risk their lives for a war they'd already won?"

He turned to look at her. That haunted expression she'd only glimpsed from time to time was solidly in place. "I've asked myself that more times than I can count. Ambition? Bloodlust? I don't know. Over three hundred Americans were killed in those last few hours, and another three thousand were seriously wounded. I guess in the end, I was one of them, even though I tried to avoid it. And that doesn't count the French and British casualties."

Her grip on his arm tightened. She was frightened for him and for herself. "I was wrapped up in my own problems for so long, I didn't know anything about it. Adam kept me cut off from nearly everyone and everything, I didn't hear much about the world."

After a moment's hesitation, he covered her hand with his own. His touch was warm and unsettling, but she didn't pull away. "I guess we got off to a bumpy start, you and me. I've heard a lot of what happened before you left town. And I suppose I let it sway my opinion of you. At first."

Amy lifted one eyebrow. "You didn't let it show. Much." They sat in silence for a moment and she remembered his few and surprising gentle gestures—his kiss on her aching wrist, his other kiss on the back stairs—and realized that a tender heart still beat within his chest. A lot of men might have lost their humanity after everything that had happened to him. She asked, "What are you going to do now?"

"Wait to see what Whit says, I suppose. If I didn't think so well of him, I'd just leave town. Move on."

No, no, she didn't like the idea of that at all. Her heart began pounding, and she offered reassurances. "Breninger might not have told anyone else. In this town, rumors and gossip spread like head lice. You would have heard about it. And I haven't seen him around, have you?"

He sat forward again. "No, not since that one time—and the day I saw him snooping around behind your backyard." He rubbed his face. It was a weary gesture. "But I wasn't sure who it was then."

"Now we are," she replied morosely. The breeze outside stirred the lace curtains behind them, bringing in the scent of someone's new-mowed lawn and fresh air. "Still, if you've ever spent time in Virgil Tilly's place, you know that nothing gets by those men. They're worse than a bunch of old hens. And no one has mentioned him, I'd bet."

"No, I haven't heard anyone talk about him. Maybe he's trying to stay out of sight."

"Maybe."

He looked back at her, his gaze brushing over her eyes and lingering on her lips. "I hope you're right."

• • •

Shortly after midnight, Amy was reaching for the switch on the living room floor lamp when she heard a knock on the front door. She stopped, her arm halted in midair, and held her breath. She hadn't heard from Granny Mae or Jessica that evening, as she'd hoped. But Susannah's labor might have gone on a long time. At least Bax and Tom were both right upstairs.

More knocking. "Amy?"

Granny Mae. She began breathing again and hurried to the door.

Mae stood on her porch with her basket, looking older than she had when they spoke that afternoon. But her thin, white hair was still neatly anchored to her head with a tortoiseshell comb. Amy moved aside and let her in.

"I'm sorry it's so late. Cole picked me up and brought me into town. Jess thought she might as well spend the night with the Grenfells. That baby took his sweet time getting here. But he finally decided to come out and meet us."

"It's a boy?" Amy said in a hushed voice, to remind her that people in the house were sleeping.

"John Henry Grenfell. A whopping butterball of a child. He weighs nine pounds."

"I didn't expect you to come over this late. You must be dead tired."

"Better dead tired than just plain dead," she said. "How's Deirdre?"

Amy motioned her to the stairs and climbed them with a soft tread. "She took three spoons of medicine before she finally fell asleep. I came back to bring her some dinner but I couldn't rouse her. She's been awake so much so I just let her rest."

"Are you sure she's only sleeping?"

Amy stopped on the steps, alarmed. "Yes! She's even snoring."

"All right. You said she's been so ill—"

"Not near death." She frowned slightly, then put a finger to her lips and gestured at the closed doors. "Tom and Bax get up early."

Granny nodded and they continued down the hall to Deirdre's bedroom. Amy turned the knob and they looked into the dim room. She'd propped a large folding silk fan between two books to shade the lamp. Painted to resemble a peacock tail, it was made of brilliant teal silk, which gave a bluish cast to Deirdre's pale skin. But when they drew close to the bed, Granny yanked the fan away and her color didn't change.

Deirdre didn't have much in her stomach, but she'd vomited a little.

"Oh, God . . ." Amy stared in horror. "I know that smell."

"It's not hard to figure out," Granny snapped, loud again. "Everyone knows that smell. Deirdre! Wake up, honey."

"Not the vomit—that other smell. My father's office at home had that odor sometimes. He had specimens floating in glass jars with preservative. What was in that medicine? And you'd better tell me more than 'a bit of this and that'!"

Deirdre groaned but didn't move.

For the first time in Amy's memory, Mae Rumsteadt looked panicky. "Just a drip of laudanum and some whiskey—you saw what I put in it!"

"I didn't know about the laudanum. It isn't even legal anymore. It was outlawed in 1920."

"I had it left over. I only used a drip," she repeated. "Anyway, I didn't tell you to give her the whole damn bottle."

"I didn't do that!"

Granny shook her patient again and shouted at her to wake up. Amy couldn't worry about their raised voices at this point. It was an emergency. She had known fear in her life many times, but never a terror like this. If that cough remedy killed poor Deirdre, her two murderers were now standing over her bed like ghouls, not healers.

"Jessica—we need Jessica," Amy said.

Granny clapped her hands next to Deirdre's ear. Nothing. She began briskly rubbing and slapping Deirdre's wrists. "No, we don't, I can manage this. Anyway, she's at the Grenfells," she reminded her. "They have a phone but we can't call out there now. Birdeen doesn't sit at that switchboard all night long."

"Dear God, how are we going to reach her?" Just then Amy looked up to see Bax shuffle in, barefoot, wearing his undershirt and pants with one suspender pulled up on his shoulder. His hair stuck up here and there, and he had sheet wrinkles on the side of his face.

"What's going on in here?" His voice was sleep-rough and he looked a little groggy.

"Bax, we think she's dying. We need Jess."

He looked at Deirdre and, like a man accustomed to having to think fast on his feet, he straightened up and was instantly alert. He sniffed. "Has she been drinking?"

Granny scowled at him. "Drinking! Of course not—she's been sick with *this*, whatever it is, for weeks."

"I gave her cough medicine," Amy added.

"I'm not insulting her. It's that last week, when—" He shook his head. "Never mind. I'll get Dr. Jess. I can use the county car."

Amy told him how to get to the Grenfells' place. "It's a pretty easy trip over there. If you hit Richey Road, you've gone too far."

"Okay, I'll be back as soon as I can." He went back to his room and put on his boots and a shirt, then Amy heard him go down the stairs—it sounded like two at a time. In a moment the back door opened and closed.

Granny grabbed Deirdre's hands and pulled her upright in the bed, making her head roll around on her shoulders like a broken doll's. "Wake up! Come on, honey!"

"Granny Mae—" Amy began, but the old woman wouldn't let go.

A long, whimpering cry escaped from Deirdre, sounding like air leaking from a bicycle tire.

Hearing this, goose bumps crawled over Amy's scalp and arms, and she started patting Deirdre's cheeks. "Open your eyes!"

Remarkably, she did. She looked straight ahead, then glanced around and let out another small cry.

The two women continued their efforts on Deirdre but that was the most they could get from her. She was lost in some foggy world between life and death. The chemical smell wafted from her with every labored breath.

Granny released her hands and let her lie down again. Amy sank into the bedside chair, but they both stared, aghast when her body grew rigid and she began to twitch. A couple of minutes later the fit passed.

"What *is* this?" Amy asked.

The older woman wore a stricken expression. "I don't know! I've never seen anything like it."

After what seemed like hours, Jessica hurried into the room with Bax close behind. Her hair straggled from its loose braid, and she appeared almost as old and worn as Granny. She looked at Deirdre and felt for a pulse. "She's still with us but barely." She lifted her nose. "Formaldehyde. Bax said you made up some cough medicine for her. What was in it?" she asked, looking at both of them.

Amy's heart sank. She'd been right about the smell.

"I'm telling you, it was just a drop of laudanum and a splash of whiskey, with some spices—rosemary, cinnamon, a scrape of nutmeg," Granny said, huffy and defensive.

Jessica's brows rose. "Mae, where did you get the alcohol? And how much of a 'splash'?"

She straightened, her aged spine almost creaking audibly. "Probably a half cup. Almost everyone around here keeps a bottle of whiskey."

Jess sighed. "I know that. We have one too. I'm not judging you, I'm trying to figure out what's going on."

"Tilly charges so much for that highfalutin hooch he sells—"

"Except it's not hooch," Bax said. "It's Canadian, bottled by genuine distillers up there. Not cooked in someone's backwoods still."

"Listen, sonny, I don't have to take—"

Jessica dropped her bag on the floor and leaned over the bed, her eyes snapping with fire. "Mae Rumsteadt! Where did you get it?"

"Some fella came around a couple of weeks ago and offered it to me," she admitted. "I couldn't say no to his price. It seemed all right to me."

"Who?"

"I don't know, I never saw him before."

Jessica stared at her with an open mouth, and Bax groaned and took a step back. "*Son* of a bitch!" he barked to no one in particular. Then he added, "Sorry." But none of them acted like they'd heard him in the first place.

"Someone is going around town selling wood alcohol and passing it off as drinkable. It's poison, and it doesn't take much to kill a person. For God's sake, didn't you hear about Winks?" she demanded. "*That* was a couple of weeks ago."

"Of course, I did! But he'd drink anything. How could I know what that man was selling? I just thought it—I thought . . ." Granny trailed off and Amy could have sworn she seemed to wither up and age fifteen years right before her eyes.

"Did you drink any of it?" Bax asked.

"No." The old woman looked down at Deirdre and shook her head. "I swear . . ." she vowed softly. "She wanted the medicine. I never meant to hurt her."

Jessica turned to Amy, and for that single instant it seemed as though no gulf lay open between them, no years of separation. When their gazes connected, Jess was the sister she remembered from years earlier, before Cole, before Adam. "How much did she take?"

Jess plucked the bottle from the night table and handed it to Amy. There was about an inch and a half missing from the top, more than when she'd left the room late in the afternoon. "I gave her two tablespoons, but she said it wasn't working and she asked for one more. I gave that to her, and it looks like she might have taken more after I left. I thought she was asleep when I went."

Absently, Jessica pushed at her straggling hair. "That would be enough. Deirdre is a small woman and she's been ill. Get rid of this before someone else takes it by accident." She handed back the bottle and reached into her bag on the floor for her stethoscope. Putting the bell to Deirdre's chest, she listened while everyone standing around her remained silent. Amy, on the verge of tears, with her forehead furrowed and her hands interlocked tightly beneath her chin, caught Jessica's gaze as she looked across the bed at her.

Jess straightened and unhooked the earpieces.

"Jess?" Amy whispered.

"She has all the classic signs of methanol poisoning. Slow heartbeat, vomiting, lethargy. I can even smell it and Granny admits she doesn't know what kind of alcohol she put in it—"

"I believed I knew!" Granny protested. The target of three pairs of angry-eyed glares, she withdrew like a turtle into its carapace.

"—and I suspect Deirdre took even more than you gave her, Amy."

"She had some kind of fit before you got here. But she didn't drink all that much. You can help her, can't you?"

She sighed. "No. I just don't have access to what I'd need, a hospital setting and an IV drip of sodium bicarbonate. It's a fairly new treatment but it's had reasonable success. She's alive so she *might* survive this. Even if she does she could have complications, and she's still sick with whatever she had to begin with. I wish you had called me sooner about that."

"I wanted to, but she wouldn't agree to it," Amy said.

"It's true," Bax added. "I heard it myself."

"All right. It's after two in the morning. I'm going to spend the rest of the night at the apartment over my office. If there are any big changes, come and get me. Otherwise, I'll be over in a few hours. Amy, you'll stay with her?"

"Of course."

"I'll take you, Doc," Bax said. And then to Granny, he added, "Mae, I'll want to talk to you later about the man who sold you that moonshine. Whit and I have been working on the problem."

Mae nodded, and her shoulders drooped with defeat.

Amy noticed that for the moment, Bax seemed to have forgotten he wasn't even sure if he still worked for the sheriff's office.

But he was a hero in her eyes. Tom had slept through the entire ordeal.

After everyone filed out, she cleaned up Deirdre and then sat in the chair next her bed, prepared to finish out the long night beside her.

CHAPTER THIRTEEN

Whit motioned Bax into the chair across from his desk. "When I learned it was true, I sat you down to hear what you had to say. The letter from the War Department and your explanation satisfied me. I'd like you to stay on."

The relief Bax felt was so profound, so visceral, it equaled the sense of freedom he experienced the day he walked out of Fort Leavenworth, dressed in a cheap suit and carrying his few belongings a paper bag. "Thanks, Whit. I appreciate your faith in me."

"There's work to do, and I need help with it," he said, tipping him a wink. "Now, how's the Gifford woman?"

"Still alive. I left before I learned anything more than that. Doc Jessica is there now, and I'm going to talk to Mae Rumsteadt this morning to try to learn more about whoever she bought that moonshine from. I think I might know." He tapped the edge of the letter with his index finger.

"Okay, let me know what you find out. I've got these county bulletins to go over." He fanned a short stack of papers at him.

"Anything interesting today?"

"I haven't looked at them yet, but they're usually the regular stuff—new laws, missing persons, bank robbers, other fugitives. Not nearly as much fun as talking to Granny Mae."

Bax gave him a wry look, then stood and put out his hand. "Thanks again, Whit." He was bone tired from running around half the night, but he was grateful to have his job and another man's trust.

As for Milo Breninger, he'd blackmailed his last victim. Bax would make certain of it.

• • •

"Miss Tabitha, those men are back," Elsa whispered.

Tabbie lifted heavy lids to see her maid standing over her. She lay languid in the semigloom of her bedroom, the curtains drawn to shut out the afternoon sun, with a cold washcloth on her forehead. She wore only a pearl-gray dressing gown. "Oh, sweet Adeline," she complained in a groan. "Have they no decency? What time is it?"

"Just after six o'clock. They're sorry to trouble you."

She pulled off the washcloth. "Yes, aren't they always? Send them away, Elsa."

"I tried, but this time they brought a Vigilance Reserve policeman with them. That Mr. Rinehart insisted on speaking to you."

"The Vigilance Reserve!" Her headache pounded so hard, it felt as if it would blow out her eyes at any moment. She caught a glimpse of herself in her dresser mirror and saw that her hair was wilted and crushed. "This harassment is beyond the limits of civility. It's despicable. Tell Mr. Rinehart that I'm ill and bed-bound. They are not welcome here. I don't know where Harlan is, I don't know what he's done, and if they don't stop bothering me, I'll call Mayor Baker's office and file a complaint. He's been a guest in my cousin's home many times, and this new police reserve business he created is his pet project. They're supposed to protect citizens, not bully them."

"All right, I'll try. Shouldn't you have dinner soon? You haven't eaten since this morning. It might make you feel better."

Tabbie had managed to entice Elsa to return after promising her a raise, but there were just the two of them here. Her maid now also cooked for her.

"Get rid of them first, Elsa," she pleaded. "Then . . . then maybe some toast and tea."

Elsa expressed her concern in a grumbled, half-audible comment about Tabitha's welfare and the thoughtless monsters who were her persecutors.

Tabbie lay there, waiting for the sound of the front door closing, which she would take to mean that dreadful lawyer, his bumbling assistant, and the volunteer policeman had gone. She hadn't seen or heard from Harlan since that one night he sneaked into the house, gave her money to keep the house running for a while, had his way with her, and faded back into the night. Not a single word. He had been gone nearly three months, and Tabbie was at wit's end. No longer an amusing conversation piece to their friends, she'd begun to notice a decline in social invitations, but it was just as well. Having to appear alone at those functions was difficult enough. To be the object of curiosity, speculation, amusement, and undisguised gossip was too much. If Harlan ever came back, they would have to rebuild their lives, start over. But she had a feeling that life as she'd known it with him would never be the same. Then what would become of her?

They didn't own this house; it was mortgaged. If the payments weren't made, the bank would foreclose and she would be forced to go—where? Back to the relatives who had been so eager to unburden themselves of her to begin with? All of the beautiful furnishings and this home that she'd poured so much of her loving attention into just—gone?

She'd thought of suing Harlan for desertion, and she should. But that wouldn't be helpful if she didn't know where he was.

At last she was sure she'd heard the front door close. In a moment, Elsa reappeared in her bedroom.

"They're gone?"

Elsa nodded, looking as frazzled as if she'd wrestled a bearskin rug out to the front lawn. "I put my foot down and told them they were not going to bother you. What lady in your situation would not be ill and have to take to her bed?" She moved through the room, tidying the bed around Tabbie and collecting cast-off garments. "They might not have been happy, or believed that you know nothing of Mr. Monroe's whereabouts. I went out on a limb and told them not to come back."

"Oh, bravo, Elsa!" Tabbie sat up a bit and clapped her hands, once. "Did you tell them I'll call Mayor Baker?"

"I did, ma'am. I think they understand that you are finished with polite cooperation."

"Yes, I am. Bless you, Elsa. I feel like a recluse."

"But there's no guarantee it did any good. I'm pretty certain they'll be back."

Tabbie sank back against her pillow, her fleeting sense of victory deflated. The weight of defeat pressed on her shoulders as surely as a pair of oppressive hands.

Elsa began straightening some trinkets on the dressing table and looked up into the mirror, talking to Tabbie's reflection behind her. "Forgive me for saying so, Miss Tabitha, but if I don't speak up I think I'll burst." She turned to face her employer. "There's no excuse good enough for what Mr. Monroe has done to you. To abandon you this way, a fine, loving woman of good family, and leave you holding the bag of his dirty linen to air," she said. "I'm sorry, but I just think it's awful. With no word from him, leaving you to worry—I don't think I could stay with someone who did that to me."

Tabbie sighed. "You're mixing your metaphors, Elsa. But I know what you mean."

The maid gave Tabbie a blank look, and she knew the woman had no idea what a metaphor was. She was right, though. Harlan had promised this would all be over soon, and claimed to have an important, anonymous client. Even she didn't believe that nonsense. She just couldn't imagine what he was involved in, and he'd dodged most of her questions from the first day of their marriage.

Had he come up with some crazy idea? Was he already in trouble with the law and simply on the run? That last option certainly seemed possible, given the ongoing talk of financial *irregularities*.

She draped the washcloth over a glass on her night table. How could he have left her in this position? she wondered for the thousandth time. She'd become a target for the authorities, gossip, and very real trouble.

Tabitha glanced around her lovely bedroom in her lovely home and decided she couldn't stay, waiting for doom. Until now she had only dallied with the idea, but circumstances were growing worse by the day. She lurched to a sitting position. "I need to get away from here. I don't know what's coming next, but I know it won't be good."

"Where would you go?"

"I don't know—not to my relatives. It would be too easy for these people to hunt me down. I just know I can't continue to live like this. I certainly wish I knew where to find Harlan, if only to demand an explanation."

Elsa put down the hairbrush she held. She cast a couple of troubled, sidelong looks at Tabitha, as if she was mulling over something.

"What?" Tabitha asked. "What is it?"

"I don't know if I should say anything more, Miss Tabitha."

"For heaven's sake, what is it?"

Her maid put on an agonized expression. "It might only cause more trouble."

Tabbie swung her legs over the edge of the bed. The sudden movement made her head swim. "Elsa! If you don't tell me, I'll cause *you* trouble! If it affects me, speak up."

Elsa pulled in her chin and looked at her with fearful eyes. "Just before I shut the door, those men were still standing on the porch and one of them said . . . said . . ."

Tabbie scowled at her.

"It was Mr. Rinehart. I think he believed I'd already closed the door. He told the others he has information that Mr. Monroe might be in Powell Springs."

"Powell Springs—what is that? Some kind of therapeutic facility, like Battle Creek Sanitarium?"

"No, miss, it's a small town east of here."

"I wonder how they know that. And why in the world would Harlan be there?"

"I don't know. I didn't hear Mr. Rinehart mention anything about that." She cast another look at her. "But there might be more. He said that Paul Church is missing too."

"The gardener? He took my gardener with him?" She pressed two fingers to her forehead. "Ralph stopped coming here at the same time. You know how ragged the yard has become—and my roses, I think they're a lost cause." But then, everything seemed lost now, she thought. "Well, I don't think I have any choice. I'll have to find Harlan myself." When that trouble came, she would not be here.

• • •

Amy crowded beside her sister, watching as she listened again to Deirdre's lungs. She still wore the dress and apron she'd had on yesterday. Spending the night in the bedside chair had covered them with wrinkles. Jess, she noticed, had been able to change clothes.

Jessica straightened, wearing a frown. "She's consumptive. I suspected it last night but I couldn't hear a normal heartbeat because of the methanol. Now it's speeding up again and it's too fast. Her lungs are full of crackles and rales. It's a pretty distinctive sound—goopy, I guess you could call it."

Consumption. God, Amy didn't know anything about taking care of a person with tuberculosis. "I've seen it before, but the people who had it were ill for a long time, sometimes years." She stared at the patient in the bed. Her red hair was a sweaty, snarled mess and the slight gray cast to her sharply boned face made her look as if Death were in the corner of the room, waiting to claim her. "She got sick just a few weeks ago."

Jess's brows rose. "I've never seen a case in Powell Springs— oh, you mean not here."

Amy nodded, and briefly, an awkward silence opened between them.

Jess continued, "Those people you saw probably had chronic tuberculosis. Deirdre has the acute form."

"What now?"

Deirdre had floated in and out of consciousness all night, but she'd never really seemed fully aware of her surroundings. Now her eyes fluttered open again and she groped around the bed with her right hand, as if searching for something.

"Amy?" she croaked.

She clasped the seeking hand. "I'm here. What can I get for you?"

"Deirdre," Jess said, "how are you feeling?"

"Who is that? Dr. Jessica?" Her voice was thin and weak, and she seemed to be gazing right at them.

Jess blanched, and involuntarily, Amy clamped down on the hand she held. "Can't—can't you see me, Deirdre?" she asked.

"No, it's—no. Where . . ." Her voice was as thin and gray as her face. "Where is Tom?"

"Damn it," Jess uttered quietly.

Amy's blood raced through her veins. "Can you see *anything*?"

"No." The word sighed out of her.

"Tom came in this morning, Deirdre. He sat beside you for a long time before he went to work. Do you remember?"

"N-no."

Jess took a deep breath and pulled Amy aside. "Blindness is one of the effects of methanol poisoning. Winks lost his sight too just before he died. As for what now, really, between this and the tuberculosis, I don't imagine she'll last much longer," she whispered. "It's a huge battle for anyone to fight, and she was kind of frail to begin with."

"I should have insisted that she see you instead of letting her talk me into getting that cough medicine from Granny Mae." Amy fought to speak around the strangling knot that formed in her throat, and her words quivered with emotion and regret. "D-did the cough medicine kill her?"

Jessica studied her sister, a woman who had betrayed her and disappointed her in the worst possible way. Strands of her dark-blonde hair had come loose from their untidy bun and fell around her face. Exhaustion made her look almost as bad as she had the first day Jess had seen her here in the entryway. Naked worry and time had sapped the youthful spark she'd had as a young woman. What Amy really wanted to know was if she had killed Deirdre with a tablespoon and a bottle of poison. What she really sought was mercy. If Jess were vindictive, the sort of person who felt driven to get even, she could lie to Amy and watch her squirm. But regardless of what had passed between them, she couldn't do that. Her soul was not that dark, her heart not as wicked. So she gave her the truth.

She met her tired, fearful gaze with an even look. "Not really. It might have pushed her to the edge, but she would not survive her illness."

Amy's eyes closed for a moment—in relief, in gratitude—Jess wasn't sure which. She released the breath she'd been holding and nodded. "What shall I do for her?"

"All we can provide is palliative care. You know, try to keep her comfortable. People usually know when they're dying. I'll come by a couple of times a day until, well, until she doesn't need me anymore. When that time comes," and she made direct and unwavering eye contact with Amy, "all the bedding, her handkerchiefs, and so on will have to be burned."

Amy glanced at the bed then back at Jess. "Everything?"

"*Everything*. Including the mattress. All soft and porous surfaces, whatever can't be sterilized. Don't bother to wash it. Just put it out in the burn pile. You might as well get started with some things already soiled, and be sure to wash your hands with carbolic soap each time."

Amy took a deep breath and exhaled. Fatigue was painted on her face with gray strokes. "All right."

"I'll tell you one thing," Jess went on. "Granny Mae and I might have become friends and managed a truce these past few years, and I still respect some of her knowledge. But she can't go on cooking up her tonics or anything else with real drugs. I gave up trying to fight her on it because she's so stubborn and outspoken. But this . . . this is a catastrophe."

Amy swept a hand over a loose curl to push it back. "I think Bax has gone to the café to find out who sold her that moonshine."

"Good. What did you do with that bottle from last night?"

"I poured it down the bathtub drain."

"All right. I hope Mae quits this on her own, but if I have to, I'll talk to Horace about reining her in if she doesn't cooperate. She's not a chemist or a pharmacist. She's always done pretty much what she wants, but the mayor's office ought to be able to put her out of the compounding business."

"She's pretty shaken by this."

"Yes, I know." She looked at the watch pinned to her apron front. "Now I'm off to see Cole and Margaux." Glancing back at Deirdre, she added, "If anything changes here, call me. Otherwise, I'll be back late this afternoon."

Amy tipped her face down. "Thank you, Jess."

• • •

Adam paced the floor of the cabin, an unsatisfying pursuit given its small area. He had been living in this dank, grubby shack for nearly a week and he needed to find a way to catch Amy alone in the boardinghouse. Breninger had told him two men and another woman lived under that roof, too. The men would probably be gone during the day, he speculated. He kicked at a pine cone on the floor.

Speculation wasn't worth much. It had seemed like a good idea to hide out here, but he realized that he'd need to rely on Breninger and whatever other flunky he could hire to perform surveillance for him. By the time he learned of an opportunity to go to the house, everything could change. And the more people who knew about him and his plans, the higher the risk of word getting around. His chief weapon was the element of surprise.

He thought he'd been so clever, hiding that book in the back of the closet. How could he have anticipated that Amy would find it there? He paused in front of the cloudy, vine-covered window, and for a moment his certainty wobbled. Maybe he should have just let her go and been done with it. He doubted very seriously if she knew what she possessed, and this was becoming an extremely trying chore.

Then his outraged ego and fury rose again. No, by God! She must have known, otherwise she would not have taken it. She was his wife, she had sworn to honor and obey him, and nothing gave him greater pleasure than seeing her dread of igniting his anger reflected in her eyes. She was meant to be with him, to follow him, and do his bidding. Love had nothing to do with the issue. It was simply the natural order of things. His gambling debts and other miscalculations did not excuse her.

He took up his pacing again. He had no choice, he realized. He'd have to light a fire under Milo Breninger and pay him for the privilege.

Damn you, Amy, he thought bitterly. He was a busy man. He didn't have time for this. But he'd get what he wanted, no matter what it took.

• • •

When Bax stopped by the house around two o'clock, he searched the whole first floor but saw no one. Then he climbed the stairs and started looking into each open room. Over the sound of running water, he heard short, gulping sobs. He found Amy at the sink in the bathroom, scrubbing her hands with soap and a small brush as if she meant to take off her skin. She still had on the same clothes she'd worn since yesterday and her apron was dirty. He could see her reflection in the mirror. She looked like a madwoman.

"Amy?"

She glanced up at him. Her face was crumpled with her crying, but as soon as she saw him she wiped her face against the shoulder of her dress and her expression became a blank.

"What's going on?"

Taking a deep breath, plainly trying to take control of her voice, she gulped back the tears and cleared her throat. "Fred Hustad is on his way. Jessica sent for him."

He looked toward the end of the hall and saw that Deirdre's door was closed. "Where's Doc Jessica?"

"Down—down there." She inclined her head in that general direction.

Bax headed there and knocked. "Come in, Fred," he heard her call.

"Doc, it's Bax Duncan."

The sound of footsteps crossed the floor, and Jess opened the door and stepped out. She looked composed but tired. "Sorry, I thought you were Fred Hustad."

"Amy said he's on his way. So—she's gone?"

Jess nodded and shut the door behind her. "About thirty minutes ago. I'd like to keep this room closed off from the rest of the house until she can be moved."

He sighed. He'd really liked Deirdre Gifford. "She went so fast."

"That methanol pretty much finished her off. She lost her sight, like Winks did."

He flinched.

She put on a resigned face. "But she wouldn't have survived. Hasty consumption has a very poor outcome."

"I stopped by the office. Whit told me they've had a couple of deaths in Fairdale and Twelve Mile too. The news came in the mail."

Jessica shook her head in wonder. "I suppose it was bound to happen—I just wasn't expecting it here. Did you talk to Granny Mae?"

"Yeah. She's a wreck over this—she didn't want to talk to me but I finally convinced her that she's not going to jail."

"What did you find out?"

"She doesn't know who she bought that alcohol from. She'd never seen the man before, and when she described him, I couldn't hazard a guess as to his identity. But then I don't know that many people around here."

"Mae does. If she didn't recognize him, he must have been a stranger."

He rubbed a thumb over his chin. "Who's going to tell her about this?" He gestured at the closed door.

"I will." Amy walked toward them. Her eyes were still red, and her hands looked chilblained from the scrubbing. "I feel responsible."

Bax turned to Amy. She'd grown so accustomed to blame, she accepted it even if it didn't belong to her. "It was an *accident*. Nothing was intentional, was it?"

She looked over Jessica's shoulder to the four-panel door behind her. "No."

Just then, someone knocked on the front door downstairs.

"That will be Fred, I imagine," Amy said, and she turned to go meet him.

• • •

Tabitha stood on the platform to watch the porter unload her belongings from the train. He tossed them onto the baggage cart as if they were hay bales instead of her treasured Louis Vuitton luggage.

"Excuse me, *please* be careful with those trunks. There are some fragile things in them. And have them delivered to the New Cascades Hotel."

"Yes, ma'am." The porter nodded, and she stepped forward to hand him fifty cents.

"Oh, and where is the taxi stand?"

He turned one ear toward her slightly and gave her a sidelong squint. "The what, now?"

"Where can I get a taxicab?"

"There's nothing like that in Powell Springs. I've never even seen a taxicab, except once when I was in Paree during the war. Anyway, the hotel is just there, two blocks over." He pointed at a two-story brick building that shone rust-red in the sun.

She sighed and walked down the platform steps to the street. The trip out here had not taken all that long, though there were numerous stops on the way, but her day had been, and she was frazzled and tired. She looked down at her wrinkled cream ben-galine suit and realized it was probably impractical to wear for travel. It would just get dirty. But her ivory gloves and straw cloche created such a lovely ensemble. She would change clothes when she got to the hotel and hope that the wrinkles relaxed.

Her escape from the house had taken place in the dead of night, with her belongings going first. After another visit from Rinehart, this time with a real police officer, Tabitha had become so nervous she didn't want to wait any longer. Elsa arranged for her brother to take the luggage to Union Station and check it. Two hours later Tabitha followed in a taxi, in case any nosy, and poten-tially gossipy, neighbors were watching. To reward her efforts and loyalty, Tabitha had paid her maid six weeks' severance pay, plus a bonus of seventy-five dollars, a gift so handsome that Elsa wept with gratitude. Tabitha had left the hall lamp on, as she always did, to make it appear that she was still home. Then she locked up the beautiful, stately house on Park Place, and with a grief-stricken last look, climbed into the taxi that carried her to the train depot. Whether she would see it again was impossible to know.

Looking around now, she saw that Powell Springs was a humble village of a place compared to Portland. Not even Main Street was paved, and there were as many horses on the roads as cars. And dear God, was that ghastly figure perched in the horse trough a replica of the Statue of Liberty?

She had to keep her mind on why she was here. This was not a European holiday. She was here because Harlan had made it impossible for her to stay in her home, and she'd come to find him. She didn't know if he was here, but at least no one in this town knew her either.

Once she had her room, and her belongings had been brought upstairs by the bellboy and a put-out maintenance man, she had a chance to look around. By local standards, the hotel was probably the height of elegance. To Tabitha, it was adequate. At least it appeared to be new and not furnished with lumpy old castoffs from the previous century. She wouldn't have to go down the hall to a communal bathroom. But given her limited means—a galling situation in itself—she could not have afforded something more expensive in any case.

Next to a north-facing window, she settled in a chair upholstered in dark-blue rep and looked down the length of Main Street. Tomorrow, after a bath and a decent night's sleep, she'd begin her search for Harlan. If he was in this town, someone must have seen him.

CHAPTER FOURTEEN

Over the next few days following Deirdre's death, Amy, Tom, and Bax had collected everything Amy believed should be burned and taken it outside. Each had tended a fire. Now she stood over the burn pile to splash kerosene on it, then struck a match and threw it on top. Following a *foom*, flames erupted, creating a cloud of thick, gray smoke pungent with the petroleum smell of lamp oil. The last remnants of Deirdre Gifford's worldly goods were sterilized and consumed by fire. There had been no sense in saving any of the stuff like old letters or hairbrushes—Deirdre had no living relatives, no next of kin to notify that Amy was aware of.

She leaned on the handle of an upright rake. What a horrible two days it had been, with events jumbled together in her mind like scenes from a fever dream. All their clothing that would withstand boiling she had stirred in a galvanized washtub on the other side of the backyard. Those garments that would not survive such treatment were in the pile before her, along with the mattress, a wool blanket, and the flotsam of a life cut short by the surprise attack of an illness.

Jessica had insisted that they all come to her office to undergo the Mantoux test for tuberculosis to learn if they'd been infected. She included Granny Mae—most especially Granny Mae, because she cooked for the public. All of them had tested negative, thank

God. To make sure, they were to come back in a month to repeat the test.

How strange and awkward it was that Amy had peered at her sister across the great gulf of their estrangement, extending her hand for help and accepting that help without addressing the reason for their falling out. She could argue to herself that so many things had happened to derail her attempt to apologize, that the right moment kept eluding her, and that wouldn't be unreasonable. But Deirdre's death brought home to her the consequences of intentions too long delayed.

Tom Sommers had come to her yesterday after they got back from Deirdre's funeral to tell her he was moving out. While she scrubbed the floor in Deirdre's now-empty bedroom with Lysol, he stood before her torturing the hat he gripped. It was not because of the possible contagion, he said, or anything wrong with the accommodations. His hours were long and unpredictable, and for him it just made more sense to move to a cabin at the sawmill. Amy saw the real reason in his eyes—regret and a kind of grief, not just for Deirdre's death, but perhaps for the death of future possibilities and a dream held close. She believed that had Deirdre not become ill, she might have had that husband and family she'd longed for with Tom. Amy sighed and let him go with good wishes.

Fire caught the scorched, lacy edge of a valentine stuck in the burn pile, and it disappeared in a hungry blue flame. Things could change that quickly.

Amy had no illusions about her own future. But she was beginning to regret returning to Powell Springs. It had sounded like a nearly perfect, if not sensible, destination, with her inheritance and its ready-made income. Nothing had gone well since she'd come back, though. She hoped only for peace, and freedom from the infuriating, unpredictable tyrant who was her husband, although the second wish had been a childish, impractical dream. She had neither. Although she hadn't seen Adam since that evening in the hotel lobby, she had no idea where he was. He could pop out at any time. Then there was that other man, Breninger, who'd tried to swindle her out of a month of rents. Peace came at a higher price than she'd realized, and she wasn't yet sure of its full cost.

Still, even as she told herself this, the image of a tall man with dark hair and eyes the color of the fire's smoke rose in the play of the flames. At moments of unguarded reflection, he wore the expression of a weary cynic, and she understood why. But there was something more she sensed in him that extended beyond her own brief goals of security and heart's ease.

Bax had hope.

Amy envied that. She couldn't see far enough ahead to hope.

• • •

Tabitha Monroe stood outside an eatery and looked up at the ceramic tile numbers above the door, then back at the scrap of paper in her hand. Inside, customers seated at tables jabbed cutlery into midmorning meals, sipped coffee, and read their newspapers. The desk clerk in the hotel had told her that if she wanted to find someone, this place or Tilly's Soda Shop would be the best places to start, although he pointed out that Tilly's might not be a place for a lady to visit.

Here, the addresses matched, but its only identifier was the word *Café* painted in red letters on the plate glass windows.

"For heaven's sake," she said aloud.

She couldn't go in and sit at a table, waiting all day to see who walked in. There had to be a better way.

She pushed open the door and a bell rang overhead. Inside, she saw a counter with stools. Behind that another counter held a Hamilton Beach milkshake mixer, assorted glassware and crockery, and a pie and a layer cake under domes. On the wall above, a Coca-Cola calendar with an illustration of a pretty girl in a beautiful hat smiled at her. At the end of the back counter, swinging louvered doors that led to the kitchen bore signs that said *No Admittance*. Enticing scents of coffee, cream, roasting meat, potatoes, and sugar all mingled together.

But there was no one waiting tables and the diners around her stared as if she were from a distant planet. She could hear something going on in the back—sounds of frying, clanking pots, dishes.

"Excuse me," she called.

Soon, a rangy old woman pushed open the doors partway. "Just have a seat. I'll be with you in a minute."

"No, I'm not here to eat. I'm trying to find . . . something."

The woman emerged, wearing a white bib apron and a faded housedress. "Okay. I know just about everything that goes on in this town and everyone who does it."

Tabitha blinked at the woman's undignified informality. "Yes, well. A clerk at the hotel told me I should talk to Mae Rumsteadt and that someone here could direct me to her. I want to find a man."

The old woman's brows shot up. "I don't know why anyone told you that! I run this café and the only things I serve up is food and coffee."

She stared at the crone, mortified by the woman's misunderstanding. "*You're* Mae Rumsteadt?" For some reason, she had expected a homey sort, living in a charming cottage with over-stuffed furniture, ruffled curtains, teapots, cookies, and crocheted antimacassars.

"I am, missy. Who are you?"

"I-I am Mrs. Monroe."

"A married woman, and looking for a man?" She gave Tabitha a once-over.

Tabitha pressed her lips together. This was dreadful, just so dreadful. She felt the eyes of everyone present boring into her. Her own eyes flew open so wide, she thought her lashes must be tangled in her brows. What a horrible hag, and worse, she didn't even seem to realize how insulting she was. She should have just gone back to her cousin's house. Then she remembered—people were looking for her and it wouldn't be hard to trace her back to them. Plus, her family had been fairly eager to see her married off to Harlan. Oh, they'd tried to hide it but they weren't very subtle. Their relief had been palpable when she'd announced her engagement.

She swallowed and briefly shut her eyes. "Mrs. Rumsteadt—"

She waved her off. "Oh, I'm just Granny Mae to everyone. Anyway, there never was a Mr. Rumsteadt, except my daddy."

For some reason, the name Granny Mae conjured an image of a clucking chicken in Tabitha's mind. In a low voice, she said, "Please, I don't want to discuss anything in front of an audience . . ."

"Come on back to my office." Then to the customers she said, "You all go on with your meals."

Tabitha cringed, but the group did as they were told. She must have lost her mind. She'd left it on that train from Portland or perhaps dropped it while she had walked up and down the street, because she was actually listening to the old woman, too. Like a dutiful schoolgirl, she followed her into the "office," which turned out to be a big kitchen with a huge range, dried flowers and herbs dangling from the ceiling alongside braids of onions and garlic, and raw meat on a worktable. Tabitha couldn't decide if she felt as if she'd looked through the open gates of hell or into someone's most intimate space. In any event, she felt distinctly out of place. Instead of leaving, though, she stayed.

"Now, what's this really about?"

"I'm looking for my husband, Harlan Monroe. I heard a rumor that he might be here in Powell Springs. The clerk suggested I talk to you because you see just about everyone who passes through this little town." She adjusted her handbag on her arm and ran a nervous, gloved hand over her jacket lapels. "The clerk also mentioned someplace called Tilly's Soda Shop. I don't know why but he said that I might feel out of place there."

Mae considered her expensive clothes and hat again. "Ho, I can guarantee you would. It's a saloon, and not too many women hazard a trip in there."

"Do you think you've seen my husband?" Tabbie asked, trying to get the information she came for and get out.

"Nope, not around here. Up and left you, did he?"

"Not exactly, well, no, I think something bad might have happened to him on a business trip and I've decided to look for him myself."

The old woman's skeptical expression told Tabbie she wasn't buying her story, but she didn't say it.

"And truthfully, I'm hoping to find suitable lodgings for a while. I'm not sure how long, and a hotel costs more than I'd like to spend. Can you suggest something?"

"You're in trouble with the law?"

God, but the woman was tactless. Tabitha wasn't really wanted by the law. But Harlan was, and if the authorities couldn't find him, they would keep pestering her. "No, I am not! It's . . . something else."

"Oh, that's right—a man. That's why there was never a *mister* in my life. At least not one I had to answer to. Coffee?"

"No, thank you." Tabitha couldn't imagine why she stayed, but she detected a sympathetic ear in the artless, tough-hided Mae, and that kept her in the kitchen.

Mae walked to the stove and poured a cup for herself from a blue enameled pot. "All right, then. First things first. I don't know about your husband, but I believe I know the solution to one of your problems."

• • •

Amy and Bax sat in the living room after dinner. Actually, she sat on the sofa, and he was slumped so low in a chair his backside was on the edge of the cushion. His legs stretched out in front of him, crossed at the ankles. In the quiet, she heard the mantle clock ticking with slow resonance within its walnut case, and somewhere a block or two away, a dog barked.

She crocheted.

He slept. His hands were interlaced on his belly. His breathing was quiet and even, his forehead smoothed out.

The blinds were all pulled to keep out the prying eyes of Adam's hired thug, and Bax had made sure the doors were locked. Now it was just the two of them in the house, and she'd never been more aware of his presence. She had told no one about initiating divorce proceedings against Adam. It just wasn't something discussed in polite company. But her thoughts could not help but stray to the possibility of an unencumbered future, when she would be free of him and able to make a better choice, her own choice. She could imagine herself and Bax under different circumstances, but the situation didn't involve sitting in the living room, with her crocheting while he napped, like an older, staid married couple. She'd seen him awake, asleep, sober, tipsy, angry, in various states of dress, serious, and smiling. She hated to admit it to herself—she didn't want to be attracted to any man now—but there was nothing about him she really didn't like. And if he were gone, she would miss him, and mourn the chance they might have had.

Her imagination carried her upstairs with him, out of this living room. When she realized the path of her thoughts, her face grew warm. She'd never craved Adam's contact and it hadn't taken long for her to loathe it. Her experience was limited to him, but surely for all the fuss some women made in giggling, whispered conversations among themselves, there must be more to making love than what he had demonstrated. Sometimes she thought that she could have been anyone to him, any faceless, nameless female for all the attention he paid to her during those awkward, mechanical encounters.

But Bax carried a heat with him that made her wonder what it would be like to feel his hands and mouth on her bare skin. To erase the formality of landlady-boarder in the soft gray light of his bedroom, on crisp sheets that smelled of sun and fresh air, which she herself had laundered and laid. To find, if just for a while, comfort in the touch of another person. One who wouldn't yell, or hit, or belittle. A person who knew what it was like to be rejected, lonely, a casualty of his own decisions. A man of honor.

Her crochet hook moved faster and the rows of picot trim on the pillowcase she was edging increased apace.

"What are you working on there?"

Torn between her daydream and concentrating on her project, she nearly jumped off the sofa at the sound of his voice.

"I thought you were asleep!"

He pushed himself upright. "I was. Now I'm awake. What is that?" He nodded at her crocheting.

She put down the pillowcase. The action of the hook was making her wrist ache. "Nothing special."

"My mother used to do some kind of needlework. I was a boy—I didn't pay much attention to what it was. It might have been knitting or some kind of sewing—probably knitting. She made our socks."

"You've never tried to reach her in all these years?"

"Nope. I never went back to Cedar Mill after that first time. I wasn't as brave as you are."

"Brave! What makes you think I'm brave? I came to Powell Springs to hide."

He stood up and sat on the sofa, leaving about a foot of space between them. "So did I. But you knew what might happen when you got here, and you came anyway. I'd thought my family would be glad to see me. Of course, you didn't spend time in prison."

"Hmh," she huffed thoughtfully, smoothing the lace edging against her knee. "I did, but it was a different kind than you experienced. And *no one* was glad to see me."

The clock ticked four or five times in the silence.

"I am."

Her head came up and she caught his gaze. It was as if he could see past all of the hurts and lies and posturing she'd once done to find the terrified girl inside. With a fingertip, he reached out and stroked the back of her hand, leaving a trail of what felt like invisible sparks, a match striking emery on the side of a matchbox.

"I think it took a lot of courage to come back to a place where you knew you would be, uh—"

"Shunned?"

"Well, yeah. Most people wouldn't do that."

"I came back only because I inherited this house. But I've been here long enough to get a different view of what I did to my sister and . . ."

He pulled her hand into his and rubbed his thumb lightly over the space between her thumb and forefinger. She realized she was leaning toward him. Then he worked his way up to her forearm, running the backs of his fingers over the soft, tender part. Goose bumps erupted there and she looked away from the drowsy intensity she saw in his face. "You're a beautiful woman, you know."

No one had told her that in years. And she didn't believe it was true anymore. "Pfft. I was once, maybe. A long time ago."

"You still are."

"I went to see Daniel Parmenter," she said, as if he'd willed the admission from her. Her pulse thumped up and down the side of her throat.

"Really?" He brought her hand to his mouth and put a kiss in her palm. She'd never felt anything like that before.

"Oh—um, yes. I told him I want to file for divorce." She had trouble staying on the subject with him making her attention stray. "He—he's begun the paperwork." What would he say? Would he want to escape from her, and treat her the way people treated divorced women? Open season on damaged goods?

"It's about time."

She felt the tip of his tongue on her hand and it was as if an electric wire had branded her. She pulled her hand away and he searched her face, looking for what, she didn't know. But he found it apparently, because he took her into his arms and kissed her, a slow, lazy invasion of her senses that touched off a fire in her.

How could she feel so close to this man, someone she never laid eyes on until a few months ago, when her own husband had been a stranger by comparison? Bax was not merely attractive and very male. She felt comfortable with him, a new experience for her. Cole was also attractive and very male, but his heart had never been in their courtship, and now she knew that had been because he'd never stopped loving Jessica. And he had never been hers. Those two were meant to be together.

With steady pressure, Bax pushed her back against the cushions with her head resting on a needlepoint feather pillow, until he lay half on her and half on the sofa. His arms around her kept her from tumbling to the floor while he laid a line of kisses that began just behind her ear and on down her throat. She was certain he must feel her heartbeat throbbing there. The scent of him, leather and denim and his own chemistry, filled her head and drew her in as deftly as the feel of his warm mouth on her. Finally she looped her arms around him and arched her neck against his touch, thrilled by the fierce tenderness of his ministrations and the heated length of him pressed against her thigh. He wedged his knee between her legs and instinctively, she bore down against it.

In the back of Bax's mind, the dual-voiced enemy of impetuous behavior—logic and reason—called to him with a warning that he must have lost his mind. Lying here, kissing Amy, and running his hand up her ribs to her breast and covering its soft curve with eager fingers, what the hell did he think he was doing? He was trying to make love with her, so logic and reason could just shut the hell up. He hadn't lain with a woman in months and she was no ordinary female. She was soft and tenderhearted, and as thorny as she had been, he'd wanted to do this the first week she'd gotten here. But a vulnerable woman with an uncertain future? He didn't know all the legal ins and outs of divorce, but what if Jacobsen, or the law, fought her? And what if the good people of Powell Springs heard about his history and weren't as accommodating as Whit Gannon? Then what? He didn't feel like he could tell her about that yet. Not until he knew for sure.

He pulled back and gazed at her half-shuttered eyes and flushed cheeks, hairpins falling out, and felt her breath coming swiftly. "Amy."

Her eyes flew open, and she looked at him. He propped himself up on one elbow. "This isn't right. Not now. Not yet." God, it was agonizing. Why was doing the right thing always so damned agonizing? With great regret and no little discomfort, he sat up and pulled her with him.

She exhaled like a suddenly deflated paper bag. "Why, because I'm married?"

"No. Well, partly, but not for a reason that simple. I don't want to take advantage of you. You're still lost and hurting. You don't need me to make things worse. If we made love, it would change everything between us. Complicate things."

She looked down at her lap. "I see."

He put his index finger under her chin. "No, maybe not. I don't know how the town will take it if word gets out about me. Where would that leave us?"

A flash of apprehension crossed her face, followed by resignation. "You're right, of course." She wriggled away from his arm around her shoulders.

His expression was wry. "If you're mad at me now, think of how you'd feel if things don't go right for us. You'd hate me as much as you do Jacobsen."

She whipped her gaze back to him. "I couldn't hate *anyone* as much as I hate him." Rising to her feet, she smoothed her dress and left the room.

CHAPTER FIFTEEN

Amy climbed the back steps to the kitchen, her flower basket filled with snapdragons and greenery, still sparkling with lingering raindrops, to arrange in a bouquet. It was nice to have a yard with flowers again. The colors were beautiful—pink, deep crimson, bright yellow—and the stems of laurel would be a pretty complement when she gathered them all in the china vase she'd found in the sideboard. It would look good on the table in the entry. Maybe Mrs. Monroe wouldn't think they were so uncultured, after all.

Mae had sent the woman to her the day before. Tabitha Monroe wasn't running away from something, as Amy had been, but toward something. She said her husband was missing and the authorities had been no help. So she'd decided to come to Powell Springs based on a flimsy rumor, desperate to find him. She'd be along soon and had hired a boy to bring her luggage from the hotel.

Grabbing a paring knife from a kitchen drawer, she stood at the sink nipping off a leaf here, a wilted bloom there, when she heard footsteps on the same back steps she had just climbed. The instant she heard the rattle of the doorknob she remembered that she hadn't thrown the lock. Now Bax would come in and give her a well-deserved reminder about keeping the doors secure.

"Well, Amy, I don't suppose you expected to see me again."

Still holding the knife, she turned her head to stare at the man in her kitchen, unable to believe her eyes. He carried a large suitcase, which he dropped with a thud. Her heart beat so hard she heard it throbbing in her ears, and for a moment she couldn't speak. She couldn't even breathe.

Her wind came back in fits and starts. Tucking the blade into her apron pocket, she demanded, "What—what do you want, Adam?" She forced false courage into her tone, although she knew it was a stupid question. His expression mirrored her thought, but his eyes shone with a strange feral gleam she had not seen before. He looked unkempt, with a three- or four-day beard and red-rimmed eyes. His clothes were rumpled, as if he'd been living in a cold-water flophouse. Or a tent.

He crossed the floor like a lightning bolt and grabbed her wrist. It was the same one he'd gripped and broken in the past, and she winced. "Did you really think you could just walk away from me, from our marriage, and that I'd let you go? It took a bit of doing, but I tracked you down. I'm surprised you'd have the nerve to come back here."

She worked to maintain a brave face even though terror flooded her veins and her hands turned icy. "Let go of my arm. You have no right to barge in here. Do you realize the deputy sheriff lives here? He'll be home any moment."

He scowled. "He's not here now, and you know damn well that as your husband, I have every right in the world. I can take you away, or I can move in here. I heard about that deputy, and the little romance you've got going with him. That ends now. He'll answer to me and I'll throw him out myself. Now you and I are going to talk." He began pulling her toward the living room, the site of his fussy, determined courting so long ago.

She pulled back. The adrenaline rushing through her dulled the pain in her arm. She almost blurted out that she had begun divorce proceedings, but started didn't mean finished. And she knew that information would only escalate the level of his anger. "We are not going to talk. There is no romance with anyone, and I have nothing to say to you. Besides, we're not alone here. There is another boarder—"

His expression grew more threatening. "No there isn't. Milo Breninger has done a good job of keeping an eye on you, even though it's cost me a fortune. One of your lodgers moved out, and the other one is in a new grave at the cemetery. And now your husband is moving in."

She gaped at him. How long had Breninger been spying on her? And how much more did Adam know?

"Adam, don't you realize how unwelcome you are in this town?"

"No more unwelcome than you are, I'm sure. Let's not forget your participation in that drama between Braddock and your sister."

Frantic, she scrabbled for excuses. "You can't move in here. There is no space."

"Of course there is—in your room." His smile was sly. "Besides, Laura Donaldson likes me. She always thought I could walk on water."

She nearly bit off her tongue. He didn't know as much as she thought. Obviously, he didn't realize that she owned this house. Her thoughts raced. "Mrs. Donaldson isn't here, either. But I'm expecting a new tenant this morning!"

"You used to be a much better liar, Amy. Now, we're going to straighten out some things." Still clamping her arm, he pulled her along, stopping once to backhand her, then started heading for the main stairs.

Amy's ears rang, and for a moment lights flashed in her head. She tasted blood where her teeth had cut into her lip.

But she knew what he meant, straighten some things out.

He was finally going to kill her. He was going to take her upstairs and beat her to death, and no one would be here to stop him. All the things left unsaid and unsolved in her life, all the wrongs she had hoped to mend and make right, the tiny spark of hope that Bax gave her—it would all be lost when he punched her insensible, broke her bones, and kicked her after he'd thrown her on the floor. If he used something like a lamp or a table leg again, this time there would be nothing left of her face or head. And she wept inside, in terror, and for the opportunities wasted because of her own selfish foolishness.

But she couldn't let him drag her like a cow to the slaughter-house, without trying to save herself. She pulled hard against his grip on her arm, the pain making sweat pop out on her forehead, but she couldn't get free. Then she remembered the knife in her apron and closed her hand on the blade's hilt in the pocket.

Just as she was about to raise the knife over her head and stab him in the arm the doorbell rang. She tucked the knife away again.

"Who's that?" he whispered, glaring at the door.

"I told you, I'm waiting for a new lodger," Amy replied, unable to hide the relief in her voice.

He shook his head and kept trying to pull her up the stairs. "Shut up!"

"I said I'd be here. If I don't answer, it will seem like something is wrong!"

The bell rang again, followed by knocking.

Right now, Amy didn't care who was on the other side of that door, as long it was someone who wouldn't make things worse, like that Breninger devil.

Adam dithered for an instant. "Get rid of whoever it is." That gave Amy a chance to wrench her arm free with a sickening crack, but she barely felt it. She ran to the door, her hair loose and flying around her shoulders. She swiped at the blood pouring down her chin, then turned the knob and opened it wide.

"Mrs. Jacobsen! My goodness, are you all right? I was afraid I'd confused our meeting time," the woman said.

"No, no, please come in." She stepped back and inclined her head toward Adam, hoping to indicate a problem.

"I'm so glad to be moving into such a charming—" Mrs. Monroe hesitated in the entryway, looking Amy up and down, at the drops of blood on the bodice of her dress. Then she glanced at the stairs and the color left her face.

"Harlan!" she shrieked.

"Who?" Amy asked, confounded.

"Tabitha—" He looked poleaxed, and stared at them both with his jaw hanging.

"What!" Amy blurted, and gazed at Adam.

"That is my husband!" Tabitha Monroe pointed an accusing finger at him.

"Husband!"

"What are you doing here, Harlan?" Mrs. Monroe demanded. "Is this where you've been all these months while I've been fending off lawyers and the police in Portland because of your scheming? With this—this woman?"

Amy recognized her implication and her blood heated up another twenty degrees. "Now, just a minute. I have been married to Adam for four miserable years!"

Mrs. Monroe swung on her. "Who is Adam?"

"He is!" She pointed at the guilty party. "Who is Harlan?"

Adam froze on the bottom step and stared at them, looking for all the world like a rabbit cornered by a pair of starving wolves. Without warning, he reached into his jacket, pulled out a small silver revolver, and pointed it at both of them.

"I'm leaving," he said, wild-eyed but keeping his voice low, menacing. "You two are not going to make any more noise about this. May God help me for ever getting involved with either of you, you ungrateful, complaining bitches." He came down the one step and circled them in a wide arc, keeping the gun trained on them. Moving toward the open front door, he kept his back to it so he could watch them while the women stared at him, paralyzed. He was so unstable, Amy knew he could shoot them both.

Suddenly, Bax Duncan's frame filled the doorway and Adam backed up against him. Bax grabbed Adam's gun arm and twisted it in its socket until he dropped the weapon.

It went off when it hit the floor and skidded across the hardwood. Mrs. Monroe screamed. Bax wrestled Adam to his knees and reached for the manacles hanging from his gun belt. Adam put up a furious struggle, swearing, spitting, and kicking—he snarled and even tried to bite Bax.

"Stop it!" Bax roared at him. He whacked Adam hard in the face with his heavy suede gloves and pulled Adam's head up by the hair and bashed it once on the floor. Then he put a knee in his back and forced him facedown over the threshold to keep him still. Adam, a soft man accustomed to a soft life, was ultimately no match for someone of Bax's size and lean-muscled build. "Amy, call Whit at the office, right away."

She wobbled on jelly legs to the telephone in the hallway. "Birdeen, this is Amy. Get Sheriff Gannon over to my house right away."

"Is it serious?" the operator asked.

"Yes, of course it's serious! It's a desperate emergency!" she snapped and hung up.

When she came back to the living room, Bax said, "You'd better see to your guest, there."

She turned to Tabitha Monroe and saw her lying on the floor. The sleeve of her lovely ivory suit was ripped at the upper arm and blood soaked the fabric. "Oh, dear heaven," she said, horror-struck, and knelt beside her. "Mrs. Monroe—Tabitha! Can you hear me?"

Tabitha murmured something, and began crying weakly.

Remembering the knife in her apron pocket, Amy cut open the sleeve to determine the severity of her injury. Fortunately, it was just a nasty graze—no bullet was lodged there. She reached up to grab a needlepoint feather pillow from the sofa and pushed it under the woman's head. "You'll be all right, Tabitha. Your suit is ruined, and you're going to have a scar, but my sister will take care of this. She's a physician."

Her own wrist gave a tremendous throb, and she looked at it. The joint was swelling at a rapid rate. She glanced at Adam, still on the floor under Bax's knee. Four years of rage over beatings and abuse boiled over in her and she crawled on her own knees to look at him.

"You horrible, disgusting bastard!" she barked. "You married another woman at the same time you were married to me? I don't know what kind of trouble you're in besides bigamy, but I hope you're thrown in jail and never see daylight in this life! And you broke my wrist again!"

She stood up and Adam grumbled, turning his face away from her. It took every bit of self-control she possessed to stop herself from kicking him in the head.

Bax could hardly believe what he'd walked in on, but he was glad his timing had been right. He caught a glimpse of Amy's lip and the blood running down her chin. He knew Jacobsen had hit her and anger as hot as a Bessemer furnace flared up in him. Images of his mother with a black eye, with a busted lip, her face covered with bruises crossed his mind. His hands closed around the pencil neck above his knee and he squeezed. "By God, you sniveling coward, I'll kill you for this—"

Outside, the putt-putt of a Model T announced Whit's arrival, and Bax looked over his shoulder to see the sheriff unfold his tall frame as he got out of the car. He took a deep breath and relaxed his grip. It was a good thing Whit's timing was right, as well.

Whit climbed the porch steps. "What the hell happened here?"

"I'm not even sure. I walked up to the front door and this guy was backing out with a gun trained on Amy and that woman over there on the rug. He seems to be married to both of them."

Whit pushed over the captive slightly with his foot so he could get a good look at him. "Well, I'll be damned—Adam Jacobsen."

"According to her," Bax nodded at Tabitha, "he's in trouble for some other things too. Police are looking for him somewhere."

"In Portland," Amy put in.

"Portland, huh?" Whit leaned closer to get a better look at Adam, and then straightened to study Tabitha, too. A flash of comprehension lit up his face. "I knew it! These are the two I saw on the street in Portland that day coming out of that shop. Remember?"

"Yeah," Bax realized. "You thought you knew him."

"And I do. I think I've gotten some information about this in the office. We've got our work cut out for us, trying to unravel this mess."

Outside, a few neighbors had begun to gather, probably attracted by the gunshot, all the yelling, and the sheriff's car. It made a bizarre scene, Adam straddling the threshold with his legs sticking out on the front porch.

"All right, on your feet, Jacobsen," Whit said, and they hauled Adam upright. Most of the fight had gone out of him, but they had to drag him along when he went completely limp and uncooperative.

The spectators parted to let them through, and then closed around them again. Not much happened in this small town, but when something did, it was always a sensation.

"Amy," Bax called. "I'll be right back to pick up both of you and take you to the doc's office."

She nodded and waved him on with her good arm. "Go on. We'll be waiting."

• • •

Jessica dabbed antiseptic on Amy's chin, making her hiss from the sting. Then gently she pulled Amy's lips away from her teeth to look at the damage. "Not too bad. Was Adam wearing a ring when he hit you? Your main injury is external, and you're already beginning to bruise."

Amy shrugged with drooping shoulders. She sat on a stool at the worktable in Jessica's back office. "I don't know. It all happened so fast. And it's my fault. Bax warned me to make sure I kept the doors locked. I came in from the backyard with a basket of flowers, and I forgot. Adam walked right in a minute later. He must have been watching to make sure he caught me alone."

Jessica let out a small whoosh. She walked to her glass cabinet and took out an aspirin powder, then mixed it in a glass of water. "Here," she said, handing the glass to Amy. "Swish this around in your mouth, then swallow it. It'll help with the pain."

Amy scowled at the taste and had trouble keeping the water in her mouth due to her swollen lip. "Ugh."

"Yes, sorry about that. Let's see your arm."

Amy held it out and Jess felt carefully along the break, using her touch to find the fracture. "Hmm, this feels odd."

"It's been broken before. But it wasn't set properly so it didn't heal well."

Jess sighed. "Amy . . ."

"How is Tabitha?" she asked, deflecting any other questions or comments. Now wasn't the time.

Her sister took the hint. "She'll be all right, I think. I gave her a sedative and put two sutures in that flesh wound. She told me she married Adam two years ago. He must have created an entirely different life and identity while he was still living with you. They have—or had—a house on Park Place. She thinks the bank will probably foreclose on it."

"Park Place," Amy repeated dully. "I saw that street once. I lived in a grubby little dump in Slabtown and worked as a dishwasher." Her memory skimmed along the images of all the grubby little dumps she'd occupied since leaving Powell Springs the first time.

"Apparently she has social connections he wanted. He worked as a secretary to Robert Burton. Now the police suspect him of embezzlement, and she's not married to him at all. At least that's what I've heard so far."

"How lucky for her." That she felt a sense of betrayal could be considered strange in light of how much she despised him. But of all the things he had done, and those she suspected him of doing, this was too fantastic for her to have envisioned. "She was supposed to come and board at the house. I hope she doesn't still plan on that. It's not her fault, but I don't want that kind of reminder living under the same roof with me."

Jessica went to a drawer and brought out two splints and rolls of bandage. "I don't imagine she'd want that either." She walked down the hall to the waiting room. "Bax, I can use your help now."

Alarm flooded Amy. "Help? What are you going to do, amputate?" She eyed the splints. "Is that a bite stick?"

Bax appeared in the back office and Jessica chuckled. "Don't be silly. The last time this was set, were there two people to do it?"

"No, just some old drunken sawbones. I think he'd lost his license for too many deaths on the operating table."

"Hmm, well, that's probably why it didn't heal correctly. Bax, hold Amy's upper arm tight so that it can't move, especially down near her elbow. I'm going to pull on her hand to reduce the fracture."

"Okay." He tried a couple of different grips. Finally he stood behind her and held her in a bear hug.

Jessica quirked her brows and smiled. She looked at Amy. "Ready?"

She took a deep breath and nodded, not knowing if this would be excruciating or just average torture.

Her sister gave her hand a mighty pull. She gritted her teeth and tears sprang to her eyes.

"Good! All right, Bax, you stay put. I can use an extra pair of hands." She sandwiched Amy's arm between two splints, one on the top and one on the bottom. "Now, if you'll hold these just like this—"

He replaced Jess's grasp with his own. She grabbed the bandages and began winding them over the wooden slats. When they were fixed, she nodded. "I've got it now."

"Uh, I'll just be out in front if you need anything," he said and backed away from Amy with obvious reluctance.

When Jessica finished, she brought out a sling and adjusted it to fit. "This isn't bad. I think it should be all right in about three or four weeks."

"Three or four weeks," Amy moaned. "There's laundry to do and cooking, and all sorts of things."

"I guess you'll need help. There's always Mrs. Monroe."

"I don't even know what her real name is. Her marriage to 'Harlan' isn't legal. Anyway, does she really seem like the type who would have anything to do with those kinds of chores? She had a *maid* in Portland."

Jessica gave her a sour look. "She doesn't now."

• • •

Bax delivered Tabitha Pratt to the New Cascades Hotel and saw her as far as the lobby. She'd had nothing to else wear after leaving Doc Jessica's office but her torn, bloodied clothes, and she attracted a lot of attention when she tottered to the front desk like a sleepwalker. She asked that the kitchen bring her a cup of broth and toast, and didn't speak again, even when Bax offered to see her to her room.

He went back to pick up Amy and they drove to the house in near silence. Both women had had quite a shock, he knew. Hell, even he was unnerved.

Only by simple chance had he come to the house. "How's the arm?"

"Oh, it's no worse than the last time. At least I know it will knit properly now. And it's my left wrist and not my right."

He nodded, but didn't say anything more. Amy seemed strangely unaffected considering what had happened today. Most women he'd known would be railing and upset, cursing both Jacobsen and Miss Pratt.

"How about if I stop by Granny Mae's and get her to put a dinner together for us? I know she'd be happy to do it."

Amy nodded. "Yes, that would be nice. Maybe she has meatloaf or something else that would be easy for me to eat with just a fork."

"Okay, I'll see about it." He pulled up to the café and parked. "Do you want to eat here or shall I go get it?"

"I think I'd like to go home. You know she'll just press me for all the details if I go in."

"Right." He left her in the car and ran inside.

Mae was accommodating but she wanted to interrogate Bax, too. He was able to put her off. When he got back to the car, Amy said, "That smells wonderful. What did she give you?"

"She had the meatloaf you asked for, and put in mashed potatoes, gravy, rolls, pie. You know, all good stuff. I asked her to put meals together for us for the next two or three weeks. I'll just pick them up from her. She might be a pain in the ass sometimes, but she's a great cook." He gave her a sidelong glance. "Almost as great as you."

Amy rolled her eyes and didn't respond. They got back to the house and he helped her inside, bringing the basket with him. Not much had been disturbed during her scuffle with Adam. It had been a horrible day, but she'd be fine. She would get over it. Then she walked into the living room.

There was Tabitha Monroe's blood on the rug. Amy began to shake. Her heart beat so fast and hard, it felt as if a litter of rabbits were trapped in her chest. She stared at the stain, and the whole experience began flying past her mind's eye.

"Amy, where do you keep the silverw . . ."

She heard Bax's voice but she couldn't tear her gaze away to look at him. Her feet felt anchored to the rug.

"Amy? Are you all right?" He sounded so far away, as if she were trying to hear him over a churning, swift-moving river. She felt his hands close on her shoulders. "Amy!"

Finally she lifted her eyes to his face and words poured out, one tumbling over the other, churning like that water. "He was going to kill me. He was going to drag me upstairs and beat me with a stick of firewood or a chair leg! He hit me like that before. But this—I would have had worse than a broken arm or broken ribs. This time, this—when he was finished, I would be dead and even my own sister wouldn't have recognized me. My skull would be crushed. My face gone. If—if Tabitha hadn't come to the door when she did—if you h-hadn't come home, I'd be dead! I'd be dead." Tears poured down her face, and she trembled like a tired, old dog gazing up at the barrel of a shotgun aimed at its head.

Bax stared at her, and she saw her own horror and heartache mirrored in his face. "Jesus God," he muttered and closed his arms around her. Shudders worked their way through her and gave way to wracking sobs. She clung to him with her uninjured arm, wailing out years of suppressed fear and cruel domination against his shoulder. He tipped his head down to hers and hugged her to keep her from being swept away with the current of her living nightmare. "Jesus God."

• • •

That night after Bax coaxed her into letting him feed her from a fork, he followed Amy into her bedroom and helped her change into her nightgown. Then he propped her arm on a pillow and lay down beside her on top of the coverlet, fully dressed except for his boots. She tossed as much as her arm would allow, unable to sleep, until finally he got up and gave her two shots of his Canadian whiskey. That seemed to settle her. When she whimpered, he stroked her hair until she quieted. "Try to sleep," he whispered. At last she burrowed against him, her head on his chest, his arm around her, and her splinted arm across his stomach.

For himself, Bax found little peace. Amy's terror was contagious. He'd seen war and its abominations, he'd been wounded, hovered in a purgatory of dire illness, and had turned away the Pale Horse. But nothing compared to what she'd described today, and the pure dumb luck of his arrival—what if he hadn't gotten here when he did? What if Tabitha Pratt had not chosen that moment to ring the doorbell? Amy's description of what would have happened did not seem like an exaggeration. In the presence of authority and facing a jail cell, Adam Jacobsen had folded up and cried like a five-year-old. But when he could overpower someone smaller or weaker, he turned into a monster. Now in the cool, dim light of a waning moon, Bax grabbed the whiskey bottle from the night table and took a long drink himself.

After a while, he drifted into the shadow world of dreams and reality, but always mindful of his current task. Amy was strong. She had to be to survive the years she'd been stuck with Jacobsen. He hoped she was strong enough to overcome this.

• • •

In the morning when Amy woke, Bax had gone but he left her a note on her night table telling her he'd check in once or twice during the day, as his schedule allowed. Careful of her splinted arm, she rolled toward the side where he'd slept and pulled his pillow against her nose, inhaling his scent in the bedding. She wished he was still lying beside her. She'd had a difficult night, but she knew it would have been completely intolerable if Bax hadn't been with her. Through the mist of her pain and the horror of the day's events, she'd felt his tender touch in her hair, the back of his finger stroking her cheek, comforting her. For all the battering her emotions had taken lately, the idea of life without Bax had become equally unendurable. She found herself listening for him when he came home—still through the back door, because he'd once told her that he *couldn't* use the front door. She'd never learned why. He could make her laugh, something she didn't do much of anymore. He made her aware of what it might be like to become a ripe, mature woman in every way, something she felt she'd never really known. And perhaps his best attribute was his tender heart.

Lying next to him in the night had felt like the most natural thing in the world, like she belonged in his bed. When he was with her, she wasn't afraid.

Amy had fallen in love with Baxter Duncan, the man who offered her a ride into town when it was raining. The man she had so rudely snubbed. He knew the worst about her but still treated her with respect and dignity. He had every reason to be bitter and mad at the world, but he still found goodness in it, and in her.

Later that afternoon, Whit came to tell Amy what he had learned about Adam.

He sat at the kitchen table with a cup of coffee and a pitcher of cream. The sun gleamed through the back porch windows.

"You didn't have to go to all this trouble, Amy. Especially not with your broken wing and all." He took a sip and brushed off his silver mustache.

"Truly, Whit, it's fine. I make coffee throughout the day. Or I did, when more people were living here."

"You haven't heard from Tom Sommers?"

"No, after Deirdre died, I think he didn't want to be reminded of it. I believe he cared about her more than I realized. As far as I know, he's living at the sawmill."

Whit stirred the coffee again, then plunged ahead. "I hope you don't mind, but I told this story to Mrs.—Miss Pratt first. We still have Adam in custody. He's basically a yellow-belly coward, so he's been willing to tell us everything, hoping that he'll seem cooperative. He has quite a history, as far as I've been able to piece it together. Here's what I've figured out so far: he *has* led a double life in Portland. He lived in that fancy house up near Washington Park with Tabitha Pratt, and took on the alias of Harlan Monroe. They were married in a big church wedding a couple of years ago, but of course, it wasn't legal. She didn't know it was all a fake."

Amy studied the pattern in the woven tablecloth, trying to conceal her humiliation. "I asked him where he went, but he'd never really say. If I asked too many questions, well, Adam has a bad temper." She gestured at her splinted arm. "He came home at least five or six times a week, but sometimes I was at work. I didn't always see him."

"Well, he had a job with Robert Burton, that wealthy timber-man with the mansion in the Portland hills. Adam even had an office in his house and he was making pretty good money. But he embezzled more from the old man. They're still trying to figure out how much, but probably thousands. That's one thing he has confessed to."

She stared at him, open-mouthed. All those backbreaking hours she spent washing dishes at the restaurant, and he made her beg for her own money to buy anything for herself. Her temper began to fry like a pan of bacon. "I—I never knew any of this!"

He nodded. "I didn't think so. He would have worked hard to keep those two lives separate, and I'll bet it was a tricky chore. Plus, the police have learned he was probably using that money to buy bootleg whiskey from Canada. He would take his wife's—uh, that is, Tabitha Monroe's—gardeners with him to load the goods into his car. One night a few months ago, something went wrong, and one of the gardeners was shot and killed. The other one took off running, but recently he went to the police to tell them about it. I guess he was afraid he might be next. That was when Adam left Portland. But he did go back to Park Place at least once and told Tabitha that he was working on some special project. She admits she didn't believe it."

Amy's stomach felt as if it had dropped to her shoes. To think that all of this was going on and she had no idea. "This is incredible. I feel so stupid."

Whit patted her hand. "Don't. No one could have guessed something as crazy as this. What's that saying? Truth is stranger than fiction?"

"This certainly is."

"All the lawyers and police working on this haven't been able to find out what he did with the money, though."

Amy thought back to the day she left, and what she found in the closet. She straightened. "Wait! I might be able to help with that." She climbed the back stairs from the kitchen and hurried to her bedroom to pull out the book she had hidden in her chest of drawers. She rummaged around and found it tucked between the cuts of fabric, just where she'd left it. Pounding back down the stairs, she held it out to Whit.

"I found this under a floorboard in the house I left in Portland. I didn't know what it was, but I recognized Adam's handwriting. I took it as a kind of insurance. I thought if he went to that much trouble to hide it from me, it must be valuable. I've never been able to make any sense of it, but maybe the answer is in here."

Whit pushed aside his coffee cup and thumbed through the pages. "Maybe. It's a bunch of numbers and dates—it might lead to solving the mystery." He looked up. "Anyway, when you left he hired that Milo Breninger to find you. He gave the bum your photograph and three hundred dollars down payment."

"Down payment? How much did he promise him?"

"In the end, he paid him a thousand dollars." She could only stare at Whit. The figure was beyond comprehension.

"We think he's still around here someplace, since he's been blackmailing you and trying to knock the pilings out from under Bax."

"Oh, God—"

"Just keep locking your doors. We'll get him."

CHAPTER SIXTEEN

A few days later, Amy shrugged into a dress that was easiest to put on, brushed her hair, and left her house for the New Cascades Hotel. It was a sunny day, one that promised to be warm but not with the blasting heat that would come later in the summer. This weather was kind to flowers and the lawn. When she walked into the hotel lobby, this time she wasn't worried about who she might see. The man she feared most was sitting in Whit Gannon's jail until arrangements could be finalized to move him to the county jail in downtown Portland. But she could hardly believe the reason she was here. The old Amy, the selfish, shortsighted Amy, would never have dreamed of making the offer she was about to make.

She approached the front desk, where a bored clerk was trying to balance a pencil vertically on the end of his finger.

"Excuse me."

He looked up, startled, and the pencil clattered to the floor. "Uh, yes, ma'am! How can I help you?"

"I'd like to see Tabitha Pratt-Monroe. Could you please call her room and tell her that Amy"—she stalled here—"Amy Jacobsen is here?"

"Yes, ma'am." He fumbled through a register and did as she asked. "She said to please come up. Room two ten." Although the hotel had only two floors, it featured the most modern conveniences, including an elevator. She stepped into the car when the doors opened and was taken to the second floor. It was nice here, she thought, walking down the rug-covered hall. She had certainly seen much, much worse.

At room 210 she stopped and knocked on the door. After a moment it opened a crack and she looked at a two-inch-wide section of face. Apparently satisfied with her identity, Tabitha opened the door wider to let her in.

The two women looked at each other. They both wore slings, and both of them were protecting their left arms. Tabitha wore an expensive pink satin dressing gown.

"I understand you spoke with Sheriff Gannon," Amy said. Tabitha nodded. Then to breach the awkward moment, she added, "We're a sight, aren't we?"

Tabitha sighed and nodded. "We are, we are. Please, Amy, come and sit." She motioned to a brocade sofa.

When they were settled, Amy came to one of the points of her visit. "I'm so sorry for what happened yesterday. I had no idea that Adam would simply walk into my kitchen. And God knows, I never meant for this to happen." She gestured at their arms. "But more than anything, I want to thank you. You saved my life."

Tabitha put a hand to her chest. "*I* did?"

"If you hadn't come to the door when you did, I'm sure I would be dead now. You interrupted Adam and gave me a chance to break away from him." She went on to explain briefly what had happened, and what she knew would happen. Tabitha gaped at her.

"I never knew that side of him. He could be impatient, and he always tried to make me think less of myself, which I suppose now, reflected what he really thought of me. But, sweet Adeline, the past twenty-four hours have staggered me. I left behind a comfortable life that was built on larceny and lies." Her chin trembled briefly, and she stared at her lap. "I'm not even a married woman."

Amy understood what she really meant. She gave her an even look. "Consider yourself fortunate. I *am* married to him and all he has done is drag me through the mud behind him. He made me work as a dishwasher and turn my pay over to him, and that was while he was living part-time with you." Another moment of silence fell.

"But," she went on, "I didn't come here to review Adam Jacobsen's numerous shortcomings. I'm wondering if you have plans—somewhere to go."

Tabitha hung her head. "Yes, and not really. I haven't contacted my cousin to tell him about this. I lived with him and his family before I—before the wedding. I taught school but I was considered an old maid without any other resources or suitable prospects. They thought they would be stuck with me forever, I think. And they were so obviously relieved to be rid of me. Now I'll have to go back."

Amy touched her hand. "No, you won't. You can still come to my house and board with me. I realize it's an odd situation, probably the strangest anyone ever heard of. But as I said, you saved my life. Powell Springs isn't as grand or glamorous as Portland can be. It's a mostly rural community, but growing, and it's safe here, usually. We do have societies and women's leagues, if you're interested. I used to be. No one knows you here. You don't have a reputation or a past to live down. And it seems to me that it would beat living with relatives who aren't very eager to have you back."

"You would do that for me?"

The old Amy would not have . . . "Oh, we'll have tongues wagging for a while—the two wives of Adam Jacobsen, or Harlan Monroe. But they'll settle down after a while and get used to us.

I can't promise what the future holds, but if you're interested in a peaceful existence, you'll have that. You might even be able to get a teaching job again."

Tabitha's eyes welled up with tears. "How very kind of you," she said in a choked voice. "Can I think about it?"

"Of course. I'm not going anywhere. Let me know." She stood up and smiled at her. Tabitha rose as well, and saw her to the door.

"Harlan should be horsewhipped for what he did to you."

"He certainly left a lot of casualties in his wake," Amy said. "But I'll survive. You will too."

Amy Layton Jacobsen left the hotel knowing that she had finally grown up.

• • •

Just as she reached the house, Amy saw a car pull up and recognized Daniel Parmenter getting out.

He lifted a hand in greeting. "Mrs.—Miss—Amy, it's good to see you." They met on the front walk.

"Mr. Parmenter, it's nice to see you, too. I hear you've been busy these days."

He looked very dignified, as he usually did. "I'm on my way to the courthouse in Portland but I wanted to come by and check on something we talked about recently. Of course I heard about your terrible incident the other day." He gestured at her arm.

This couldn't be good, she thought. This house—she couldn't lose this house. But there was no point in avoiding whatever he had to say. "Please—come in. Thank you for dropping by. I've just been to the hotel to visit Tabitha Pratt."

"The two of you have had some bad luck."

"I'm still alive, though," she said, and unlocked the door.

She led the way to the dining room. "Have a seat. I'm sorry about bringing you to the table, but—" She hadn't had the rug taken out and she couldn't bear to look at the bloodstain and be reminded constantly about that horrible day. The memory was too new, too raw.

"No need for explanations." He pulled out a chair and sat at the table. She sat across from him. "Now then. After our last meeting, I began the paperwork to get your legal action against Adam Jacobsen moving. I did some research about property ownership and inheritances, that sort of thing."

She froze. No, no, no—she couldn't possibly have to share this house with Adam now, not after everything that had happened, not with him headed to jail. "He's under arrest."

"Yes, well, that's not the issue." He sat forward in his chair and put his elbow on the table.

"Issue?"

"You said you were married in Multnomah County. When you married him, did you sign anything? A license, any sort of document?"

She sat up. "No, now that you mention it. There was nothing."

"Did a judge or a justice of the peace perform the ceremony? Were you married by a clergyman?"

"Well, yes, Adam performed the ceremony himself. He is an ordained minister." She dropped the corner of her mouth and added, "As hard as that is to believe now."

"Yes, I remember that he was Mr. Mumford's predecessor." He didn't add what they both already knew. He was Mumford's predecessor due to the social disgrace that made them leave town together. "Were there witnesses? Even strangers pulled in from the street?"

She shook her head, and she stared at him. "No one except us."

"Where did this take place?"

"In the office at his home just before—before we eloped."

"The reason I'm asking is because I sent my law clerk to Public Records to research the specifics of your marriage. He couldn't find anything."

"What?"

"I've requested a special search, but I have a feeling that your wedding was never formalized. You never saw a license or a certificate?"

"No. What does all this mean?"

"Well, if Jacobsen performed the ceremony himself, there were no witnesses, and no papers were signed, you were never legally married to him."

"What!" Here came that throbbing pulse in her ears again. "Never married? All this time?"

"No. Of course, this simplifies matters. There is no common-law marriage in Oregon, so even that isn't a consideration. On the other hand, certain aspects of this are probably very distressing."

Her brain *whirled* with the distress of it. "Um, yes, I . . ."

"And just to clarify, you said there are no children."

"No . . ."

"We might see that as a good thing."

"I certainly do."

He rose from his chair. "As I said, I've requested a special records search, but I have a strong suspicion that it will turn up nothing. I hate to rush off, but it's a trek to Portland and back."

She stood up, too. "Thank you, Mr. Parmenter. I appreciate your efforts. Of course, you'll let me know what I owe you."

They walked toward the front door. "We won't worry about that now. I'll be in touch soon."

She nodded and opened the door for him. Once he was outside, she locked it again.

She went back to the dining room and sat down. Why had she never thought to question Adam about the lack of marriage licenses and certificates? All these years, she thought again. She could have walked away at any time. She hadn't needed to stay with him and take the abuse and the beatings and the poverty. Amy had only recently come to realize how selfish and immature she had been. But she believed that he actually topped her in that department. He had referred to her as his wife, used her like one, ordered her around and made her obey like one. But she was not his wife, not now, not ever. And he'd taken from her that one thing that was hers to give only once. It might be a new day, 1922. But some things stayed the same. Some things still had value, to her anyway.

Not married. *Never* married. Just like Tabitha Pratt. She was free of him and he had no legal claim on her. But he'd stolen from her something she could never get back.

Then bitter tears began to flow.

• • •

"Right. Thanks, Paul. We'll be right there." Whit hung the earpiece back on the telephone.

"Where are we going?" Bax asked. He'd just walked in from seeing Jacobsen being hauled away by two armed guards the county had sent from the courthouse. They were taking no chances—they'd shackled their prisoner, hand and foot, to restraints built into the backseat. Bax had glimpsed him just once in his high-society clothes when Whit had pointed him out in Portland. Jacobsen looked pretty bad by the time they turned him over. Both he and Whit were glad to see him go.

"Paul McCoy said he's got a stranger holed up in his barn with a couple of jugs of moonshine. He was working in his field out near the Braddocks' horse farm when the guy came by and tried to sell him some of the stuff. I talked to him a week ago to let him know we were looking for someone like that. Paul chased him into the barn with a shotgun and locked the doors. Now if the fool doesn't set fire to the inside or figure out an escape route, I think we might have our man."

"For a quiet town, we've had a lot of business in this cell lately," Bax observed.

Whit jammed his hat on his head. "Yeah, and I'd like to see it slow down. I'm not as young as I used to be. I'm getting tired of gallivanting around the countryside. Let's go."

They drove out over dry roads, past Cole's place, and just beyond the horse farm. When they reached Paul McCoy's berry farm, he met them in the yard, holding his shotgun across the crook of his arm. His overalls were worn to thread at the knees and his shirt was missing a cuff on one sleeve. Paul's wife had died five years earlier, and he and his three high school–age sons weren't all that particular about such things as new clothes and haircuts.

The flat, well-tended field of berry bushes stretched out behind him, green and healthy-looking under the sun. They got all of his attention.

"I've got my boys watching the barn. If that son of a bitch tries to escape, they'll run him down with the tractor."

Bax handed a shotgun to Whit. "All right, we'll get him." He made it sound as if they were cornering a rattlesnake in a bedroom, or trying to get a skunk out from under the house. "Do you think he has a weapon?"

"Nah, just that kerosene he's passing off as liquor."

"And you've never seen him before."

"Nope. He's a stranger to me, and you know I've lived around here my whole life."

"Got any livestock in there?"

"No, the chickens are all out pecking around under the filbert trees."

"Here's what I want the boys to do. Get some grass that's dry enough to burn but just green enough to make some smoke. Twist it into torches and light them. Fill some buckets with water to dunk them in when they get to be too short." He glanced up at the trees to determine the wind direction. "Great, it's an east wind day, so we'll have them stand on the east side of the barn."

"Damn, Whit, I don't want to burn down the barn."

"We won't. Trust me, I've used this before. It's better than shooting the walls full of holes."

Paul conceded that point.

When everything was ready, Whit motioned to one of the boys to rattle the door on the east side of the barn. Then they lit the torches. The amount of smoke was impressive. The object, he said, was to make the criminal believe the barn might be about to catch fire.

"Come on out, mister. You're surrounded and we've got a bad fire here. If you don't save yourself, we might not be able to save you, either."

It took several attempts, but at last the smoke flushed out their suspect. The barn wasn't very big and it hadn't taken a huge effort to fill it with smoke. A man flung open that east side door and stumbled out, coughing and with eyes streaming.

Whit grabbed him and they opened the big doors to let the barn air out. "Your days of selling your poison are over."

Bax closed in, and when he saw who Whit had by the scruff, he was surprised—not because he wouldn't expect it of the man. He'd sell his own mother's eyes if the price was right. But he'd tried to alter his appearance. Usually a fan of cheap, gaudy suits, he wore a pair of beat-up denims that were too short and a blue gingham shirt. He even had a red bandana tied around his neck. He'd cut off most of his hair—with hedge shears by the looks of it—and what was left had been dyed with what seemed to be black shoe polish.

"Breninger!" If he hadn't done so much harm to so many people, Bax would be laughing, he looked that ridiculous. No wonder he hadn't recognized the description Granny Mae gave him.

"*This* is him?" Whit asked.

"Yeah, but just barely. He doesn't usually look like this."

"Go piss yourself, Duncan."

"You have your own experience with that? Well, your wealthy benefactor is off to the county jail in Portland, and it looks like you'll be following him."

"For what? Selling whiskey?"

Whit said, "If I wanted to make a point, I could. Manufacturing alcohol is illegal, in case you hadn't heard. But this is for first-degree manslaughter. This isn't whiskey, and you know it."

He actually had the nerve to look insulted. "There's nothing wrong with it!"

"Really? Let's see you drink some of it. I'll go into the barn and find it for you."

He grumbled but didn't say anything more.

"Okay, Paul," Whit called to the farmer. "Thanks for your help."

The man raised a hand in farewell, and they loaded Breninger into the back of the Ford.

• • •

"Amy?"

She stood in the kitchen and was surprised to hear Bax's voice coming from the living room. This was the second time now that he'd used the front door.

She met him in the dining room. He looked so handsome standing there, dark hair and lashes, long legs in jeans that fit him so well it should be a crime to look that good. He was the same as always, and yet not. Something was different. "Hi, Bax." She felt a little bashful around him now that she'd admitted to herself that she loved him. But now there was that other problem, the matter of her marriage. Or nonmarriage. And that weighed heavily upon her.

"How is your arm?" he asked.

"It's going to be a long three weeks. It's hard trying to do things with just my right arm, although if I had to break anything, I'm glad it wasn't that one."

He lifted his face slightly and sniffed. "Is that coffee I smell?"

"It's just ready now."

"Come on. I have something to tell you."

She held back and felt her smile fade. "Bad?"

He grinned at her. "I can see why you might think so, considering everything that's happened. But no, you'll like this."

Intrigued, she followed him into the kitchen.

"Go on, sit down," he said. "I'll get the coffee. Some for you, too, right?"

Without waiting for her answer, he grabbed two cups from the pile of clean dishes draining beside the sink. "How are you washing this stuff?"

She pulled out a chair and sighed. "One at a time. It's slow business."

"I'll try to help." He poured their coffee and put the pot on a trivet that sat on the table.

"Never mind about that now. What's your news?"

"We've got Milo Breninger sitting in jail."

"Oh! You caught him!" she crowed.

"For manslaughter, yes. And if you're willing to press charges, we can slap him with blackmail too."

"I certainly will. You should, as well."

His smile faded. "That brings me to my other news." He looked so serious, her heart dropped and she put down the cream pitcher.

"Bad?" she repeated. She couldn't help her pessimism. Things had gone well lately, but other things had gone so horribly wrong she didn't know what to expect next.

Briefly, he held up a hand. "The day I came home and found Jacobsen here, I meant to tell you then. That was why I'd dropped by in the middle of the day. But when I got here, well, you know better than anyone what happened next."

She watched his face, but didn't say anything.

"Anyway, ever since prison and being banished from my family's home, I've felt like I had a sign hanging around my neck, telling everyone what had happened to me."

Amy knew that feeling. Very well.

"When I came to Powell Springs and got this job, I really felt like things were turning around for me. I was respected again and people didn't know what had happened to me at the end of the war." He raked a hand through his hair. "Then Milo Breninger showed up."

Guilt swamped Amy. "He showed up because of me. Adam hired him to find me. And he found you."

He waved that off. "It was such a long shot. Really, what were the chances that Jacobsen would hire the very same bastard who knew me too, and send him to a small town in East Multnomah County? A million to one. A billion."

"Maybe."

"Breninger isn't just greedy. He's vindictive too. In that way, those two men are alike."

She exhaled. It was true. Revenge was a big part of what they did.

"So, the new life I was just getting started, the honorable one, looked like it was about to fall down around my ankles when he showed up. And the chances were slim to none that he should have found me." He dumped two spoonfuls of sugar into his coffee. "But sometimes bad luck just sticks to a person like flypaper. You know what happened next."

"Oh, Bax," she mourned.

"But the reason that I came home that day was to tell you that Whit heard from the War Department."

She sat up straighter. "And?"

"The charges and the imprisonment are still on my military record. So is the sentence. That's not going to change. But they show that I was released early due to some vague reason. Anyway, it was good enough for Whit."

"I'm so glad for you."

"You're not the only one." He stirred his coffee. "I didn't tell you sooner because I was worried about what people would think if they learned of it. But after everything that's happened, I realized it doesn't matter. I've been dragging that anchor around with me for long enough."

"Is that the reason you've started using the front door?"

He put his elbows on the table and folded his hands under his chin. "I didn't think you'd remember I said that. Yeah, it is. I suppose it was dumb, but I couldn't make myself do it before. I wasn't, well, good enough I suppose."

Not good enough. She thought for a moment before she responded. "I think we all have our reasons for doing things or feeling a particular way. They might not always be logical reasons, but it can be hard to overcome them." She gazed off to the yard beyond the back porch windows.

He tipped his head and studied her face. "Has something new happened?"

"Hmm? No, not really." She turned her eyes toward him again. "I went to the hotel to see Tabitha Pratt. I asked her if she'd like to board here instead of going back to Portland. She said what little family she has there won't be thrilled to see her again."

A slight frown crossed his forehead. "I didn't realize you're still going to take in boarders."

"Well, yes. You and I can't live here alone. People will make all sorts of wrong assumptions. Then, I need the income to pay the taxes on this house and so on. I came back to Powell Springs to make a new life for myself too. Since Adam and that odious Breninger are out of the picture, I won't have to look over my shoulder every time I step outside."

"But, I thought—I was hoping—" He stared at her.

"What?"

"Nothing. I have to get back to work. I've left Whit with most of the job lately." He stood up and took his coffee cup to the sink. Then he turned and headed for the front door. "I'll see you later."

CHAPTER SEVENTEEN

The next couple of weeks between Amy and Bax were oddly tense. She caught him watching her when he didn't think she knew it. The friendly give-and-take they had enjoyed devolved to the stiffer, more curt relationship of their early days. He still went to Mae's to pick up their meals for them, which she appreciated enormously. Otherwise he retreated to his bedroom or disappeared for hours at a time and she didn't know where he was.

Tabitha Pratt, whose companionship she had been hoping for, finally arrived at the decision to return to Portland. She'd talked to her family and they were already aware of what had happened to her. It was disastrous, but they urged her to come home. She thanked Amy for her generous, kindhearted offer, explaining that in times of trouble, family, complete with foibles and missteps, was the most important safe harbor a person could have.

Her observation made Amy's heart clench. Now that she'd worked to discourage Bax, she had only an unhappy boarder and a still-offended family. Jessica had been wonderful about taking care of her, but although she saw Cole working in his blacksmith shop now and then, he wouldn't even make eye contact with her. She couldn't blame him, but it was uncomfortable just the same.

But before Tabitha left, Amy asked if she would stop by so that they might say a proper good-bye. The afternoon her train was leaving, Tabitha rang her doorbell again.

Amy answered the door and smiled when she saw her on her porch. "Do come in, Tabitha. There is *no one* here this time." Tabitha smiled back, and Amy noticed that her sling was missing. "Your arm is better."

"Yes, thank heavens." She stepped into the entryway. "Being a one-winged bird makes for difficult flying."

Amy almost laughed. "That's certainly true. I'm getting really tired of this, but my sister tells me she can take it off later this afternoon. I'll be her last patient of the day."

The other woman, dressed in a lovely French blue suit, bone shoes and gloves, and a stylish hat decorated with a silk hydrangea, took Amy's hand in her own. "I want to thank you again for your courtesy. We're in such a peculiar situation, you and I. I truly doubt that many people have found themselves faced with something quite like this."

"I spoke with my attorney a couple of weeks ago. I—I discovered that I wasn't married to Adam either."

Tabitha's jaw fell. "Sweet Adeline!"

Briefly, Amy explained the highlights of her wedding. "I was young and foolish, and it didn't even occur to me at the time, or until Mr. Parmenter mentioned it, that I'd never seen or signed a license or a certificate. Nothing."

"We are two smart women. I cannot believe we were both duped by a man who, frankly, was nothing remarkable. It's been a very humbling experience."

Amy couldn't help but laugh. "I will miss you, Tabitha. I really will. And now for the real reason I asked you over. I have a little celebration for us both."

Tabitha looked intrigued, but a bit wary. Amy couldn't blame her. So far a couple of really bad things had happened to her in this house. "That day, Adam brought his suitcase with him. He was planning to just move in."

Tabitha shook her head at his gall.

"In the chaos, I completely forgot about it until I found it in the hall closet yesterday. I looked through it. There wasn't much in it except his clothes, and this." Amy extended her good hand to show her a wad of cash.

Her eyes dilated. "Goodness, how much is that?"

"Eight thousand dollars. Now, I suppose if I were feeling altruistic, I would turn this over to the authorities. But they don't know about it, and I decided there is a charity that would put it to better use: Former Wives of Jacobsen-Monroe. Come over here."

Amy walked to the dining room with Tabitha following. With her to witness, Amy counted out the money, eighty one-hundred-dollar bills, and gave her half. "I hate to make you carry this on the train. Put it somewhere safe."

Tabitha stared at the cash. "I-I don't know what to say. This means so much. It will make such a difference."

"I think so too. Even though he never would have wanted to, Adam is helping us, even as he sits in jail." She put an arm around the former Mrs. Monroe and gave her a hug. Tabitha tucked the money into her purse.

"I'll find a better place for it when I stop by the hotel to check out."

"All right. And now, if you're interested, there's one more thing for us to do. We need to go out to the backyard."

This time Tabitha didn't hesitate. "Let's go."

Amy led the way down the stairs and out to the burn pile in the corner of the backyard. She had already stoked the fire and set out a can of kerosene a safe distance from the heat.

A pile of clothes was heaped beside an expensive leather suitcase. "Are you interested?" Amy asked.

Tabitha picked up a monogrammed shirt. "Definitely. I gave him this. I get to go first." Amy hadn't even noticed the different initials. Tabitha threw it into the flames.

"He always got to wear much better clothes than I did. How could I have been so stupid?" Amy wondered again.

"The time for self-recrimination has passed, Amy. Build that bonfire."

They each tossed items onto pile. When the flames began to smother under the fabric, she poured kerosene at the base and the fire sprang to life again.

"Oh, dear," Amy laughed when they were finished, "I'm afraid we're going to smell like smoke."

"It was worth it. This is the best day I've had in six months. What about the suitcase? Do you think it will catch?"

"We'll make sure it does." Together, they threw it on top of the mound. The fire roared to life by itself, as if hell had opened a trapdoor to help.

At last they reached the end of their fuel. "Well, I know I feel better," Tabitha said. "It won't be easy going back, but thanks to you, I have some freedom now." She studied the almost healed bruise on Amy's chin. "You know, that Baxter is a very nice man. And he cares about you a lot."

Startled, she asked, "How do you know?"

"I wasn't unconscious that day in your sister's office. I saw the way he looked at you and hovered around you." She put a hand on Amy's good arm, and the sun fell gently upon their shoulders. "If you are condemning yourself for the same reason I did, stop it. I realized that none of this was my fault. I was told what I believed to be the truth, as you were. My family even approved. We have a long time left on this earth, God willing, and what's the point of wasting it by regretting the past? We need to move forward, move on. Really good men don't come along more than once or twice in a lifetime. Believe me, I know. I'm still waiting to meet one of my own."

Amy's eyes burned with unshed tears, and she nodded, unable to speak for a moment.

Tabitha added, "Your roses are lovely, by the way. I'm no expert, but I know quality when I see it."

• • •

Amy arrived at Jessica's office at four thirty, enough time, she believed, to have her splint removed and to take care of one other piece of business. The waiting room was empty and she could hear the voices coming up the hallway.

"All right, Barbara. Take this prescription to the pharmacy and we'll get this thyroid problem under control."

"But *pig* thyroid?" Barbara sounded doubtful.

"It's the most up-to-date treatment available. It's a tremendous advancement. You'll lose weight, be warmer, and generally feel much better."

"Thank you, Dr. Layton."

"Check back with me in a couple of weeks to let me know how you're feeling. If you have any trouble, get in touch with me sooner."

Barbara, a woman Amy didn't know, walked through the waiting room, heavyset with a puffy face. When the door closed behind her, Jessica came out and said, "Ready to get that thing off?"

"Dear God, yes. But before we do that, I was wondering if we could talk for a minute."

"Well, sure, okay. Come to the back."

"Is Cole working next door?"

"Yes, I think so. Why?"

"Do you think he would come over too?"

Jessica winced. "I don't know, Amy. I'm not sure he's ready to listen to anything."

Amy gave her an importuning look.

"All right. I'll *try*. But I can't promise."

She went out the front door, and Amy sat down to wait and to work up a case of nerves that turned her hands icy and made her insides jump. This would not be easy. After what seemed like an hour, she heard voices outside the door, her sister's and the low, grumbling tones of a man. She took a deep breath and stood.

Cole gave her a look that could have dropped her like a deer rifle. He stood in a defensive position, with his arms crossed.

"I'm sorry to drag you away from your work, Cole." He just stared at her.

And so she began. "In 1917, I did a horrible, horrible thing. I tried to separate you two with a calculating lie, and I almost succeeded. I'm so glad that ultimately, I failed."

She took a deep breath and went on. "Jess, I was always closer to our mother than you were, just like you were more of a daddy's girl. Mama taught me to cook and keep house, to sew, to do all the things a woman is expected to know to make a good wife. I didn't know how to do anything else. Mama raised me to be just like her—useful, domestic, modest, and ladylike. When she died, I felt so lost, so alone. I'm not blaming you now, but I used to. You had a better connection with our father, with your interest in science and all that. Compared to me, I thought you were wild and anything but ladylike. You liked catching bugs and studying pond water under Father's microscope. I was left out." She looked at Cole and felt her face flame under his stern, unforgiving glare that made this confession no easier. "And you had Cole, even from the time we were schoolgirls. I always had a crush on you," she said to him. "When Adam caught you two down by the creek in the grass, fooling around, and told his own father, I thought for sure that Daddy would lower the boom on you. But he didn't. He just got mad at Adam and his father for making too much of what you had done."

"I was in trouble with Daddy. So was Cole. He just didn't want those busybody Jacobsens to know," Jessica said.

Cole shifted his weight from one hip to the other as if it were all he could do to stand here and listen to her. "Are we going to get to the point of all this pretty soon? I have work to do."

Amy pushed a strand of hair behind her ear with a shaking hand.

Jessica nudged him with her elbow and he let out a long, exasperated sigh.

Amy swallowed, wishing she could sit down but knowing she couldn't. She had to stand before her judges. "Then you went back east to school with the promise that you'd come home and join his practice. Except you didn't. You kept stalling. You stayed in New York to work for the public health department, and I decided that you didn't deserve Cole and couldn't give him the kind of domestic life he deserved. So I sent you that telegram."

"Ah, yes—the telegram," Cole said. "Wasn't that a great day? After I received mine from Jess, I went to Tilly's and got so drunk he wouldn't let me sit in the saloon any longer. He put me on his back porch in the rain with a bucket and an old horse blanket."

There was no need to rehash that particular detail. Spiteful, spoiled, and angry, Amy had forged a telegram to send to Jessica, making it look as if it had come from Cole. In it, she'd written that he wanted Jessica for his wife but he refused to wait one more day. Jessica, furious and hurt, had wired him back and told him not to wait. Then Amy had begun her campaign to win Cole. Shortly after, she wrote to Jessica to report that he was courting her.

But Amy had not won the prize she believed she had. Although she had anticipated a proposal, she knew that Cole did not care about her the way he loved Jessica.

"When you discovered what I'd done, and Adam came calling on me at Mrs. Donaldson's house, we decided to run away together. Socially, we were both ruined in Powell Springs. And we were both cowards."

Her motive now sounded so shallow and trivial, it was no better than the feeble excuse of an adolescent. But she was forthright and candid. "If it helps at all, I believe I paid for my disloyalty many times over when I ran away with Adam. You probably know that he beat me for the majority of our marriage. Somehow, I was fortunate enough not to lose any teeth or break any bones in my face. He did break my ribs, though, and this arm, twice. I visited Dan Parmenter to file for divorce a few weeks ago, and while he was doing preliminary research for my case, he learned that Adam and I were never legally married. I didn't know it. Adam performed some kind of rain dance in his office the night we left, but no papers were signed or filed. I could have left anytime. I just didn't realize it.

"Saying that I'm sorry isn't much, considering what I did. But you are all the family I have. To be cast adrift alone in the world with no one to turn to is the most desolate feeling on earth. Jess, you and I would have had this conversation the night you invited me to dinner. I dressed up and walked to the hotel. But when I got there, I saw Adam in the lobby and I panicked."

She paused and swallowed.

"If you find mercy in your hearts for me, I will be most grateful. If you can't, I understand." She turned to her sister, who was wiping her eyes with a handkerchief. "Now if it's all right with you, Jess, I'd like to get this thing off my arm."

Cole, still as handsome as she remembered him, with his rugged, slightly wild appearance, unfolded his arms and approached Amy. He sighed, kissed her on the cheek, and walked out the door. She shot a glance at Jess, who nodded. "It will be all right," she said in a near whisper. "He won't say it, but he's forgiving you."

"And you?"

"Of course I do. You are my sister, and in the end everything worked out, even better than I had hoped."

Jess went about cutting off the bandages and removing the splints. She moved those healing hands over the bones, gently, checking for proper alignment. "How does it feel?"

Very gingerly, Amy flexed her wrist. "Kind of stiff. And a little tender."

"Take it easy with it. No lifting or chopping kindling, that kind of thing."

"No, I know better."

"And your chin?" She leaned in for a closer look. "The bruise is practically gone. Did the inside of your mouth heal?"

Amy nodded.

Suddenly, Jessica threw her arms open and enfolded her in a warm, loving embrace. Her scent was familiar, vanilla and carbolic. Anyone else would think it was a wretched combination, but Amy would know her sister anywhere by that smell alone. "Despite what happened between us, it makes my heart ache to think of you helpless against that bastard's abuse. I have missed you so much. And you need to meet Margaux. I want her to know her aunt."

The tears flowed again, this time in joy and relief. The situation was like Amy's broken wrist. It wasn't 100 percent, but with time and care, it would be good again.

• • •

Jessica closed the office and gave Amy a ride back to the house. "We'll talk soon. And we'll have dinner at the hotel, all of us."

Amy smiled and nodded, and kissed her sister's cheek. "Yes, we will." She got out and walked up her front steps, her heart feeling lighter than it had for a long time. Taking out her key, she opened the door and caught the whiff of a meal. When she came in, she found Bax sitting at the dining room table alone, eating what looked like roast beef.

He glanced up and went back to his dinner. "When is the new boarder moving in?" he asked around a bite of roast.

"She went back to Portland this afternoon. There won't be any more boarders."

He poked at the green peas rolling around on the plate. "Yeah? Why not? I thought you wanted the money—and a new life."

She pulled out a chair next to him and sat down.

"You'll have to get your own plate. I didn't know where you were or what time you'd be back, so I went ahead without you. Not like it's any of my business."

Amy sighed. He was mad. She thought he was hurt, too. "I had my splint taken off."

He looked at her arm. He almost smiled but caught himself in time, she thought. "Does it feel okay?"

"It's a little tender. Jess said I have to be careful with it. No chopping wood."

"Hah. That's not a problem, is it."

"Bax, I need to talk to you."

"What, more good news?"

"Before you give up on me, I want you to understand what happened. If you can put your hostility aside for a moment, that will help."

He threw his fork on his plate. "All right. What do I need to understand?"

Once again, she relayed the information she'd gotten from Daniel Parmenter about her nonmarriage. She didn't know how else to think of it. She seemed to have his attention now.

"You were *never* married to him? There wasn't an annulment or something?"

She breathed an impatient sigh. "This is exactly the kind of reaction I worried about. Somehow being married, even to a bigamous, lying thief, is better than just being damaged goods."

Bax frowned. He was outraged. "That's not what I meant at all. Don't put words in my mouth!"

Color flamed in her cheeks and she frowned back at him. "I told you the ceremony was nothing but a performance that Adam put on, and you want to know if it was annulled. There was no marriage. What else am I supposed to think?"

"It matters to you, not to me! Do you really think that you'd be more virginal if the wedding had been real?"

She sat back with a stunned look on her face, as if he'd back-handed her. Instantly, he felt like shit. He realized that was exactly what she was thinking.

"Amy, listen. You were tricked. You were slapped around, abused, and treated like a slave. Isn't that about right?"

She nodded, and big tears rolled down her face.

"That's what I care about, not whether your name is on the county rolls in some dusty registration book. Do you suppose that I'm a virgin? I've *never* been married."

First, she looked horrified, then she tucked her upper lip down, trying not to laugh. "But that's different. You're a man."

"Sounds like a double standard to me. Those things aren't important to me. I know you have a good heart. I've seen it in action. You took care of Deirdre before she died. You offered Tabitha Pratt a place to live when I would have expected the two of you to fight like wet cats in a pillowcase, considering the situation."

"I found some money in that suitcase Adam brought here with him. I split it with her."

"Now see? Those are the things that matter."

"Then we went outside and burned everything else that was in it and the suitcase too."

"Did you dance around the bonfire?"

This time she did laugh. "No. But we had a good time."

"I'll bet you did, and I'm sorry I missed it. You love your sister, I know you do." He took her face between his hands and gazed into her green eyes. "And I love you." He kissed her with great care, mindful of her mouth and healing chin.

"Bax," she said with a small, quivering voice, "I fell in love with you the first week I was here."

He caught her gaze and searched her face, unsure of what he sought. Not the truth. He could see that already. Permission? Mutual passion? Peace? He believed he saw all of those, too. None of the other women he'd known, not even Polly, had set fire to his heart and desire the way that Amy did. Maybe his experiences and the passing years had colored his view. Or made it clearer. He only knew that he was grateful she had come along at this point in his life, not earlier. Some things were just worth waiting for. His love for her didn't make him forget his earlier hardships, but it rounded off their sharp edges. He scattered soft kisses on her face, across her cheeks and eyelids, and felt the flutter of her lashes against his lips. A whisper of floral scent rose from her skin and filled his head.

"I-I should put that food in the icebox."

"Leave it. This is our moment. Let the world roll by without us for now." He pushed out his chair and stood up, pulling her to her feet with him.

Amy let him, not out of fear this time, but because she trusted him. He pressed her body to his long torso. This was the first time he'd really held her. Her arms looped around his waist, and his around her shoulders. The match felt precisely right. With her face pressed against his collar, she smelled the clean scent of laundry soap and his ineffable maleness.

He pressed his forehead to hers. "Marry me, Amy. I want you to be my wife. We each deserve something better than we've had. Maybe we had to earn it, but now it's our turn." He kissed her, his touch soft, demanding. "It's our time."

"It is," she said, feeling both languid and aroused, as if all that held her up were his arms and the strength of his words.

"Will you, then? You'll marry me?"

"Yes. And you will be my first and only husband."

"When? I want to do this right."

"Saturday."

He pulled back. "Really? Don't women need more time for the dress and all that ballyhoo? You didn't get it the first time."

"I have my mother's wedding gown. I've kept it in my trunk for a long time. It just needs a couple of alterations. I can do that. I'll talk to the hotel manager tomorrow and ask about a nice dinner in their dining room."

"This is Tuesday. If we're doing this on Saturday, we'd better get on with it. I'll put some stuff together and go stay at the office." He disentangled her arms from his waist, and she looked up at him, puzzled.

"What? Why?"

He took her hands in his. "Amy, the next time I come back into this house, it will be as your husband."

"Ohh, Bax. But there's no bathroom or anything there."

"It'll be all right. And I'm sure Whit and Em won't mind letting me spend Friday night at their house."

She watched him climb the stairs and in a few moments, come back down with an army kit bag. Her heart was torn between loving him even more for what he was doing, and the misery of barely seeing him for the next few days.

Amy walked him to the front door, and in the low, golden light of early evening, he sank his hands into her hair and kissed her as if he were leaving for the war again. "God, I'm going to miss you so much."

She buried her face against his neck, not caring that old Mrs. Beech was walking by with her cocker spaniel. "I'll miss you more."

He chuckled. "Oh, no, no, I'm not getting dragged into that debate. We'd be standing here for hours." He kissed her again, and a low, anguished sound rose from his throat. "That wouldn't be so bad, but I doubt that I'd be content with it." He nipped at her earlobe with a gentle bite.

Shivers flew through Amy and she laughed. "I'll talk to you tomorrow?"

"You'd better believe it." He bounced down the front steps and turned to give her a last look. She swore she saw his whole heart in his eyes, and it was just for her.

CHAPTER EIGHTEEN

Due to their tight schedule, Bax and Amy decided to keep the wedding plans small and simple. Only family and close friends would be invited to the ceremony. In their case, that wouldn't involve many people. Mr. Mumford agreed to conduct the ceremony on such short notice as long as it could take place in the afternoon. His morning was already scheduled with a funeral.

"How did this come about?" Jess asked when Amy stopped by her office to tell her the news on Wednesday. They sat at her worktable, drinking coffee during one of Jessica's rare quiet moments.

"Bax proposed and I said yes."

Her sister gave her a wry look. "But with less than a week to plan the wedding? Amy, you aren't, um, pregnant—"

"Jess, no!" She sighed. "Although I guess I can see why people might think that."

"Yes, and about anyone, not just you."

Amy shook her head and stirred her coffee. "He proposed the same night you took the cast off my arm. I think we were two souls bumping around in a dark place for a long time. We finally found each other." She had told no one about his past. If he wanted to, it was his business to do so. "When we did, it was like the sun came out, despite Adam, and the blackmail, and—"

"Blackmail!"

"That Milo Breninger, he extorted money from me to keep him from telling Adam that I was having a romance with Bax. And that was before anything happened between us. I had to pay him. I didn't know what would happen if Adam believed a story like that. In the end, he told Adam anyway and that was how he showed up in my kitchen. I guess."

"Have you heard anything more about either of them? Adam or Breninger?" Jessica asked, pushing a tongue blade out of the way.

"Not really. They're both sitting in jail while the police sort out their crimes. Adam—I feel like I never knew him at all. He had at least one other identity and was involved in a lot of things I didn't know about." Amy looked down at her lap. "I can't believe I was so blind. But then again, he taught me early on not to question him. And I could have avoided all of it if I hadn't been so selfish. It was a hard lesson."

"It was," Jess agreed quietly. "But it's behind us now. When enough time has passed, that episode will fade in people's memories."

Amy pushed her chair back. "Well, I have a lot to do before Saturday, so I'd better get to it. I-I haven't spoken to Susannah. But if you do, will you tell her that she and Tanner are invited to the wedding? I'm sure she won't come, but I want to include her."

Jess stood up. "I'll tell her."

Amy nodded and kissed her sister's cheek. "Thanks, Jessie."

• • •

The short days flew by. Amy and Bax met at the café every evening for dinner. She wouldn't have minded cooking for them, but he was sticking to his promise that he would not cross her threshold again until he carried her over it in his arms and she was Mrs. Amy Duncan. Now that the evenings were long and mild, he walked her home and they strolled down the street, hand in hand. For Amy, this was the sort of romantic courtship that she hadn't known before. Adam's importunities all those years ago had been nothing more than a calculated act, shifted, she realized, to Amy from Jessica when she rejected him. Flowers and overblown speeches about her beauty and virtue—they'd all been self-serving. In Jess, he'd discovered a woman too independent and strong-willed to be taken in by his maneuvering. Amy, though, had been a perfect victim: vulnerable, with an outsized but extremely fragile ego. She'd eaten up his blandishments with a serving spoon.

But Bax . . . she felt as if they'd known each other for years. They were comfortable together, and yet a heat burned just below the surface between them that made her glad their wedding was a few days away, instead of months.

On Friday evening, he walked her up to her front porch. They sat on the wicker settee that overlooked the street. "Well, Amy, this is it. Tomorrow night, I don't think we'll be sitting out here listening to the frogs."

Ducking her head, she smiled and actually felt herself blush. "No."

"Any second thoughts?"

Her head came up and she looked at him. He was sincere. She could see a shadow of apprehension in his eyes, but she had to ask anyway. "My God, Bax, are you *serious*?"

He shrugged. "The decision was kind of hasty."

"No—no second thoughts." A shiver went through her. She feared the answer but knew she had to ask the question. "What about *you*?"

He smiled and put his palm to her cheek. "Amy, don't you know?" He placed soft kisses on her eyelids and temples. "You made my life good again. I can't even remember how long it's been since my life was good. If Whit hadn't come along when he did that day Jacobsen was here, I really think I would have killed him. I had my hands around his neck when I heard Whit's car pull up. Every night since you got here, I'd lie awake, knowing you were just on the other side of the wall—the only time I felt more alone was when I was in prison and looking at the world beyond the barred windows. Every hour I'm waiting for you seems like a year. I *need* you by my side."

Her throat tightened but she let out the breath she'd been holding. No one had ever told her something that passionate. No one had been her ally for years. With a small cry she flung herself into his lap and his arms, and didn't care if all the neighbors saw them. "It's the same for me. Why do you think I chose tomorrow for the date? I didn't want to wait months for something that feels so right. People might talk—even Jess asked me if I'm expecting—but they're talking about me anyway. The dress is ready, the dinner is arranged at the hotel, we've got Mr. Mumford. But I'd marry you if I had to wear a flour sack and stand in a field with peanut butter sandwiches for the guests if that's all we had."

He gave her a big grin and took her hand. "That reminds me—I know the bride's family usually pays for the wedding, but we aren't children. I haven't given you anything toward this except for reserving the bridal suite at the hotel. I have a little in the bank, you know. Is Dr. Jess covering this?"

"Adam is paying."

He turned a bit gray in the face, and she felt guilty about her choice of words. She went on to remind him about the money she found and divided with Tabitha.

"I didn't know it was that much!"

"Now, do you feel compelled to turn me in to the authorities for taking it?"

He laughed, then lifted her hand to his mouth and kissed it. "Taking what? I don't know what you're talking about. You never told me anything."

Dusk settled over them as they sat there. Finally he said, "I'd better let you get on with whatever you need to do. We have a party to host tomorrow afternoon." He winked at her and got to his feet.

She laughed and wondered how, after all this time and everything she'd been through, she'd gotten so lucky. Maybe Bax had been right when he said it was their time, their turn. "Whit is going to be your best man?"

"Yup. Em is going to get me put together properly so that I'm presentable. Doc Jessica is standing up for you?"

"Yes. I'm so grateful that she forgave me and that I have her back in my life again. I guess I didn't deserve her before." She paused. "Do you think I'll ever meet your family?"

He sighed. "Someday. Maybe. After the old man is dead."

"Do they know about us?"

"Nope. Hell, they don't even know about me. You're my family now." He took her into his arms. "Speaking of which, you'd better get your fooling around in right now, lady. Tomorrow, I'm a married man."

His kiss was slow and leisurely, only hinting at a suppressed urgency that she had yet to see in him. He ran his hands up her back and one slipped around to her ribs, creeping higher toward her breast. Now she *did* care what neighbors might think if they saw this. She clutched his fingers in her own. "Bax, this is no one's business but ours. We're on the porch."

A boy flying past on his bicycle howled out a catcall when he saw them. "Sorry," he muttered sheepishly, and then yelled at the kid, "Don't you wish!"

"Bax!"

He grasped her upper arms and looked into her eyes. "Tomorrow."

She nodded. "Tomorrow."

Then, with a quick peck on her mouth, he was down the front stairs and gone.

• • •

The next day, under a brilliant blue-chrome sky, Jessica and Cole picked up Amy in Jess's car because it had a backseat. They both looked very nice, and Cole actually smiled at her and carried her overnight bag down to the trunk of the car. She'd spent an hour soaking in the tub with a bar of sweet almond soap. Her hair she had washed the night before to make sure it would be dry by this morning so she could weave it into a braided chignon.

"You look beautiful, Amy," Jessica said. "Mama's dress worked out so well for you." The cream-colored lace gown with its gossamer veil made Amy feel like a princess on her way to marry her prince. She had even splurged on a pair of shoes to match. Bax had told her that Em was arranging for Amy's bouquet. The group would be small—Granny Mae, Cole and Jess, Whit and Em, and Susannah and Tanner, if they decided to come. Maybe one or two others.

A light July breeze stirred the poplar and graceful birches surrounding the small church, and the blooms of daisies bobbed in the gentle currents of wind. Amy looked around but she didn't see the county sheriff's car that would have carried Whit, Em, and Bax. A nervous jolt shuddered through her chest to her stomach.

Any second thoughts?

She remembered Bax's question from the night before. She glanced at every form in the church, looking for the right one. It took her eyes a moment to adjust to the dim church from bright daylight, but once they did, she found Bax up near the altar and relief swept through her. He looked so handsome in a suit. She'd never seen him in one before. Em was waiting in the foyer with a simple but lovely bouquet of white carnations and pink roses tied with a wide satin ribbon. Her red hair was twisted into an elegant upswept style and she wore a hat that matched her moss-green dress.

"Aren't you a pretty bride!" she said. She handed the flowers to Amy and they carried a whiff of spice and sweetness.

"Thank you, Em, for everything. Bax told me you would supervise him to make sure he was dressed properly."

Em lowered her voice. "Don't ever let him know I told you, but the poor man was so nervous, he lost his breakfast as soon as he ate it. This means an awful lot to him." She smiled. "So do you."

"Oh, dear. I hope he's all right." Amy peeked into the church. "Where's Whit?"

Em sighed. "That's the bad news. He got called out to Fairdale on a report about a still someone set up on Luke Becker's property. He dropped us off but he felt like he had to go. Whit has known that old man and his wife for years."

"So he won't make it?"

"He said he'd try, but we might have to find someone else to stand in for him. But don't worry about that—we'll work it all out. This is your day, yours and Bax's."

Amy caught Jessica's eye where she stood chatting with Granny Mae, and the three held a short conference.

"Do you think Cole might fill in?" Em asked. "I don't suppose he knows Bax very well."

"It looks like Whit won't be back? Mae mentioned the situation, of course. All right, I'll do something." She turned to her sister. "You just go about your job of being the bride."

After that, the few guests settled in the pews and Birdeen Lyons, who also served as the church organist, struck up the opening bars of Mendelssohn's Wedding March on the panting old pump organ. At that sound, Amy clutched her bouquet in a stranglehold of emotion and began her short walk to the altar, where Bax was waiting for her with a sprig of lily of the valley on his lapel. There was no one to give her away, but that didn't matter. Amy was her own person now, making her own decisions.

Although she caught a quick, vague glimpse of Cole standing beside Bax, the rest of the brief, dignified ceremony was a joyous blur. Jessica pried the bouquet out of Amy's nervous grip, and Bax held both of her hands in his. She made the appropriate responses when prompted, but she saw and heard only her husband. He gazed straight into her eyes and promised his life to her, come what may, good times and bad. When Amy repeated her vows, tears streaked her face and she clutched his hands.

"Kiss your bride, young man," Mr. Mumford instructed.

Bax lifted Amy's veil and gave her a bashful kiss. She smiled, both at him and to herself. This was not the same man she'd lain with on the sofa, caressing with feverish urgency. But he *was* her husband now; she knew the rest would come later this evening.

Mumford put his hands on their shoulders to turn them around to face their guests. "Friends—Mr. and Mrs. Baxter Duncan."

Jessica gave her a handkerchief and they all applauded. Cole shook Bax's hand. "Congratulations. I think you've got a great future ahead of you."

Amy looked at Cole and nodded wordless thanks to him. She appreciated the kindness of his gesture, and knew that he made it with sincerity.

The small group crowded around them to offer their best wishes, and suddenly Amy found herself facing Susannah Grenfell, Cole's former sister-in-law and a woman she had once used in her shameful scheme to win Cole away from Jessica. Certainly, she liked Susannah, but her primary aim had been to convince her that Amy was the better choice. Susannah had believed only that she had a good friend. Discovering the truth, and at just about the same time the army had notified Susannah that her husband was presumed dead on the Western Front in France, had left her disillusioned and numb. Amy planned to apologize to her, just as she had to Jess and Cole. But with all that had happened lately, she hadn't had the chance yet. Amy swallowed. She wasn't sure if Susannah and Tanner had come to celebrate with them or to censure her. She couldn't imagine that Susannah would create a scene at a social gathering like this, but people sometimes did strange things.

"Amy," Susannah greeted her with a hesitant smile. She carried John Henry in her arms and he slept on, despite the celebration going on around him. "I hope you've found what you sought for so long." She glanced at Tanner, the man she'd married after she'd been declared a widow, and gave him a loving gaze. "I want you to be as happy as we are."

Amy released a quiet breath and her eyes grew teary again. "Thank you both for coming today. It means a lot to me, and to

Bax." She kissed Susannah, then Tanner leaned in to peck her cheek.

"Come on, people," Granny Mae called from the back. "Let's get this party started. Everyone over to the New Cascades."

"Still bossy as ever," Amy murmured to Bax. Granny Mae wore a navy-blue dress, and this was one of the few times that Amy had seen the old woman without her apron. Deirdre's death had knocked the wind out of her for a while, but she'd bounced back, for the most part. In some ways she wasn't quite as cocksure as before, but that was a relief.

Bax took her arm. "What are we having for dinner?"

"Do you really care?" Amy asked, giving him a mischievous look. "I'd have thought your mind would have carried you beyond the reception."

He grinned down at her. "Hey, I have to stoke up for afterward. I didn't get much to eat this morning."

They emerged from the doors of the church into the afternoon sun and the bell in the steeple rang out to announce them. "Oh, I wasn't expecting that!" Amy said, looking up.

"I think Em arranged for that with her boys and Mr. Mumford," Jessica said, standing just behind her elbow.

Bax and Amy were pelted with rice, and laughing, he grabbed her hand and pulled her away from the steps in the general direction of the hotel.

• • •

After a wonderful dinner, happy toasts of illicit champagne, and servings of cake, Bax and Amy slipped away from their guests under a hail of good wishes and threats of a shivaree to their room on the second floor. Bax opened the door and then swept Amy into his arms and carried her in.

"Can I take off my tie and jacket now?" he asked, setting her on her feet. "I've been wearing this getup all day and I'm not really a necktie sort of man."

"Yes, take them off," she said, "but you should know that you look very handsome in dressy clothes."

"You might see me decked out like a store-window dummy once in a while in the future, but not often."

She shook her head and unpinned her veil, draping it over a chair. "Just like Cole and Tanner," she said, quirking a brow at him. "Even Whit was wearing a tie when he showed up, and he'd been out on business." She kicked off her shoes and sank onto the sofa, pleasantly tired from the excitement and complete happiness of the long day.

He waved that off. "He just went to check on the Beckers. It wasn't like digging a ditch." He slouched beside her and took her into his arms, so that they were half sitting, half reclining. "Anyway, I didn't bring you up here to talk about men's furnishings." He nuzzled her ear and sent a wave of delicious shivers across her shoulders and over her scalp.

"No," she whispered, "you didn't." She gazed into his handsome face and any shyness she'd felt began to melt away. Then she admitted, "When I got to the church and I didn't see the county car, I thought . . ."

"Thought what?"

"Well, maybe you changed your mind."

He gave her a serious look. "Amy—as if I could." He slid from the sofa to his knees in front of her. "I promise I will love you and protect you, no matter what." He put the flat of her hand over his heart and covered it with his own. "I'll never lie to you or play you false. I'll keep you first in my heart and my head. I won't abandon you and I'll always be faithful to you. You're stuck with me."

Amy's throat grew tight and she almost wept. His pledge was even more meaningful and poignant than the vows they'd exchanged at the wedding. "And I have never loved anyone as much as I love you," she said, studying the lean line of his jaw. He leaned forward and kissed her then, with more heat than she had ever known, leaving her breathless from his pledge and his lips. He smelled of soap and fresh-cut grass.

He stood up and pulled her with him, turning her around. "Damn, you've got enough buttons on this dress to lock up a bank vault. How did you get into it?"

"Jess fastened me in when she and Cole came to pick me up."

He made an impatient noise, and then as if by magic, her dress suddenly dropped off her shoulders, puddling around her ankles. He turned her around, and she stood before him in her white stockings and almost-transparent chemise with its strategically placed lace insets. His brows rose and he exhaled. He pulled a pin from her hair, and then another, letting them drop to the hardwood floor. With the last pin gone, her hair fell out of the elaborate style it had taken her an hour to construct and tumbled over her shoulders.

He combed his fingers through the braids to loosen them and muttered, "God, I'm glad you haven't bobbed your hair. A woman as beautiful as you should have long hair."

"Would you hate it if I did?" She had no plans to cut her hair. She was only curious.

"No. I want you to do what makes you happy." His gaze swept over her again. "I didn't marry you for your hair. But—" He gestured at it and sighed. She smiled.

With a featherlight touch, he skimmed the side of her breast and her eyes closed briefly at the sensation. Taking her hand, he pressed a kiss into it before he led her to the small adjoining bed-room.

Pushing her back against the blue jacquard bedspread, he tugged his shirt off over his head and was down to his draw-ers before she had the chance to reach out and participate. He climbed over her and rolled her up against him. He planted kisses along her hairline, as soft and fluttering as the first one he'd put on her wrist that long-ago afternoon in the backyard. His breath stirred her eyelashes and she was electrified—she swore she could feel every sensation in her body. Her own breathing, her heart, the blood pumping through her veins. The sweetness of his lips moved over hers, now with an aching hunger. The hint of arousal that she'd known only with Bax now raged like a grass fire, melt-ing her, turning her to thick, warm honey. She was no innocent, but all of this was new to her.

He gripped her backside with both hands and pulled her tight against him. She nestled her hips against his and felt the hard length of him. When she pushed harder, he groaned and buried his mouth against her throat. Then he edged away enough to fit his hand between them and unbuttoned the bottom of her che-mise, which wasn't much more than ribbons of lace and diapha-nous chiffon. She had made it herself and in a hurry, especially for this day.

"You won't tear the fabric, will you?" she whispered.

"No, honey, why would I do that? I want to see this on you again." Then Bax looked at her and she saw in his eyes that he realized why she worried. "I would never do that to you."

When he touched the slick center of her and stroked her most sensitive place she drew a sharp, surprised breath. It was as if he'd touched her with a live lamp cord. A moan sounded in her throat.

Instinctively she reached for him, too. Snaking a hand into his fly, she found him hot and smooth under her fingers, and much more than she expected.

"God, woman, you're merciless," he mumbled. Amy felt empowered—an equal partner—in a new and completely different way. She wasn't frightened or burdened with a sense of duty that made her want to shrink from his touch. Bax desired her and she wanted him. He rolled out of her grip and stood to strip off the underwear. His long torso and backside had not a spare ounce of fat and she could see his muscles flex beneath his skin. His strength, and his contrast to her own softness, added fuel to her desire. Behind him the late-day sun gleamed through the filter of the lace curtains on the window, and he was outlined with rich gold light that highlighted all the red and blue strands usually unnoticeable in his dark hair.

Bax was a man—a true man, physically and morally. His touch was gentle as he teased off her stockings and slipped her camisole straps off her shoulders, then bared her to his view. His hands and mouth were everywhere on her then, tender, urgent, passionate. She responded in kind. Lips and tongues met and moved on to explore, only to return and meet again.

"All those years alone," he said, his breath coming fast, "all that time was the sentence I served to have you. And you were worth every minute."

"You're my reward for paying the consequences of every bad thing I did and have lived through," she said against his chest.

Bax took her then in one heat-fueled stroke, his body covering hers, their hips reaching for the other. Her breath whooshed out of her, the sensation was that intense and unexpected. So primal and visceral was their joining that words had no use or meaning now. She felt as if she'd lost the power of coherent speech. All of her attention was concentrated on the core of her femaleness, being ministered to by her husband with darts of flame, pushing her ever closer to a completion she had never known before. Feeling as if her soul and body were on the knife-edge of being split in two, when that explosion came she realized that she was being forged in a conflagration that would join her to Bax.

Bax had already guessed that fulfillment she should have experienced with a man would be new to her. He was pleased, knowing that he was the one to give it to her. But the muscle contractions surrounding him in her wet, warm flesh took every other thought from his head except finding his own release. He'd held back to make sure he satisfied her first because he knew he wouldn't be able to maintain control any longer than that. Now with her writhing and sobbing beneath him, he held her tighter and sank deeper into her and the completion he needed.

Sweat-soaked and exhausted, they both lay boneless and relaxed.

He kissed her again. "Are you okay? No aches or pains?"

She said nothing but smiled at him with a dreamy languor that told him what he wanted to know. He sighed and rolled them to their sides, still joined.

• • •

An hour later, Bax slept on his stomach while Amy lay with her head propped on her hand and studied him in the waning daylight. The scars that she had glimpsed just one time now were fully visible. She traced around them with a light fingertip. They obviously had faded over the years, so she could only guess how horrific they must have looked early on, because they were very vivid even now. She wondered how on earth he'd survived them.

He had another on the back of his shoulder; it must be the one he'd suffered first. It made her heart ache to think of everything he'd been through, but it also swelled with love for him. She'd told him the truth when she'd said she had never cared as much about anyone as she did him. But no other man had shown her the kind of devotion and genuine love that he did. He had become her heartbeat.

Of course she'd adored her mother, and losing her at such a young age had been devastating. But somewhere along the way, a piece of her she'd needed to make her a complete person seemed to have gotten lost. Certainly time and experience had done their job on her, but it was Bax who'd really given it back to her. She no longer automatically thought of herself first. Just when that had changed, she wasn't sure.

She did know that she liked this new Amy much better.

CHAPTER NINETEEN

Because they woke and made love twice more in the moonlit darkness, Amy and Bax were still asleep the next morning when a loud, persistent knock sounded on their hotel door.

"God, what? Is the place on fire?" Bax groaned. He lay naked under the sheet, wrapped around Amy, who at some point had slipped into her white batiste nightgown. Groping for the alarm clock on the nightstand, he looked at it. "Nine fifteen? If someone has rethought that idea of a shivaree, there's going to be a big problem."

More pounding. "Bax!" came a muffled voice from the other side of the door.

"What *is* that?" Amy asked, pushing at her hair.

"Damn it," he groused, and disentangled himself from her arms and legs. "Who the hell would do this to a man the day after his wedding?" He pushed away the sheet and grabbed the bedspread from the floor. During the night it had slid off, and now he wrapped it around his waist, holding it in place with one hand at his side. It trailed behind him like a coronation robe, and she couldn't help but laugh.

"You look so elegant, Your Majesty."

He gave her a dry look and trudged to the door. "Can't a man have twenty-four hours with his new bride?" he barked at the wood panel before he opened it a crack.

He saw Horace Cookson, Powell Springs's mayor, standing in the hall. He was dressed in overalls and a plain cotton shirt. Obviously, he'd been working on his farm, not in his office. It was Sunday, after all. "Bax, I'm sorry as hell to interrupt, I truly am. But there's an emergency at the Becker place."

"What, today? Horace, Whit was out there just yesterday. I think he's got it taken care of."

"No, he's out there again—*now*. He's been injured, and Luke and Emily Becker are being held hostage in their own house. There's no one left to ask."

Bax stared at him. "How do you know all this?"

"Emily managed to call Birdeen just before the men got into the house. Then Birdeen heard a commotion and the line went dead. Frankly, I don't know what the situation is right now."

"How many men?"

"I'm not sure, maybe two or three."

"Where is Whit? In the house? Outside?"

"Outside I think, but I'm not sure."

Bax raked his free hand through his hair. "All right. But I can't manage this alone. I need to deputize men to go with me, starting with you."

"Me! Bax, I'm not so young anymore."

He ignored the protest. "And you're going to round up Cole, Tanner, and anyone else you can think of. We need a raid. Oh, and get Virgil Tilly too. This affects him as much as anyone else. I don't care if he has to close up, because if he won't come along, I'll close him up for good!"

Horace seemed to be trying to edge away, having delivered his message. "Well, okay, but—"

"Look, Horace, I need help with this and you have thirty minutes to get this done. Meet me at the office in half an hour, and I don't want to hear any more *yeah, buts*. I need help, and I'm only one man. We're all spread thin. Now get going and I'll see you there."

Amy had crept out of bed to stand against the wall beside the doorframe, unseen by the mayor. Bax felt her presence there before he closed the door.

"I can't help it. I *have* to go."

Amy nodded but her heart sank under the weight of an old companion—fear. Not for herself, but for her husband. She gripped his forearm. "Bax, please, I know you have to do this, but if no one shows up to help you, *please*, I'm begging you, don't go alone. There can't be any sort of raid with just one person."

He took her into his embrace, kissed her forehead, and sighed. "I'm sorry, honey. I never imagined this might happen. I've been thinking for a while that we just don't have enough men. We ought to at least have reserve personnel. The town is growing and this part of the county is wide and empty. We can't be everywhere. Either the smaller towns like Fairdale and Twelve Mile need to add their own staff or we need to expand. But none of that is going to happen today." He hugged her extra tight. "Right now, I've got to leave. You can wait for me here if you want, or you can go home."

"I'll go home. I don't want to sit here by myself, not knowing anything." She picked up her veil from the chair where she'd left it yesterday. "I'll call Em too. She's probably crazy with worry."

He released her and walked back into the bedroom where he'd left his everyday clothes in his kit bag. At least the suite had its own bathroom so they didn't have to make trips down the hall. Amy watched him go, thinking no man wearing a bedspread ever looked so gallant.

• • •

Bax walked Amy home under a clear sky that promised to turn hot later in the day. Their parting was emotional and heart wrenching. He had expected to spend this morning eating breakfast with his new wife in the hotel dining room and carrying her across the threshold of the house—and beyond. Instead, he left her on the front porch with a knot in his throat and a rock in his stomach, hoping this wouldn't be the last time he saw her.

She flung herself into his arms with a choked-back sob. "You *have* to come back to me! I'm going to be selfish again. I want my husband home and in one safe piece."

He buried his face against her shoulder for a moment, inhaling the scent of her and swallowing hard to stop the tears that threatened him. He wanted the same thing she did. "I'll be back. I swear it," he promised, his voice cracking. "Hang on to that. I'll be back." Then he pulled her arms loose and turned to go, jogging to the office every step of the way.

Now, twenty minutes after they hurried out of the New Cascades, he had buckled his gun belt, pinned on his badge, and he paced the office floor, waiting for someone to show up. Periodically he checked the gun cabinet out of nervous anticipation. He'd taken out a shotgun and a rifle, not knowing which he'd need. He couldn't arm everyone but there were a couple of sidearms to spare. He was in a bind because Whit had the Model T and unless someone with a vehicle showed up soon, he'd have to borrow Whit's horse. That wasn't practical in this case, and in fact, was becoming less practical with every passing year. And he had no details about the situation beyond what sketchy information Horace had given him.

Just as he was about to get Birdeen on the telephone and try to track down the man, he heard cars pull up outside. Rushing to the window, he saw Cole and Jessica, in their truck. She carried her doctor's bag and he had a rifle. Bax was very pleased to see Paul McCoy and his three boys in the bed, all armed. Tanner had come, too, in the 1917 Corbitt truck he'd recently acquired. Horace and Virgil were in the back of the Corbitt. They were the weak links in the chain, and Bax wasn't sure how much help they'd be, but a show of numbers was important.

He met them all outside. "Thanks, everyone, for coming. Tanner, I need you to be my ride. Doc Jess, I imagine you know you'll keep a *very* safe distance, but we might need you."

"That's my intention," she replied, catching a disapproving look from Cole. "Yes, I already know you didn't want me to come along."

"What's going on, Bax?" Paul asked. "Is this the same skunk you and Whit smoked out of my barn?"

"No, he's in jail in Portland. I don't know who these guys are but Whit and I tore down a still we found on Luke Becker's land a while back. It might be whoever put it up to begin with."

"I didn't do anything wrong. I don't know why you wanted me along," Virgil groused. Neither did Bax—the man couldn't even manage a barroom scrape in his own saloon. But he thought that Virgil Tilly owed Whit this gesture for letting him keep the saloon.

"It's not a work detail or a chain gang, Virgil. It's called helping your neighbor," Cole threw in, as if reading Bax's thoughts. "None of us are here as punishment—what the hell is wrong with you? Whit has let you stay in business all this time when he could have forced you to sell ice cream to old ladies and kids. Now he needs us."

"Do you have a plan for this?" Virgil asked. It sounded like an accusation.

No, but Bax wished he did. This wasn't like organizing an assault against a known enemy in an identifiable uniform. He had no surveillance or intelligence to work from. This was a different kind of battle. "I'm making it up as I go along. If I thought it would do any good, I'd make Granny Mae come with us. She played a part in this too, even though she didn't mean to."

"Oh, Bax, you know she feels horrible about that," Doc Jess said.

"Yeah, but it sure didn't help things. Anyway, that doesn't matter now. We've got to go rescue the Beckers and find Whit. And hope everything turns out well. I haven't even been married for twenty-four hours. I'd like to see my wife again."

There was a general shuffling of feet and murmurs of agreement.

"And Horace, you and I are going to have a talk when this is all over."

The mayor looked alarmed. "Wha—me! Why?"

"We need you to talk to the county about getting more help for us."

With a quick speech, he deputized all of them, which he stressed was a temporary situation. "All right, people. Saddle up and let's get this done."

They all piled back into the vehicles and headed east toward Fairdale. Tanner's truck led the way since this was Bax's party.

When they pulled into the long road that led to the Beckers' place, Bax said, "Keep your eyes open for Whit. He might be out here somewhere." At last they spotted the county car parked where the road met the weeds, but no one was inside. "Wait a minute."

Bax jumped out and looked in the window. Nothing. Then he came around to the passenger side and found Whit, gray-faced on the ground beside the door. He was alive and conscious, but something was wrong. Bax crouched beside him. "Whit! Are you shot?"

"No, burned. But I'm glad to see that help is here."

Bax motioned to Jessica, who took a quick look around before jumping out to join them. Cole was right behind her.

"What happened?" Bax asked.

"Luke called me and said he thought it was the same bastards who were here before. I came out to run them off, but they started shooting. They didn't hit me, but I fired back and hit their boiler. It exploded and hot mash came flying toward me. They just laughed."

Bax cringed and watched while Jessica cut holes in his clothes to look at the burns. "You think they're in the house?"

"Yeah. They went running down that hill and headed straight for the back door. It wouldn't be hard to overpower two older people who aren't expecting that kind of trouble."

"How many are there?"

"Two, I'm pretty sure. But I didn't get a good enough look to tell you much about them. They've got to be cleared out. They can't keep squatting here and harassing these people."

"Horace says Birdeen got a call from Mrs. Becker and that there was some scuffle in the house, then she got cut off."

"Maybe, I wasn't sure. I was out here."

"What do you think?" Bax asked Jess.

"Looks like second-degree burns at most, but they're bad enough," she replied, distracted and harried. "I need to get him to my office so I can get a better look and start treatment."

"You'll have to take him back in the county car. Do you think you can manage on your own?"

"I'll manage. I've done harder things and you all need to stay here."

"I could go with you," Virgil piped up.

"Tilly, I can take out your appendix but I can't put a spine in your back, even if you come to my office. You'll have to find one of your own," she snapped. Cole and Bax looked at each other over her head and laughed, even though there wasn't much funny about the situation.

Virgil slumped in his seat, wearing an expression of injured dignity.

"She's a firecracker, isn't she." Cole murmured.

"Okay, can you two give me a hand here?" she asked.

"I can walk, Doc Jess," Whit protested.

"*Your* spine works just great, Whit. A little help won't be a bad thing." She turned to Bax. "I'm going to stop and pick up Em and Amy, and take them back to the office. That's where we'll all be, so if you should call, get us there. Otherwise, you two"—she nodded at Bax and her own husband—"meet us there."

Bax and Cole both looked around to make sure no one was pointing a gun at them, then boosted Whit into the backseat.

They and the McCoy men directed her in backing up so she could use the two trucks as shields until she could get turned around and headed back down the road.

Once she was safely on her way, they faced their next task. "How should we go about this?" Cole asked, as if wondering out loud.

Paul McCoy and his sons joined the conference. "If there's just the two of 'em, they can't cover every window and door. There are more of us than them. We could distract 'em by trying to talk them out, while some of us check for unlocked sashes and try the doors."

"Sounds as good as anything else," Cole said, and Bax agreed. "But I think we ought to get only a little closer with the trucks and not park them in plain sight. And be careful—remember there are two old people in there who won't be able to move as fast as everyone else."

Everyone agreed with that.

They piled back into the vehicles and drove to a bend in the road heavy with shrubs and blackberry brambles, just beyond which was the house. A lot of whispering and hand signals passed between the men, and they moved forward into an uncertain situation.

• • •

Amy did her best to stay busy but she wandered to the front and back windows so often she accomplished almost nothing. She was standing in the kitchen, trying to decide if she should bake a cake or bread when she heard a car horn out front. Running to the door, she saw the county car and her heart leaped in her chest until she realized her sister was driving and someone was in the backseat.

"Oh, God," she moaned. She grabbed the house key from its hook next to the telephone in the kitchen, then hurried out the front door, slamming it behind her.

When she got closer and saw Whit, a flash of raw panic burned through her. "Where's Bax?" she yelled.

"Get in," Jess called back. "He's still with everyone else at the Beckers' place, but Whit's hurt. We've got to stop and pick up Em."

"Whit, is it serious in Fairdale?" Amy asked, getting into the car before turning around completely in her seat. All she saw were holes cut here and there in his clothes and some angry-looking blisters on his face and neck.

"If it's all the same to you, Amy, I'd rather explain this just once more. Can we wait till we pick up Em?"

"Oh, of course, I'm so sorry!" She turned around again, grateful that he didn't seem to be seriously hurt and wishing that he'd brought Bax with him. Would these problems never end?

When they got to Whit's house, a tidy little white house with a yard full of flowers and a neatly trimmed lawn—a sure sign of a woman's touch since Amy last saw his place—his wife came running out of the house, much the way Amy had.

"Sweet Jesus!" Em screeched and hurried to the car, her red hair flying behind her. "Whitney!" She almost pulled off the backseat door to get to him, then climbed onto the seat on her knees.

"Shut the door, Em, we're going to my office. The men know we'll all be gathered there." The midday sun glared off the hood of the car as Jessica pulled away.

"What happened?" Em asked.

"All right, now listen carefully because you're all going to have to repeat it when someone else asks. I'm only going to tell this one more time today," he said, his face showing a little more color now that his wife was with him. Hers was ghastly pale, making her freckles pop out like paint specks. So he explained again what had occurred and commented that he hoped Bax could take care of the problem once and for all since it kept coming back. He added that Bax should be all right because he had so many people with him, while Whit had gone alone.

The women got him into Jess's office, careful to avoid touching any of his obvious burns, and Amy sat on the sofa in the back office to wait for word of her own husband.

• • •

"You might as well give it up," Bax called to the house from the shelter of a large oak that grew in the front yard. "If you don't, we'll just storm the house and shoot you on the spot."

While he talked, one by one his posse slipped off to surround the house and check for possible entrances, using the cover of the shrubbery as much as they could. He didn't expect his order to be followed, but he kept talking anyway.

Then he noticed Paul McCoy in the yard, waving his arms to get Bax's attention. He made a semicircular motion toward the front of the house with his pointed finger, but Bax wasn't sure what he meant. Just then, the front door opened and two men emerged with their hands on their heads, being prodded along by Cole and Tanner.

"I'll be damned," Bax uttered, and felt a rush of gratitude for the two men and their willingness to help. He didn't know the details of how they'd gotten in—right now he was more interested in finding out who they'd caught.

"What about the Beckers?" Bax asked.

"Mrs. Becker is a little shaken up, but they're fine," Tanner said, just as the older couple emerged from the house.

"We sure do want to thank you boys," Luke said. He gestured at the two criminals, now surrounded by the rest of the posse and forced to sit on the ground with their hands tied behind them with clothesline they'd gotten in the house. "After you and Whit took out their still, they came back and waved a shotgun at my wife when she told them to get off our land. Emily doesn't scare easy, but she's not one to argue with a gun pointed at her face." The couple still held hands, and Bax could see Mrs. Becker's faded but vibrant beauty in the fine bones of her face and her fresh-snow white hair. She was nearly as tall as Doc Jess. "I called Whit and he came out. I guess you know what happened after that."

"I'm glad you're both all right," Bax said, then looked over at the two offenders. "I didn't think it would be that easy to sneak up on them."

"Just because they're lawbreakers doesn't make 'em smart," Paul McCoy observed.

"True. Let's see who we've got here."

One man he'd seen in Powell Springs a couple of times, but hadn't thought much of. He might have been the one Granny Mae talked to. The other, though, the *other*—

"By God! Tom Sommers?"

Cole shrugged. "Yeah. Isn't that something?"

Bax felt like a gaffed salmon, his astonishment was so complete and unnerving. He'd lived under the same roof with the man, had sympathized with him when Deirdre died—hell, he'd even been sorry to see him move out of Amy's house. Now he felt altogether defrauded. Then another thought occurred to him. "All those nights you claimed you were working late at the saw-mill? You were making methanol?"

Sommers looked up at him with an expression that could have frozen the blood in Bax's veins. "So what? It paid better than that shit job at the mill."

"What about Deirdre?"

"What about her? I didn't kill her. That old woman did." How could Bax, how could all of them, have been so deceived? Well, he had to admit, the guy had two completely different personalities. Even Adam Jacobsen wasn't all that different from Harlan Monroe. Monroe just owned a better wardrobe and put on better manners, according to what he'd heard from Tabitha Pratt.

Bax was so furious, he was afraid if Sommers said anything more, he'd kick the man in the head. "All right, tie them to Cole's truck bed and bring them in. We'll get this sorted out in town."

Luke and Emily shook everyone's hands, and invited them all to an outdoor picnic sometime this summer. "We'll have a grand time. My Emily is a good cook, so you won't starve." To Bax, he added, "I heard you just got married yesterday. I'm sorry we had to drag you away from your gal. I still remember the day Emily and I got married."

She gave him a wry look. "Yes, he was furious with me but he married me anyway."

"Well, I was supposed to marry your sister, and you tricked me good, but we don't need to tell the world about that again. Anyway, it all worked out. We got four kids out of the deal, didn't we?"

She actually blushed and murmured to him, "That was the easiest part."

Cole and Bax stared at them, open-mouthed, and then at each other. Bax was itching with curiosity over that story. He'd have to ask around about it.

Luke gave them a quizzical look. "Say, are you two boys related?"

"Bax is my brother-in-law," Cole answered. Bax glanced away and smiled, filled with a true sense of family and homecoming.

"We'll get out of your hair," Bax said. "I hope this is the end of the problem for you."

"Don't we all? Thanks again, boys," Luke said. "We'll be in touch about that picnic." He put an arm around his wife's waist and waved to them as they dragged the prisoners away.

Would that be him and Amy in forty years? Bax wondered as they pulled out. Would he still be able to make her blush and giggle? They were off to a great start. He just needed to be able to spend some time with her.

• • •

Amy had actually dozed off on that sofa in Jessica's private office when she woke to the sound of a commotion out front. She sprang upright and got to her feet in time to see both Cole and Bax coming down the hallway from the waiting room.

With an incoherent cry, she threw herself into his arms. "You're all right?" she asked, raining kisses on his face. "Tell me you're all right!"

Cole chuckled and moved around them to see his own wife.

"Yes, but what a story I have to tell you." Bax sat down on the sofa and patted the place next to him. She sat too, cuddling up so tight he was pushed to the corner, and listened to the story of Tom Sommers and his new occupation. She stared at him the way he supposed he'd stared at Sommers.

"*Really?* I can hardly believe it. He didn't seem like that kind of man at all."

"Yeah, that's what makes him even more creepy and dangerous than that stupid Jacobsen. He was heartless and incompetent. Sommers is just plain evil. I don't know the whole story yet. I left Tilly in charge of the two prisoners. He can get them dinner from Mae's and sit there the whole damned night as far as I'm concerned." He told her about his whiny helplessness and Jessica's comment to him about finding a spine. She laughed.

"Yes, Jessie doesn't pull any punches when she's mad."

He nodded in the general direction of Jessica's surgery. "What about Whit?"

"She says he'll be fine but he'll have to take it easy for a couple of days. Some of those burns are as big as my palm, so he'll be better off hanging around in his nightshirt for a while."

Bax sighed. "I guess I'll have a couple of long days ahead of me too. But I talked to Horace about getting us more help. He said he's up for reelection in November but he's not going to run again. He wants to retire to his dairy farm and let someone else have the responsibility now."

"Hmm, I think I know someone who might be just right for the job."

"Not *me!*"

"No, no, not you. We'll have to see what happens."

He paused for a moment, then asked, "Do you know Luke and Emily Becker?"

"Just in passing. Why?"

He played with her hand, lacing and unlacing their fingers. "They've been together for forty years, and he mentioned that she tricked him into marrying her. He was supposed to marry her sister."

She sat up a bit straighter. "I've never heard about that! I'll have to do a little checking. Just out of curiosity, you understand."

"Well, yeah, I'm curious too. Be looking for an invitation from them for a summer picnic. They want to thank everyone who helped them today." He turned her wedding ring on her finger. "We've come a long way over these months, you and I. Together and separately."

"I suppose we have," she agreed quietly.

"I came to Powell Springs looking for a home, one where no one knew about my past. It came out and I'm still here. You came back to Powell Springs because it's the only home you know. People already knew about your past, you overcame it and got your family back. We found each other. And today, Cole referred to me as his brother-in-law. I lost my childhood family and found my real one."

"My luck changed when I changed," she said simply.

"My luck changed when I found you." He reached up and pushed a blonde strand away from her eyes.

They looked into each other's eyes and his mouth took hers sweetly at first, then hungrily. She looped one arm around his neck and put her other hand on the back of his head.

"I think you two had better go home." Bax and Amy both jumped and saw Cole standing in the doorway. Amy ducked her head, and Bax laughed, feeling his face get hot. "It's okay. You got dragged out of your hotel room early this morning, probably dog-tired from no sleep, and had to go assemble a posse to catch some bad guys. You weren't supposed to spend your day like that."

Bax pulled himself out of the soft cushions and dragged Amy up with him. "As a point of fact, we were not. We were supposed to be enjoying each other's company privately," he said with great specificity. "And that's what we're going to do now."

Cole laughed and gave him a playful punch in the shoulder.

Bax stopped to see Whit where he lay on one of the two beds in the back of the clinic. They were hidden behind hospital screens and served as recovery beds for Jess's occasional surgical cases. He just wanted to make sure for himself that the man would be all right. Em sat beside him, her handkerchief balled up in her hand.

"Oh, hell, I'm a tough old cuss. I'll be fine. Doc Jess gave me a little shot of something for the pain and will send some pills home with me so I can sleep."

Bax could tell. His words were a little slurred, and Bax had had enough painkillers in military hospitals to know the feeling.

Whit's arms were wrapped here and there with white bandages, and a sheet covered the rest of him, so Bax couldn't tell how much damage had been done. But his face sported a few blisters that looked angry and painful. Maybe worst of all for Whit, Doc Jess had shaved off part of his luxurious silver mustache. "Did Cole tell you who we caught?"

He nodded. "Every time I think I've seen it all, I get surprised."

"Well, you take it easy. I've got Tilly watching the suspects in their cells, and I'll be back there tomorrow. You know, he's sort of useless for anything except selling beer."

"Huh, that's not news. I've known him all my life and I don't think he's going to improve now."

Bax gripped Whit's uninjured hand and patted Em's shoulder. Amy patted Whit's shoulder and gave Em a big hug. "You be sure to let us know if you need anything." Em nodded and gave them a wobbly smile.

After bidding good-bye to Jess and Cole, they walked out into the summer sun toward home, holding hands. "Do you remember the first day I saw you?" Amy asked.

"Yes. You hated my guts on sight."

"No, I didn't. I was terrified of you. You were driving a county sheriff's car and I was worried that Adam had every local jurisdiction looking for me to drag me back to Portland. I wanted that ride you offered in the worst way. I'd been walking for miles in the rain and mud, and I was soaked right through."

"Jacobsen didn't have that kind of authority or power to send police after you," Bax scoffed. Then he said, "I suppose you didn't know that at the time."

"No, I didn't." She looked around at the bright day and gestured at the sky. "But look how time changes things."

"And look how love has changed us." He stopped and kissed her again, right there on the street, in front of God and Powell Springs, and anything else watching.

"Oh, my." She giggled and they picked up their pace, heading for home.

EPILOGUE

Bax stood in front of Whit's desk and considered a photograph of Em that sat on his bookcase. "Do you two have plans for Christmas?" he asked.

"I don't think so. This year the boys are going out to the Grenfells' farm for Christmas vacation."

"Come to our place. Cole and Jess will be there with Margaux and whatever little passenger she's carrying in her this time. Tanner and Susannah will be there anyway with the kids, so you can spend Christmas with them. Mae will probably stop by, and I've got Nate Cameron scheduled to watch the office."

Whit smiled. "That sounds great. I know Em gets a little blue when they're gone, but Tanner raised those boys for five years while Em was working. They all got a little attached."

"That's okay, it's like having extra family, aunts and uncles and so on."

"It is." He glanced out his office window. "You know, it looks like it might snow out there pretty soon. Have those cars been delivered yet?"

"No, but I got a call from the dealer. They'll be here first thing in the morning."

"Okay, good."

In November, and at the urging of many, Whit Gannon ran unopposed for the office of mayor of Powell Springs. Deputy Bax Duncan was now Sheriff Bax Duncan, and between the two of them, they'd been able to make quite a few improvements in the month that he'd had the job. After Whit recovered, he and Bax sat down to discuss what they thought the department needed and which of those needs stood the best chance of being answered first. They were able to get three new cars and hire another two full-time deputies. Bax bought the old Model T for Amy and had it repainted so she wouldn't have to drive around with the county's emblem on the doors.

Horace retired to his farm and after many years was able to devote all of his time to his dairy cows. There was even a reliable rumor going around that he'd started courting Birdeen Lyons. After all those years of working together, it wasn't really surprising.

Amy replaced the rug in the living room, the one that had been stained the day that Adam Jacobsen walked into the kitchen. Both he and Milo Breninger had been tried and convicted for some crimes, although others were still under investigation. While those were pending, they sat in prison at the Oregon State Penitentiary, awaiting the court's pleasure.

As for Bax and Amy, he was headed home right now to a glass of whiskey and a great dinner. He didn't know what she would be cooking, but she hadn't missed yet. He could see that she was right about her mother's training—she loved working around the house, just as much as Jess hated it.

"Okay, Whit, I'm off for home. I'll bet Em is waiting for you too."

"Yeah, she is. She likes my new hours a whole lot better than the old ones. I'm there every night unless there's a council meeting."

Bax shrugged back into his Woolrich coat—the east wind was howling down the Columbia River Gorge again—and walked out, waving at Birdeen on his way to the door.

When he pulled up to the house, he saw Amy in a heavy shawl, standing on the porch waiting for him, as she always did when she knew what time he'd be there. He came up the steps and his face was icy from the stiff wind.

"Oh, come inside and sit by the stove! It's going to be frigid tonight." He looked at her, rosy from the cold, her hair pulled up into a loose knot, and he thought she'd never been more beautiful.

He took her into his arms and she slipped hers around his waist inside his coat. She gave him an arch look. "I guess that means I'll have to put the down quilt on the bed. Or wear that old flannel granny gown."

He laughed and kissed her. "I'll help you look for the quilt."

"I thought you might want to do that." She disentangled her arms.

"What's for dinner?" he asked, following her back to the kitchen.

"Something good. Do you really care? You eat anything I put in front of you."

He shook his head. "I don't care. I know it will be great. I have you. And I'm home."

ABOUT THE AUTHOR

Alexis Harrington is the award-winning author of over a dozen novels, including the international bestseller *The Irish Bride.* She spent twelve years working as an administrative manager in civil engineering offices before she became a full-time novelist. When she isn't writing, she enjoys jewelry making, needlework, embroidery, cooking, and entertaining friends. She lives in her native Pacific Northwest, near the Columbia River, with a variety of pets who do their best to distract her while she is working.